Spirits Unbound

The Dragon's Dream Saga, Book 4

D.C. Fergerson

The Dragon's Dream Saga

Project Phoenix

Heaven's Crest

The Pendragon Codex

Spirits Unbound

Shadows of Olympus

Fated Alliance

Helen of Seattle

The Dragon's Dream

ISBN: 9781087256078

Spirits Unbound

DEDICATION

To Cat and Leanna, my girls.
To Catherine, for giving me my light. We miss you.

IN MEMORIAM

A beach in Maui would have been a better place for Cora to drink herself to death. Instead, she wound up in the Free State of Texas. For a land that prided itself on freedom, they sure had a lot of checkpoints on the way to Schulenburg, an hour west of Houston. Weary from the road, she stopped into a bar called Taphouse a little after ten o'clock. By midnight, she was putting a dent in the second bottle of whiskey, and all the prying eyes stopped annoying her.

Only a day removed from yet another funeral, the wound was still raw. She opted to teleport into Oklahoma and rent a car from the Native people there. The time on the road had the opposite effect of what she was looking for. Instead of peace of mind, she found herself mired in thoughts on a long, lonely trip. Her eyes were still sore from crying most of the way there.

Every checkpoint officer took one look at her caramel skin touched with a hint of red and she was out of the car, patted down, and asked for her documents. They always suspected her of something. Her papers were fake, but that was beside the point. She didn't like being stereotyped.

By the time she arrived in Schulenburg, days later than she intended, all she wanted was to forget. She wanted to forget Lucius. The damned dragon could keep his stupid war. Forget

Julian with his pompous, aristocratic demeanor and his stupid, claustrophobic undersea research facility. More than anything, she wanted to forget what it felt like to lose. The whiskey hadn't done its job yet, but at least it hurt a lot less. Between the country music, the noisy crowd, and the smell of industrial cleaner on wood, her head hurt more than anything.

Even in a booth at the darkest corner of the bar, far removed from the Friday night crowd, trouble still found its way to her. From the second that two deputies walked into Taphouse, she knew they were coming for her. After a brief conversation with the bartender and a few glances shot her way, they did not disappoint. The lead deputy was tall and broad-shouldered, with blue eyes as vacant as the podunk town's motel. She looked up and smiled.

"Evenin', boys," she said, her words coming out slurred. "Something wrong?"

The big deputy turned his head as though he were checking for someone. His head settled on Cora, but he looked around her. It was an obnoxious, rookie tactic guys like him used to make their prey feel lesser. He showed he was so powerful and strong that he didn't need to watch her every move as though she were a threat. He was wrong.

"Good evening, ma'am," he replied. "I understand you arrived in town earlier."

"I did," Cora nodded.

"I've been working the front desk at the sheriff's office, and I don't recall seeing you today," he said, head surveying the room.

Cora raised an eyebrow. "I didn't have any crimes to report, except maybe that these whiskey bottles are 32 cred a piece. That's some bullshit."

The deputy didn't find her amusing. He locked eyes with her and put his hands on his hips, another attempt to intimidate her. "Ma'am, if you are a traveler in the State of Texas, you are required to notify the sheriff's office when you take up residence here."

Cora sipped straight from the bottle. It didn't make sense to refill her glass every two minutes. She wiped her mouth with the sleeve of her brown bomber jacket and looked up.

"I'm not taking up residence," Cora replied. "I'm just passing through."

"I spoke with Mr. Maynard at Towne Inn, he says you got a room there," the deputy replied.

"Well, he shouldn't advertise as a 'no-tell motel' if he's going to run his mouth to you guys," she replied, tripping on her words. "So, what did he say I did, anyway? Being a red girl in his pretty white hotel a crime?"

Over his shoulder, the other deputy looked nervous. A smaller version of the corn-fed, hay-bailing, all-state wrestler his mama made, this deputy was fresh. By his baby face, Cora guessed twenty-two.

The big deputy motioned toward the door with his head. "Why don't we step outside? We have a few questions we'd like to ask you."

"Are we talking about a few minutes, or should I settle my tab?" Cora asked.

"Why don't you settle up, ma'am?" he replied. He kept it friendly, even as the threat loomed over that she wasn't going to be allowed to leave anytime soon.

A smirk crept up Cora's mouth. She needed to get to the sheriff's office, but she didn't imagine it would be like this. Either way, it suited her purposes. She screwed the cap on her bottle and tucked it into a red duffle bag on the seat beside her. After she zipped it up, she lifted her wrist and swiped a finger across the face of her silver bracelet. A holographic screen projected to the back of her hand. With a few swipes and gestures on the screen, she walked to the bar. The bartender came over with a hesitant, cautious step.

"Hey, asshole, thanks for calling the boys in brown," she said with a smile. "What do I owe you?"

"Seventy-two fifty, ma'am," he said with a nod.

The smile left Cora's face. "It was thirty-two a bottle."

The bartender nodded. "Plus tax."

"Texas doesn't have taxes," Cora replied.

He shrugged. "It does for you."

Cora shook her head. The money didn't matter. She could buy the whole building six times over and not have her bank account feel a tickle. The principle of it, though, that really got to her. Texas wasn't exactly a haven for any meta-human, but she hadn't imagined treatment this bad even in the Southern Confederacy. With another swipe, she'd sent the funds from her screen to a register beside the bartender. After raising a middle finger to wave goodbye, she let the deputies follow her outside.

The night air was humid enough to chew on. Within five steps into the parking lot, Cora noticed two deputy's vehicles. Another pair of jocks in brown uniforms leaned against the hood of one car. It was going to be a pretty wild night, after all.

"I'd like you to place your hands against the hood of the car right here, ma'am," the big deputy came up beside her and pointed to his car.

She set her bag on the hood and leaned forward, opening her legs about shoulder-width apart. The younger deputy went to work on her, patting down her ribs, waist, and hips. The big guy pulled out a scan-gun from way-back, checking both her wrists for an IdentChip. Next, he'd have the young guy check her neck. She'd had this conversation a dozen times in the past twenty-four hours.

"Derrick, check her neck for a barcode, will you?" he said.

Cora rolled her eyes. "You won't find one. Natives don't believe in poisoning their bodies with technology and implants."

"That so?" he replied. He turned his head to Derrick. The deputy swept her long, black locks up from her shoulders and checked her neck.

The two other deputies sauntered over, presumably for moral support. They were interchangeable, the same buzzcut, same clean shaven face, same stocky frame. The only difference was their eyes, one had blue while the other had brown.

"What's the deal?" the brown-eyed deputy said, keeping his voice low.

The big guy shrugged. "No chip, no barcode. Says Injuns don't like tech."

"Injuns? Seriously? There's a few million of us spread across seven tribes," Cora huffed.

Derrick continued his work unabated, though Cora was pretty sure he'd have found something by now or he was never going to. She clicked her tongue and turned her head over her shoulder.

"Are we on a freakin' date, buddy? I've had boyfriends less handsy," she said, annoyed.

The blue-eyed deputy was the only one to smile. He nodded to his colleagues. "Feisty one."

Derrick looked to his superior and froze. With a nod from the big guy, he stepped away from Cora. The big man walked in front of Cora's view and picked up her duffle bag. He started to rifle through, but his face soured. Whatever he saw gave him pause. He set the bag back down.

"Are your papers in here, ma'am?" he asked.

"My back pocket," she replied. "Am I actually being accused of something here, guys? I mean, you know I would have shown my papers to at least five checkpoints before now, and I needed them to sign for my motel room."

The big deputy glanced over her shoulder, back at good old Derrick. He went right to task, fishing through the back pocket of her jeans to fetch a small, leatherbound book.

"I swear, Derrick, you keep this up and you'll be making me breakfast," she warned.

Derrick came around to the front of the vehicle and joined the big guy. He handed off the book, pages of lies cooked up by Gideon, too accurate a forgery to be detectable by the antiquated technology Texas agencies were still using. As it was, being techless was enough of a headache for law enforcement in the most advanced metropolitan areas, these brave souls didn't stand a chance.

You see the way they look at you.

The old voice of Sitting Bull spoke in her mind.

You know what they mean to do.

5

"Not now," Cora whispered to herself. "Be quiet."

"Come again?" the deputy said. His eyes narrowed.

Cora returned the look with a dismissive wave. "Nothing at all. I was talking to the errant spirit wandering around inside my head."

"Spirits?" the deputy responded, alarmed. He went from confused to mad like flipping a switch. The file said Texans were a superstitious group.

"Look, I'll tell you what," Cora huffed. "You want to arrest me? Let's just go. Cuff me and let's get on with it."

The big guy leaned against the hood, getting himself comfortable. He smiled for the first time, and it annoyed her more than anything. She wanted to slap the smug look right off his face.

"Why? Have you done something we should be arresting you for?" he asked.

"You don't seem like friends to Natives," Cora replied. "Isn't that good enough?"

The big guy's face turned dark, his brow digging in. "Never met an Injun that was friendly to Texans. Maybe you need to take a message back to your people about visiting here."

Whether it was the look, the drawl, or the feeling in the air, the temperature changed. Cora cocked her head and stared him right in the eye.

"You don't want to do this," she said. Plea or warning, it could have been either.

With a simple gesture of his head, the big guy directed Derrick to her back. The other deputies behind him spaced out, trying to form a half-circle around her.

Derrick grabbed her wrist. In her drunken haze, muscle memory took over. She wriggled out of his grip and switched positions, holding him by the wrist instead. Lifting his arm, she wheeled under until she was behind him. Caught off-guard by her swift movement, Derrick's momentum carried him off balance, tipping forward. With a little guidance, Cora released him into the hood. His knees caught the chrome bumper, while the top of the grill dug into his stomach, doubling him over before he slid off

6

and slammed into the ground.

"Shit," Cora sighed. She backed away from the deputies, hands raised in surrender. The spike in adrenaline made her body's regeneration eat away at the whiskey. Clarity of mind was returning to her. She pointed at Derrick's crumpled body, moaning on the ground. "I didn't mean that."

The big guy stalked toward her, pulling his baton from off his hip. "Oh, you're in for a world of hurt, girl."

There wouldn't be any negotiation for mercy. Fighting back was the worst of all choices. She still had a mission here, and killing police officers was not part of it. She turned her arms from surrender to covering her face as the trio came at her, batons raised. The first one struck at the side of her knee with enough force to make it give out. She collapsed to the other knee, using a hand to catch herself as the second hit battered down between her shoulder blades.

Between the booze and taking beatings far worse, Cora knew she could endure. Somewhere in the distance, a black raven watched on. His feelings of concern and wanting to act on her behalf filled her mind across their connection. She struggled to restrain him and herself. The next blow caught her right above her exposed eye. Hot, blood trickled down her face from her eyebrow.

"Ooh, that one cracked her open," the big guy hooted.

"C'mon, Derrick, get you some!" one of the deputies called out.

A hit came from the side, striking her ribs. Another blow smashed into her opposite hip. As Cora took one brutal strike after another, images filled her mind. If this was any other Native woman, the damage would take days to weeks to heal. The fact that they showed no signs of stopping made her sore bones scream for revenge. She held on a little longer, determined to hold back. One of these morons had to have the sense to restrain themselves short of killing her outside a bar in public. The next hit across the back of her head knocked that thought, and any desire to contain herself, right from her mind.

Dizzy and seeing spots, Cora felt the warm ball of energy centered in her gut and pulled from it. Twinkles of orange light coalesced into both hands. The beating stopped. She opened her eyes for the first time since it started. On shaky legs, she stood up, eyes fixed to the big guy. His jaw hung open at the sight of her pulling together a Stunbomb in each hand. The other deputies backed away from her, more panicked than he was.

"I think you've gone far enough," Cora said, gritting her teeth. "I'm barely holding all this energy in."

"She's an Injun witch!" a deputy shouted behind her.

Cora smiled, amused by their terror. "You need to arrest me. Now. Before this gets worse."

The big guy gathered himself, still staring in awe. His hand crept toward the service pistol at his hip.

"I wouldn't do that," Cora warned. "Hexes. Curses. You don't know what I might be capable of."

"Can't do anything if you're dead!" he shouted back, grabbing his gun.

She didn't expect him to call her bluff, but his vacant eyes didn't get that way from critical thinking. She crushed the energy balls in her hand to dust, pulling the energy back inside her. She never intended on using it, anyway. She stepped forward as he pulled out the weapon and took aim. He was slow and lumbering, and she was on him before he leveled the pistol against her. Disarming him and breaking his hand in the process would have been easy, but he had three buddies, and one of them would make her use lethal force if she didn't put an end to things with her next move. She put her left palm against the barrel of his gun. He froze. Her eyes still locked to his, she nodded.

"Pull it," Cora said, eyes fixed to his. Her tone grim and serious, she did more than dare him. She insisted he fire.

Faced with the reality of the situation, the big guy hesitated.

"Do it!" Cora yelled.

He startled and pulled the trigger. The roar of the shot deafened her. Cora reeled back, clutching her hand as she spun around and dropped to her knees. A trail of blood followed her the whole way around. Ringing in her ear made everyone sound distant.

"Oh, shit, you really shot her, Bobby!" Derrick yelled. He sounded more frightened than anything.

Cora clenched her jaw. The bar emptied out, with people piling through the door to see what was unfolding. At least now she had witnesses. Maybe one of them wouldn't tolerate the cold-blooded murder of an unarmed woman in a parking lot. Maybe the whole crowd would cheer them on. Either way, she forced herself to pivot back toward the big guy and stand up.

She held out her clutched hand, with a hole in it large enough to push her finger through. The pounding of her heart and the white-hot adrenaline surged through her, making her sweat even as she felt cold. The big guy grimaced at the aftermath of what he'd done. Cora continued to hold it out, to force him to see. He couldn't take his eyes off it. Before his eyes, the diameter of the wound shrank. His mouth fell open again. He let his weapon arm fall to his side as every muscle went slack. If he pissed himself in that moment, she wouldn't have been surprised.

The hole in her hand filled itself in. Two severed halves of her metacarpal bones knitted back together, regrew muscle in the surrounding area, and caramel skin closed over top of it. Within less than a minute, with all of the deputies and patrons watching, Cora's wound healed. She put her wrists together and held them out as an offering.

"Now, will you just arrest me? I'll go willingly."

The big guy cleared his throat, trying to find the words to say. "Derrick...Derrick, go ahead and cuff her."

Derrick approached her as if she were a snarling dog. She set her hands behind her back and let him do his thing. Cora whipped her head to the side, throwing her hair in front of her face. People were recording with their Arcadias. While it worked in her favor to keep these yahoos honest, she didn't want her face on GNN tonight. The big guy took her bag while Derrick loaded her into the back of his car. She got comfortable in the roomy backseat and waited for the big guy to get in the front.

"Get on your radio right now and wake the sheriff," Cora said.

"What? Why?" he asked.

Cora sat back in the seat and stared out the window. "I'm only going to talk to Sheriff Earp."

LOCKUP

As far as jail cells went, this one wasn't too bad. It was quaint, with a way-back charm, like something out of the 20th. Cora held an ice pack to her head. The big guy had intended it for the bruises she'd received, but those wounds healed before the deputies finished with her fingerprints. Her skin had returned to smooth caramel, free from the purple blemishes those idiots had left. The booze, expenditure of magic, and her regenerative abilities, though, packed a headache that kicked like a mule.

It took two long hours before the sheriff showed up. Beneath the brim of his cowboy hat, tired and wary eyes fixed on her before turning his head to the front desk. He fit the part of Wild West sheriff to perfection, complete with the long duster jacket and handlebar mustache. His boots made a heavy, jangling sound as he stepped forward. He whispered to his men, out of view behind the desk, gesturing his thumb at her.

Cora waited patiently for his arrival. She'd made enough ruckus for one night already, and by morning, she'd be the talk of Schulenburg. The sheriff rubbed the sleep from his eyes, shaking his head every step of the way to her closet-sized cell. He glanced to his side, grabbed a metal folding chair and held it up.

"Am I going to need this, ma'am?" he asked.

"Oh, you'll want to sit down for this, for sure," Cora replied.

She sat on her cot and pressed her back to the wall. "Unless you meant you want to hit me with it. Your boys already went into the red zone with the unnecessary force. That didn't go well for either of us."

The sheriff glanced over his shoulder, back toward the front desk. He turned back and sighed. "That's not how we do things here, ma'am."

Cora set her hands on her hips and put on a mock southern drawl. "Well, I guess folks 'round here don't take kind to Injuns."

"Alright," he said, rolling his shoulders. He unfolded the chair and sat down, close enough to the bars she could reach out and grab him. He smelled like sawdust and dad's cologne. "We can talk about that. First, why don't you tell me why you're in here?"

Her eyes went to the ceiling, trying to recount the evening's festivities. "First, I went to a place called Taphouse and drank a bottle and a half of whiskey. Then, your deputies wanted to know what I'm doing in town. So, we had an old-fashioned nightstick beating in the parking lot until it started to hurt. At that point, I started glowing, so they stopped. Then the big guy shot me in the hand, but I calmed him down enough that they stuck me in a cell instead of murdering me."

"Glowing?" he asked, shifting uncomfortably in his seat. Of all the things she said, that was what he heard. "You have magic powers?"

"You could say that," Cora replied. "Your men were not in any danger unless they tried anything above an ass-whoopin'. I can take those like no one's business."

"You know practicing magic in the Free State of Texas is forbidden?" he asked.

"Well, your boys laid into me pretty hard until I showed my powers off," Cora replied. "Probably would have killed me if I hadn't, truth be told. The big, dumb one shot me in the hand."

"Yeah, I heard some ravings about that, didn't make much sense. There's a couple problems I have with this story, ma'am. For someone beat half to death, you heal up pretty quick," the sheriff said, motioning up and down her frame. "You also seem awfully clear-headed for someone that drank two bottles of whiskey."

Cora sighed. It was a sad truth of her regenerative abilities. If they got any stronger, she doubted she'd ever again know the sweet relief of a good buzz. "The two are related. My body regenerates."

For all the news this poor, tired man was receiving at two in the morning, he kept an even composure. Leaning in, the sheriff stared at her, studying every inch of her face.

"What's your story? Are you Apache or Aztec?" he asked.

"Neither," Cora replied. "I'm Sioux."

The sheriff shook his head. "May as well be the other side of the world. You're a long way from home, ma'am."

Cora smiled and bowed her head. "You're such a southern gentleman. Call me Cora. I'll call you George, if that's alright. Or do you prefer the formality of Sheriff Earp?"

The sheriff sat up straight and crossed his arms. "Why did you ask for me to come here, by name?"

"You wouldn't give me the clearances to cross the border and you wouldn't return my calls," Cora replied. "I had to get us face-to-face somehow."

Sheriff Earp shook his head and wagged a finger at her. "You? You're that wacko that's been calling me about some damn artifact?"

"Well, yeah," Cora shrugged. "It's yours, and I want you to have it, but I have more pressing business right now."

He got up from his chair and folded it, shaking his head in disgust. "I'm very sorry you wasted your time, ma'am. Hopefully the magistrate will go easy on you come Monday. You're just going to have to spend the weekend here."

"I'm leaving in the morning," Cora replied, standing up with him. She walked to the steel bars and locked his gaze. "I was hoping to explain all this to you before I have to go."

Sheriff Earp chuckled in spite of himself. "I don't know how you propose you're walking out of here."

"Bring me my Arcadia," Cora replied, holding out an expectant hand.

The sheriff put his hands on his hips. "You know, I don't think I will."

"I wasn't talking to you," Cora said.

The squawk of a raven echoed around the building, startling the poor sheriff half to death. The black bird appeared through a wall beside him, moving through solid matter as if he were a ghost. He swooped past the front desk before flying straight to Cora. Phasing through the bars as though they weren't there, the raven dropped a silver bracelet in Cora's palm before coming to rest on her shoulder. The sheriff reeled back and grabbed for his sidearm. Cora raised her hand, warning him to stop.

"I really think that's unwise," she said, sparkling orange dust coalescing in her open hand. "I swear, I only want to talk. The truth is, I'm only in this cell because I chose to be...to meet you. If I have to fight my way out of here, I can assure you that's much easier than it was getting in."

The big deputy came around from the desk into view, armed with a shotgun. He stalked down the hall, murderous intent in his eyes. The sheriff threw up an arm without taking his eyes off Cora. The deputy stopped in his tracks.

"Sheriff?" he said.

"Nothing to worry about just yet, Bobby," George said. "I've got things under control. Isn't that right, ma'am?"

Cora nodded. "Right as rain, Sheriff Earp. I'd just like to talk to you."

The sheriff turned his head to the deputy a few paces behind him. "Bobby, why don't you go sit back down?"

The deputy cocked his head to the side, staring at the sparkling light in her hand. He massaged his shotgun. "You sure?"

"Sure," the sheriff nodded.

Once the deputy had returned to his position at the desk, Cora crushed the ball of energy in her hand. It became twinkling dust before vanishing. She went about clasping the silver bracelet over her left wrist. With a swipe at the center, a holographic screen folded out on the back of her hand. After a couple of swipes and gestures, a beam of light projected from the device, creating a screen floating in the air. A man with long silver hair and glowing orange eyes stared at Sheriff Earp from the screen.

"This is the Dragon Lucius, of Germany," Cora said.

The sheriff took his seat and cocked an eyebrow. "I'm aware."

Cora sighed. "Everyone says that. I've got to work on this intro."

The picture changed. It was outside a restaurant, surrounded by German Polizei vehicles, siren lights flashing. Cora took a breath.

"Six months ago, an NSA team investigated the dragon's activities in Berlin. Before they could get the intel out of Germany, assassins struck. To cover their tracks, every single patron in the restaurant where the team met were massacred," Cora explained.

The sheriff held up a hand. "Why would the UNS send NSA outside the country?"

"It was strictly fact-finding and reconnaissance," Cora shook her head. "Lucius was targeting museums around the world, including multiple locations in the United Northern States. We needed to know why."

"We? You survived?" George asked.

Cora clenched her jaw. "I wasn't there. I...ended up being late. Out of the five-man team, three agents were killed, as well as eighteen innocent people."

George crossed his arms and sat back. His stoic expression hadn't given an inch. "You have my attention."

"Lucius was trying to protect a data-mining facility called Project Phoenix, south of Berlin. It contained the locations of every suspected artifact in the world, and every potential person that could wield them. An artifact, as I found out the hard way, is a historical object that conveys the thoughts, memories, and experiences of its previous owner to the person it's intended for."

"So, it's magic?" George asked.

Cora moved her head back and forth. "Of a sort. It bonds the spirit to you, but it doesn't have any power beyond that. The facility that I found out about, this Project Phoenix, was a list

Lucius was mining of his enemies, the people and objects he did not want getting together. I was on the top of that list. I destroyed the facility."

"Lucky for you," George scoffed.

Cora shrugged. "I didn't know what I was seeing at the time. It probably worked out for the best, because even if we didn't have the list, Lucius didn't, either."

The projected image changed to a wide shot from a GNN helicopter. Tanks sat on a dusty road that lead up a mountain. Video began to roll, observing the UNS Army positioned in the valley of the Wyoming Mountains.

"Lucius orchestrated a ridiculous story to the Americans after I got home," Cora said. "Still River, the Sioux diplomat that was working to end the Second Civil War, was my father. Lucius tipped the UNS government off that my father was still alive after the assassination attempt back in 2072."

George stroked his handlebar mustache and nodded. "I remember seeing him on the TV. Was the story true? Was he still alive?"

"His body remained alive on machines, but his consciousness was lost forever," Cora replied, her eyes cast down. "Lucius told the UNS my father's prophetic abilities could be theirs if they captured him. In the end, Lucius abducted me and used the standoff at Heaven's Crest between the Sioux and the UNS Army to pressure me into giving over my father to him. I escaped, but he still forced the ultimatum. I pulled the plug on my father's life support, which allowed me to end the standoff."

George took a deep breath. His eyes narrowed. Whether he thought she was crazy or he realized the gravity of the situation, his facial expressions gave nothing away. Cora shook her head and swiped over the next image. This time it was blurry, dark footage of a freak lightning storm at the top of a skyscraper in Paris.

"Two months ago," Cora began with a sigh. "I met up with several other artifact holders, and we made a play against Lucius to rescue someone imprisoned in Tour Tetriarch. The official story was that a freak lightning storm knocked out part of the Paris electrical grid due to some new technology installed in the building. In truth, we battled Lucius in his dragon form on the rooftop and narrowly escaped with our lives."

The sheriff got up from his seat and paced around in front of her cell. He shrugged his shoulders. "So, to recap, you're telling me that you're an NSA secret agent?"

"Former NSA, Arcane Unit, specialized in infiltration," Cora said. "I never formally quit, but I became a traitor to the UNS over the incident at Heaven's Crest."

George took a step forward, his face inches from the bars that separated them. "You expect me to believe this? That every major global news story for the last six months is centered around you?"

Cora shrugged her shoulders. It'd sound crazy if she hadn't lived it. She understood his doubt. "Lucius and I are the focal point of what he called a 'new cold war', as both sides vie for these artifacts. There are 687 on each side. Don't ask me what significance the number has, I don't know. The only thing I can tell you is that I know you were on the list of people on my side, and we found your artifact. I'm sure you've also been hearing about the rash of museum break-ins worldwide?"

"Also you, huh?" George asked.

"Lucius' people or mine, but yeah, one of us," she replied with a shrug. "Look, I know this is a lot, but by virtue of you being on the list, I know that means that you're a good person and you will help."

"Caw," the raven said, admiring the sheriff.

Cora stroked his back with a finger. "I know, Vincent. I like him, too."

The sheriff leaned back in his chair until the front legs came off the ground. All the while, his gaze burned a hole in her, as if he were looking for some crack that would make her story fall apart. She kept her eyes on him, waiting for some sign to satisfy him. Cora knew the truth, but it was always going to be this difficult with everyone she ever met. The story was never going to sound believable to anyone, even when she left out the truly weird parts.

"Let's say I believed you, which I don't," George said, exhaling from his nose. "I'm supposing you have some proof of what you're talking about."

Cora swiped away the screen to her Arcadia and pointed down the hall behind him. "Your boys confiscated a bag. The bottle of whiskey is mine, but the artifact is yours. If what I've seen is correct, the moment you touch it, you'll absorb the memories and experience of the person who once held it. If it's intended for you, of course."

"Of course," George replied with a smirk.

"You don't have to believe me," Cora said. "It's a two century-old pistol. I don't even know if the damn thing works. If you touch it and nothing happens, then we're done here. Make sure you're sitting down when you do it. Sometimes, the experience can be...traumatic. Also, don't do it in front of your boys. I don't want them thinking I 'dun put a hex on you.' Last thing I need is for them to start shooting at me again while I'm stuck in here."

George scoffed, holding back a laugh. "You're fully in on this."

Cora sighed, hanging her head. "The truth is...I need you."

"Come again?" George said, cocking his head. The smile left his face.

"I've lost...people. A lot of people. I would have been here days ago, but I had to bury a friend," Cora said. Tears filled her eyes, unsure if she could go on.

"I'm sorry, ma'am," George replied, shuffling his feet.

She nodded in appreciation. "I understand you've worked missing persons cases before?"

His eyes narrowed. "I have."

Cora snorted and choked the emotions back. She locked eyes with the sheriff again. "I'm going to lose someone else. An artifact holder, like you, has gone missing. My entire base is filled with mostly military personnel. I need someone that knows police procedure, someone that can help me work a missing persons case."

George crossed his arms, eyes narrowed. He was sniffing for a lie again.

"Like I said, if I'm lying, you're going to figure it out pretty quick," Cora said. "Try for me...please."

He shook his head and got up, walking down the hall. Cora overheard him ask Bobby about the bag. He returned in a few moments, a red duffle bag and a ring of keys dangling from his hand. He pushed the key into the lock on Cora's cell and froze. He turned his head to the side and met Cora's gaze.

"Any tricks-"

Cora raised her hand to silence him. "I went to pretty great lengths, including taking a beating, to sit here in this jail cell and talk with you. Texans hate everybody, but especially, Texans hate Native people. No offense, but this town, this whole territory isn't worth the effort. I wouldn't have bothered if it wasn't for you."

George sighed and turned the key. "Follow me."

He led her to the front lobby, a place she only recalled in a blurry haze that was equal parts whiskey and a concussion. Bobby was the blonde-haired deputy in his mid-twenties that played leader to the welcome posse. He looked like he joined the department when he could no longer obliterate opponents on the football field. His shoulders were wide, adorned with a thick neck and a tiny head with a sloped brow. His mouth was wide open at the sight of Cora walking free behind the sheriff.

"What's going on, George?" he guffawed.

The sheriff motioned his hand to the ground, soothing the savage beast. "Easy there, Bobby. I want to interview the lady before she goes in front of the magistrate."

George walked her between the desk and the wall, to the inner sanctum, where all the justice and paperwork got done. The computers at the desks beyond the counter were decades old, obvious from the low-tech, first generation holographic displays. Cora laughed to herself, imagining Bobby getting mad at his aging computer and trying to punch a holographic screen in Neanderthal frustration.

Past the desks to the back of the room, George brought Cora to the door of his office and motioned her inside. She walked in and sat down. Reaching over her shoulder, her finger traced down

Vincent's back. He hopped down to her knee and cocked his head, signaling her to resume the affection. It distracted the sheriff as he shut the door and rifled through the duffle bag. He made his way to the seat behind his desk, but kept looking up at the bird.

"You have it trained or something? How did it get past the bars?"

"I'd explain it to you, but if you're having trouble swallowing the artifact part, we might need to break this into baby bites," Cora replied. Her eyebrows turned up. "I wish I could make this easier, I do. Trust me when I say that after this, it's only going to get weirder."

The sheriff grumbled and shook his head, pulling items out of the bag and setting them on his desk as fast as he could grab them. Her bottle of Jack thunked onto the table, followed by an ear piece, and two folded rock shirts. His head perked up, an eyebrow cocked. The corners of his lips turned down. Cora leaned forward and peered into the bag. A lacy, pink pair of panties sat atop the contents. She giggled to herself and wadded them into her hand as she sat back.

"Sorry," she snickered. "They're not even mine. If you want to make sure a man doesn't search a bag too hard, a frilly thong usually does the trick."

George continued staring at her with a skeptical eye.

"I'm serious!" she continued, even as her smile betrayed her. "You'll find a paper bag at the bottom with a pistol in there. Your boys didn't even look past the panties, I'm telling you. It's like a live grenade, no man wants to touch them. You didn't."

George set his eyes back into the bag. "Thanks for the tip."

Digging his hand to the bottom, he pulled out a brown paper bag and set it on the desk. As if it would explode, George unrolled it slow. He peered inside as he held it open with the tip of his thumb and forefinger. With a sour look on his face, he turned back to Cora and shook his head.

"I don't even know why I'm entertaining this," he said. "You're telling me this is a magic gun from two hundred years ago? That your friends stole from a museum? When I touch it, I'm going to magically have someone else's memories transferred to me? All so I can help you fight a war against a dragon?"

Cora reached forward with a closed fist and knocked on his desk. "Three seconds. That's how far away you are from finding out if I'm telling you the truth or some drunken Native Sim-head."

He rolled his eyes and reached for the weapon, his other hand pulling the bag in the opposite direction. No sooner was it free from the bag that Sheriff George Earp snapped back against his chair. His eyes slammed shut, flitting back and forth beneath his lids as if dreaming. Every muscle locked, his grip on the holstered pistol so tight his knuckles turned white. It looked uncomfortable, something Cora could relate to. Her experience was fast and overwhelming, on the steps outside the Pentagon. She remembered young Madeline's experience a few months back, screaming and crying as she relived Joan of Arc's martyrdom by fire. She held her breath and waited to see which one George's experience would be.

When it was over, his muscles relaxed. His head dropped, hiding his eyes beneath the brim of his cowboy hat. For a moment, the silence ate at her, uncertain if he'd fallen unconscious. As though emerging from water, he let out a sudden gasp, followed by a bout of heaving coughs. At first, he tried to shake it off himself, beating at his chest with a cupped hand. As the hacking continued, he got up from his chair with greater urgency. Cora got up with him, but he raised a hand to stop her from moving near. He stumbled a single step from his desk, dropped to a knee, and coughed so hard that he got sick into his trash can.

Cora stood with her hands ready to grab something - his unconscious body, a glass of water, whatever was needed. Of the few experiences she had with witnessing artifact holders receive their gifts, none of them ended the same.

With the sheriff's purge complete, a shaky, weary hand reached up and grabbed his desk. With the other, he pressed the holstered barrel of the gun to the tile floor, using both arms to get back to his feet. He stood erect and lolled backward. Again, Cora reached across the desk for him, but he shied from her touch.

"Are you okay?" she asked. "Talk to me."

"Fine," he croaked, his voice hoarse. His free hand rubbed his temple. "Maybe just get me some water."

Cora's head darted around the room, finding a water cooler in the corner. She raced over and grabbed a paper cup, filling it as she glanced over her shoulder.

"Wyatt Earp, right?" she said. She walked over and offered him the drink. "The museum claimed it was his, though there was another in a private collection that disputes it."

"No," George said, pouring the whole cup down his throat in a single gulp. He inhaled deep, letting his breath out slow and methodical. His eyes met hers. "It was John Holliday's sidearm. Must have been some confusion."

"Who?" Cora stared at him, puzzled. It wasn't Wyatt Earp's gun, but it was an artifact all the same, belonging to an ancestor of Earp.

"You came all this way to give me this, ma'am, and you don't know anything about Wyatt Earp? 'Doc' Holliday? The Gunfight at the OK Corral?" George asked, incredulous.

"I'm a little fuzzy on the details," Cora admitted with a shrug. "But you can tell me the whole story from experience now, can't you?"

Hands still trembling, George sat back down. He sighed and met her gaze. "I know how to perform 19th century dentistry. What the hell am I going to do with that?" He tipped his chair back and stared at the ceiling. "I never married. No children. I just assumed the family line died with me. Died with a puff of smoke while I took a quiet job in a quiet town."

Cora leaned over his desk and smiled. "Not you. I need you to come with me. You're going to be a legend again."

A WORLD AWAY

Cora unscrewed the cap of her whiskey bottle. As she glanced up, George extended his arm to her, holding out his paper cup. She was more than happy to oblige. She didn't have a proper drinking buddy in a long time.

"I know," she said, getting nostalgic about her own innocence lost only a few months back. "It's a lot to take in."

He replied with a bitter laugh. "Yeah, you could say that. It's like having someone else taking up rent inside my head. Memories rolling around that aren't mine, getting crossed with ones that are."

Cora took a long swig from the bottle and nodded her understanding. "I promise you, that goes away. You learn to compartmentalize, to put that person to the side. Think of them as a confidant or an advisor, someone you can call upon the wisdom and experience of as you need it."

"You have one of these?" George asked, holding up the holstered pistol.

With a turn of her head, Vincent took off from her shoulder and flew to perch on an old-time filing cabinet. She moved her straight black hair off her left shoulder, sifting through the strands until she exposed a leather braid in her hair. It was adorned with beads and two feathers, dyed blue and yellow. The colors were less than vibrant, speaking to its age.

"You might laugh," she warned with a dark smile. History and fate had played such games with her before, rarely to comedic effect. "I carry the memories of Sitting Bull. You could say we're literally playing Cowboys and Indians right now."

George laughed and shook his head. He let a moment pass in silence, a pregnant pause before the elephant in the room tumbled from his lips. "What happens now?"

"Like I said, I need you," Cora replied. "I don't know how much time I have to find this artifact holder. He might already be dead."

"Then there's a war against Lucius?" George said with a smirk. "I can't believe I'm saying this."

Cora pointed at him with the bottle. "I'd like you to see where we are and what we're doing. I know leaving your life here behind might not seem like a great plan, but I can't understate that the fate of the world hangs on this. This entire Awakening might be about this war. Do you have family here?"

The sheriff shook his head and held out his paper cup for a refill. Perhaps it was the vulnerability created by his exposure to the artifact, but his face had become easier for Cora to read. He gave off a lonely cowboy vibe, a mixture of bittersweet satisfaction for delivering law and the sadness of having no one to share it with. Cora filled his cup and watched his expressions close.

"Why Texas?" she asked. "I mean, I know you were probably born here, but it seems like it's just a matter of time before the President has to admit this was a failed experiment and joins the Southern Confederacy. What's kept you on this sinking ship?"

George took a sip from his cup and blew out a long breath. "It's hard to explain if you're not from Texas. We're fiercely independent, you know? And we had the oil, so we figured we'd have trade for decades. Then China started mass producing power cells. By the time we realized oil was a dead market, the sharks were already circling. Aztecs in the south, Apache in the North. I couldn't just leave my people stranded, you know?"

Cora nodded. She'd heard all she needed to hear. "That's a lot to strap on your back. You're a pretty noble man. That's why I want you to come with me. All of us are there, protecting what we care about and who we love. I don't know what form this war will take, but it's already shown me some pretty ugly faces. Like I said, I've lost a lot of people."

George's eyes narrowed, as if he were trying to read her. "Was it a boyfriend?"

Cora shivered, dredging up the fresh wound. "No. A mentor. He...died in my arms a few nights ago."

"I'm very sorry," George shook his head. "I shouldn't have asked."

"It's okay," Cora said, grabbing a quick sip from the bottle. "He was old, to say the least. It was his time."

"Alright," George said. He pounded the last sip of whiskey from his paper cup and crumpled it in his hand before tossing it in the trash. He sat back in his chair, tipping until his shoulders touched the wall behind him. "Hit me. All of it. What am I getting into if I say yes?"

Her Arcadia buzzed. She tried to ignore it, to open her mouth to speak, but it buzzed again. This time, the large, flat face of the bracelet glowed red. Cora cocked an eyebrow. That was an emergency call. She held up a finger to George.

"One second, I'm so sorry," she said, rifling through her belongings on the desk. She found the earpiece and put it in. "I have to take this."

With the tap of a button on the side of her earpiece, the phone call connected.

"Oh, thank God I got a hold of you," Gideon said. The tinny, robotic voice wasn't coming from the hacker's vocal cords. Instead, it was an approximation of his voice created by a computer whenever his brain was wired into NeuralNet. Most people wouldn't notice the difference, but Cora was both sensitive and averse to technology. She would have ditched the earpiece and Arcadia in a heartbeat if it wasn't for the fact every human on Earth couldn't live without them.

"I'm kinda in the middle of a mission here," she said.

25

"I know," Gideon replied. "We have another missing person. That makes three."

The air pulled from Cora's chest. Her eyes involuntarily filled with tears. It took her a moment to catch her breath. She snorted, grabbing hold of her emotions by the throat. "Have Tesla prepare for transport immediately. Go on my signal."

"Affirmative," Gideon replied before closing the line.

Cora brushed a tear away with her forearm. She grabbed the shirts and shoved them back into the duffel bag. Her head spun as she tried to juggle the mission with her personal feelings.

"I wanted to have a long conversation with you, George. Ease you into this slow and steady. My clock just ran out. I have to get back to my base. It's far away and you'd be gone for a while. I need to know right now if you're willing to come," she said. She took a deep breath and shut her eyes. "I could come back for you if you need more time. I'd understand."

George stood up. "Looks like you got some bad news. I'm sorry for that, but you have to know I can't just let you walk out of here."

Cora pulled a huge sip off the bottle before capping it and stuffing it in the bag. "In about thirty seconds, you're not going to have a choice. I'm gone. I told you that. The only question is whether you're coming with me."

His brows cast down, stern and serious. He stepped around the table and entered her personal space. Eye to eye, ancient pistol in hand, Cora could only pray he wouldn't do something dumb. She didn't need this with her emotions so close to the surface.

"How are you planning on leaving?" he demanded.

Cora held his gaze. "Teleportation."

"Where are you going?"

"Atlantis, a repurposed military base at the bottom of the Atlantic Ocean," Cora replied. She tightened her jaw. "It's commanded by Julian Penel, who is wielding King Arthur's Excalibur. I have to get back because I just found we're now looking at a third missing person, including my artifact holder. You coming?"

George's stare lasted a moment longer before he turned for the door. "Goddammit," he said. As he walked away from Cora, he fiddled with something on his chest, out of her view. He opened the door.

"Bobby!" he shouted.

Holding his palm at waist level, a golden star badge rested in his hand. With an underhand toss, he threw it out the door. "I'm going to need you to take charge for a time, son. I don't know how long."

"Sheriff?" Bobby's voice called from the lobby. Distant as it was, Cora could still hear the confusion in his inflection.

"You heard me, boy," he raised his voice. Turning his head to Cora, he asked, "Do we need to go outside?"

Cora shook her head. "They're already tracking me. On my word, they can take me from anywhere."

George turned his attention back to the lobby. "Give it about five minutes and this office is yours. Take good care of her."

The deputy's protests muffled as the sheriff shut the door. He took a step towards Cora and sighed. "Let's go."

"Vincent," Cora called out. The raven swooped across the room and landed on her shoulder.

Grabbing hold of the strap for her bag, she slung it over her opposite shoulder and held George's free hand. He'd not relinquished his new artifact for a second since receiving it. Cora tapped the comm button on her ear.

"Echo-1, two to transport," she said.

A flash of white light and the most unsettling vertigo Cora had ever known marked the split-second teleport. She kept her eyes shut until the feeling passed. Judging by the sound beside her, George had not been so lucky. He wretched on the floor of the transport platform. As her eyes opened, she found the sheriff taking a knee next to her.

The laboratory was an open space with massive wires that crossed the floor. They led from the pad she was standing on to a computer console on the far end of the room. Behind the desk, an old man with wild white hair pounded his fist against the computer. The holographic screen projected in front of his face warped and flickered. Against the back wall, a young woman tended to a large metal box with black smoke pouring from it.

"Caw," Vincent said, flying to the pipes at the ceiling of the room. He hated being in Atlantis.

"Transport complete," the young girl said with her heavy French accent. She glanced at an illuminated panel on the smoking box. "Overload at 16 milliseconds and coil is on fire."

The old man pounded an angry fist on his computer one last time. Talking over his shoulder, he said in a thick Russian accent, "I replace coil, it explode. Nothing work right, and now American cowboy throw up on FUCKING MACHINE!"

George stood erect and faced the old man. He tipped the brim of his hat. "I do apologize, sir. I'm afraid my stomach wasn't ready for that. I'd be happy to fix the mess if you can point me in the direction of the cleaning supplies."

Cora stepped off the pad and walked toward the computer desk. "That won't be necessary. We'll get a janitor in here. Sheriff Earp, this is Doctor Vadim Tesla and Madeline Berger. Our doctor here built this technology with the help of the spirit in his artifact."

Tesla grumbled under his breath. "Useless idiot not much help at all. Coil still burn out."

The sheriff stepped off the platform and walked on shaky legs around the mass of cables that crisscrossed the room. Gym mats were affixed to the floor in spots, creating humped bridges over the high-traffic areas. George extended a hand to Tesla. At first, the old man stared at it as if he were trying to figure out what it was for. It took him a moment to realize the courtesy and shook his hand. George reached to do the same with Madeline, but she was preoccupied with the directions on the fire extinguisher.

Cora motioned to the girl. "Madeline is Tesla's assistant, holder of Joan of Arc's artifact, and a ninja. Isn't that neat?"

"A ninja?" George's brow furrowed.

"I'm not a damned ninja, mon ami," Madeline huffed, putting on a glove like an oven mitt. "My combat training is Elven, not

Japanese."

"Well, either way, she has enough tech in her to power a third-world village," Cora replied. "We'll get out of your way, though. Looks like we're still working out the kinks of the teleporter."

"It's matter-energy conversion transport!" Tesla yelled as she escorted George out of the room. Cora couldn't be bothered with the semantics. It may as well have been magic for all she understood about it.

As she took George down the metal, sickly-green colored corridors of the base, the smell of recycled air and chemicals filled her nose. The low buzz of electricity all around her had to be tuned out. She tried to focus on playing tour guide.

"Atlantis was originally intended to be a long-term undersea research facility. Now it's run run by former British Army Staff Sergeant Julian Penel. As our fearless leader explained it, the project ran into financial difficulties in the late 2050's. The Penel family, and their vast wealth, stepped in to repurpose the lab in secret," Cora explained. "With teleportation and submarine the only way in or out of the base, only a select few even know where it's located."

"You're in that much danger?" George asked.

"It's a necessary precaution to keep Lucius in the dark about where his enemies are hiding," Cora replied.

The corridor from the lab to the living quarters section of the station was a quarter mile long. Cora weaved around former British Royal Army officers that had turned rogue and joined Julian's cause. Redubbed as knights, the word meant less than the connotation. As far as Cora was concerned, a knight was a British soldier, an American jarhead, it was all the same to her. They all wore their hair buzzed close to the skin and walked with the same rigid posture they were taught in basic training.

A quick turn around a corner, and Cora made it to the computer room. At the front of the room, the tall and lanky Gideon appeared to be asleep in a reclined leather chair in the corner. A long wire wound up the side of the chair to a port behind his ear, letting her know his consciousness was still in

NeuralNet.

"Good...morning, is it?" Cora said, her face crumpled as she tried to do the math.

"Good morning, Cora," Gideon replied, his robotic voice projecting from the speakers in four corners of the room. Above him, six large-panel holovid projectors came to life, flickering on to a flat white screen. "I see you've brought our guest."

George looked around the room, as if he were unsure where his greeting should go. "Pleasure to meet you, wherever you are."

"At the moment, I'm a little bit of everywhere," Gideon said. "Cora, I'm still gathering information as it's coming in. How would you like to proceed?"

Cora walked to a nearby desk and offered George a seat. She sat beside him and kicked her legs up. She really needed sleep, but that would have to wait.

"You stay on task," Cora replied. "Bring up the interview recording and I'll get him up to speed. Oh, and while I remember - I had a little-run in with some locals in Texas. Some of them may have recorded me regenerating."

"I'll track it down and erase all videos," Gideon replied. "I have the interview queued up if you're ready."

George took off his cowboy hat and duster before sitting down. His thick, dark hair appeared almost black in the dim light of the room. He turned to Cora and nodded.

"Straight to work?" he asked.

Cora pursed her lips. "I don't know how much time we have...or if we even have any at all. I know you're tired, I'm sorry."

George held up a hand. "No apologies, ma'am. Show me where we're at."

The holovid screen came to life with a three-dimensional image of a room, not unlike the computer room, but with a long conference table. Cora sat in a black dress, beside Julian at the head of the table, flanked by others on both sides. Gideon was at the front of the room, lively outside NeuralNet and setting up various computer rigs. He stared directly at the camera.

"Alright," Cora said. She pointed to the screen. "Beside me is Julian, I mentioned him earlier. To my left, the guy in the suit with the shades is Johnny Clean. The beautiful Italian woman you couldn't have missed is Giovanna, and you already met Madeline and Tesla. Beside Julian is Michael, his right-hand man. Up front, that's Gideon and beside him is Professor Crowley. We comprise the senior staff on Atlantis. Almost every one of us is an artifact holder."

"I see," George said. He pointed to the center of the screen. A slight man with a clean-shaven face and glasses sat at the foot of the table. "Who's the little fella?"

"That's our missing man. Professor Leopold Collins," Cora replied. She crossed her arms, face dour. "We were having a funeral at sea. That's why I'm in the black dress. While we were up there, we found a small, two-person motorboat adrift. The Professor was the only passenger. He'd been plagued by dreams of the spirit in his artifact."

"He dreamed of it, without ever seeing it before?" George turned in his seat, surprised.

Cora nodded. "For some, like Madeline, their artifact appears to have a drawing power, in the form of prophetic dreams, telling them to seek it out. Only Leopold had no idea what he was looking for, or where."

George's brow furrowed. "How did he end up here?"

"He followed the feeling, or whatever instinct drew him here," Cora shrugged. "He described it like an obsession. When we found him, he was badly dehydrated. His water had run out. He wouldn't have survived another day out there."

"Right," George nodded, his brow still wrinkled. "But you said he followed the feeling, and this base is in the middle of the ocean. So again, why was he up there, adrift?"

"We had his artifact," Cora replied. "There's a vault on the base where we keep any objects we've taken, whether we know who they belong to or not."

"Who was the original owner of the artifact?" George asked. He was already in sheriff mode.

31

"The video will fill in a lot of those gaps for you," Cora said.

George sat back in his chair and stared ahead at the screen. "This video is..."

"Our attempt at interviewing him, to see if we wanted to give him his artifact," Cora replied. "First we argued among ourselves, then we brought him in."

"Alright," George said. "When was this video taken?"

"This was taken seven days ago," Cora replied. To the ceiling, she said, "Gideon, begin playback."

VETTING PROCESS

The screen started to move. The camera focused on a man in his mid-forties, with glasses and dark hair. He wore a plaid shirt and dress pants, an outfit no doubt as boring as whatever subject he taught.

"Please state your full name for me," Gideon said. He motioned to the numerous electronic devices behind him. "It helps calibrate a baseline."

Leopold sat up and cleared his throat. His voice came with a meek Irish accent. "Ah, yes, of course. Leopold Devin Collins."

"Where do you currently teach?" Gideon asked.

"Queen Mary University."

"Do you currently live at 11A Lindley Street in London?" Gideon asked, staring into his holographic computer screen.

"I do, yes," he replied.

"Are you now, or have you ever been, King of England?"

Leopold flinched, an uncomfortable smile on his face. "What? No?"

Gideon turned around to Cora and Julian and gave a thumbs up. "We're good to go. Try to keep it to one person asking questions for a bit."

Cora looked around the table, but all eyes were already staring back at her. Even Professor Crowley in the corner by the door fixed his gaze on her. He stroked his thick salt-and-pepper beard and folded his hands in front of his face.

"Alright," she said with a sigh. She looked at Leopold. "We're going to have a conversation, Leopold. What brought you here today is, well, a strange set of circumstances. We want to be certain we can trust you before we address the solution to these dreams you've been having."

Leopold returned the statement with a somber nod. "I want them to stop. That's all I want."

"I know," Cora said. She paused to collect herself. "Some of these questions may be personal. Please don't take offense, just be as truthful as you can. Let's start with a few easy questions. I noticed you wear glasses. Why?"

He shrugged and hung his head. "The same reason I never went to med school. I have an...issue with blood. Wounds. It's pretty bad. If I cut myself, I have to run and get a Stitch-Patch and look away, or I'll faint."

"Well, don't be ashamed," she replied. "I'm Native. Almost every one of us can't even think about any kind of implant without it conjuring up these horrible visions of being operated on."

Leopold's head perked up. He adjusted his glasses and leaned forward, resting his arms on the table. "Really? That's fascinating. I never heard of that. Is it a cultural thing? You're all like that?"

"Mmm-hmm," Cora replied with a smile. "The majority of us are like that, yes. As for why, I'm no scientist, but about one in four Natives has innate magical ability. The rest of us are magic-sensitive. The way my uncle explained it to me, our magic comes from the energy in our soul. When you put machines in your body, it's like putting a hole in the side of a paper cup. A part of your soul leaks out, and can't ever be filled again."

"I wasn't aware the soul was something tangible or finite," he replied. His brow raised. "I guess I have a leak, with my IdentChip, then. You don't even have one of those?"

She shook her head. "No, I wouldn't even let my mother get me a barcode tattoo."

Cora's eyes shifted to Gideon for a moment. He looked up from the readings and nodded his approval.

"Well," Leopold started, taking a deep breath. "Your people's beliefs are on the paranormal end, for sure. The question of biology for the last twenty years has been how to explain or understand the natural order of things with so much that science can't explain since The Awakening."

"You really have a love for science," Cora replied. "What made you go into teaching? You seem a little nervous around people."

Leopold avoided her gaze. "I don't mean any offense, but I don't know who any of you are, what this place even is, or why I'm being asked all these questions. You'll have to forgive me if I'm uncomfortable."

"I completely understand," Cora replied with a gentle smile. She stood up from her chair and walked around the room, resting her bottom on the table beside him. "I'm going to tell you what all this is about, and then I'm either going to let you leave, or ask you to join us."

"Join you? This looks like a military operation," Leopold looked up at her, his face a mask of confusion.

"In part, it is," Cora replied. She motioned around the room as she spoke. "As I mentioned already, I'm Cora Blake, former NSA operative, Arcane Unit. Over there, we have Julian and Michael, both former British Royal Army. Giovanna over here was an NSA liaison from Italy, and Johnny is a former CIA boogeyman. But, Doctor Tesla and Madeline aren't military...although Madeline was trained in martial arts by elves, so that's almost the same thing. Gideon is a hacker, with no affiliation to any government."

"Wanted by a few of them, actually," Gideon added with a titter.

"Ugh, you're not helping," Cora replied. She pointed to Crowley. "The Professor here, he's not military at all."

Crowley bowed his head to Leopold. He reached forward to offer his hand. "Good day, Mr. Collins. The name-"

"Robert Crowley," Leopold interrupted, shaking his hand. "I thought it was you. You used to teach at UCL in the 60's."

"Guilty as charged, lad," Crowley replied with a smile. "Have we met?"

"I visited a friend that went to UCL pretty often around that time," Leopold replied. His face soured with the memory. "I remember catching one of your lectures while waiting for her. I'd never seen a psychology class so...animated before."

A smile of perfect teeth lit up from beneath Crowley's beard. "Motion creates emotion. That's why I try to never sit down. Passion is meant for lovers and teachers."

Leopold folded his hands in his lap. "Well, I...I could never teach like that."

Crowley crossed one leg over his other. "And why do you suppose that is?"

"I'm a very private person. I mean, there's a woman," Leopold started. He shook his head. "She's a colleague. We have a date-night every week. It's never been romantic. Not even once."

"You wish it were, though?" Crowley nudged.

Leopold clicked his tongue. "Yes...I can't believe I'm telling you that."

"He has that way with everybody," Cora replied, giving a weak smile to Crowley. He bowed his head in response. "For what it's worth, if you want a girl's perspective, she feels the same."

"She does?" Leopold gasped.

Cora shrugged. "Of course she does. If you're her weekly date night, and she isn't seeing someone else, that's because she's waiting for you to tell her how you feel. You need to watch some romance holovids or something, buddy. Ease up on the documentaries."

Leopold raised a finger and wagged it. His brow furrowed. "See, now that...that was what I worried about. How much do you people know about me?"

"Everything," Gideon replied dryly. "As much as your digital fingerprint can tell."

"I think I deserve an explanation at this point," he replied, holding up his arms. He fixed his eyes on Cora. "I've been a good sport, but you went around this room and said 'former' to every military agency I can think of off the top of my head. Who are you people? Some kind of secret society?"

"Hardly. Maybe. Sort of," Cora huffed and hesitated. She looked at Gideon and nodded. A projection of Lucius appeared on the far wall.

"This is the dragon, Lucius," she started.

"I'm aware," Leopold replied.

"Alright, Mister Smarty-Pants," Cora said. "Look, Lucius and I are wrapped up in a cold war against each other. There are 687 souls on either side that will join us. For those people, there is an artifact out there with their name on it. These artifacts carry...an echo of the soul that once held it. Lucius wants to get his people together with their artifacts, and he wants to keep me from getting mine. Are you with me so far?"

"What do the artifacts have to do with the people that use them?" Leopold asked.

"We...don't understand that, yet," she replied. "Right now, Lucius knows more about this war than we do. All I know for certain is anyone in possession of an artifact is either with us...or him."

"What does this 'echo' do once the person has their artifact?" Leopold asked.

Cora swept her hair to the side, exposing her braided feathers. "Their soul joins with us, for lack of a better term. We pick up their experiences, their memories, even a portion of their voice in our head."

"That sounds terrifying," Leopold replied, his mouth agape.

Cora rested her hand on his. "It's not painful, though it can sometimes be...overwhelming," she paused and sighed. "I want to be honest with you. Lucius has marked us, imprisoning or killing anyone he can identify as a threat. We can protect you."

Leopold stared at the ceiling, as if looking for something. "You mean by hiding. I was adrift in the ocean. Unless I somehow ended up crashing into a secret island, this is one of those deep-sea research facilities they were building in the 40's, right?"

"Correct," Cora bowed her head. "No matter what your strength is, or who is in your artifact, we can help you develop those talents. You need a lab? We can build you a lab. We need all the help we can get."

He shifted in his seat and met Cora's gaze. "I want to know what has been calling to me all this time."

Cora glanced at Gideon. The hacker shrugged.

"He's been completely honest with us, as far as I can tell," Gideon said.

She stood up and faced Julian. "I'd like to bring him to the vault."

"Out of the question," Julian replied in his aristocratic British accent, so offended by the notion he stood from his chair. "Mr. Collins, I can see you are gentleman, so please take no offense," he turned his attention back to Cora. "I barely trusted you enough to show you the vault until Merlin twisted my arm."

Cora rolled her eyes. "We're really going to have this out right here? Like Mom and Dad arguing in front of the kids at the dinner table?"

"If I may?" Gideon raised a hand. "There's another solution."

Julian crossed his arms and lorded over the head of the table with rigid military posture. "I'm listening."

Gideon's finger tapped away against the desk, typing into a holographic keyboard projected there. Staring at his screen, he said, "Of the artifacts we currently have in possession, only six are not cross-referenced to the Project Phoenix database. Instead of bringing him to the vault, why don't we just bring those six objects here?"

Cora raised an eyebrow and checked Julian's reaction. He nodded.

"Seems a fair compromise," Julian said. "Michael, head for the vault. Gideon, send that list to his Arcadia."

"On it."

Michael got up and left with haste. The tension of the room relaxed, as if someone rang the lunch bell. Johnny and Giovanna got up from their chairs and circled the table to Cora. Johnny stopped by Leopold and offered a handshake.

"Nice meeting you Mr. Collins," he said. He turned his attention to Cora. "This room is a little full, we're going to duck out."

Cora nodded. She looked at Giovanna, then down at herself. "I'll be by in a little bit to return the dress."

"Take your time, patatina," Giovanna replied with a sultry, evil smile. "Maybe it will convey some good fashion sense through osmosis."

Leopold chuckled nervously. Cora laughed and shook her head. She pointed over her shoulder as the pair left the room. "You see what I have to deal with?"

"You do seem like a family," Leopold replied. His smile faded.

Their exit prompted Tesla and Madeline to follow suit. Tesla stood up and cleared his throat. "I have time-sensitive experiment I must return to."

"Of course," Cora smirked. She turned around. Professor Crowley sat in his chair beside the doorway, stroking his beard. "Would you like to leave, as well, Professor?"

"I'd quite like to stay, if that's alright," he said. "I think it will be fascinating to watch the ritual unfold, as it were. The transference of spirit from artifact to the mind. Our friend may even benefit from some counseling afterwards, to help him adjust."

"You're not turning him into one of your *students*," Julian said with a curt tone.

"Does my counsel and camaraderie with your men intimidate you, Sergeant?" Crowley asked, his voice calm and measured. "I would hate for you to have a wrong impression of me. I only offer the men wisdom in these dark times."

"That's a discussion for another time," Julian replied.

"We are a family. Just your typical dysfunctional family, as you can see," Cora commented, meeting eyes with Leopold. "Seriously, though, you are welcome to stay here and learn what we're doing. We want you to be a part of this. I'm not kidding when I say the fate of the world rests on this war. All of us feel the calling to act."

"Did that feeling," Leopold started, his voice cracking. He cleared his throat. "Did it come from getting the artifact? A calling, like the one I'm having to find this spirit from my dreams?"

Cora went to the side of the table next to Crowley and fetched a cup of water from the dispenser. She handed it to Leopold.

"No," Cora sighed, reflecting on the question. "I don't think it did. Maybe it's the fighter in me, but I see there's work to be done here. I see a group of people working to protect what they love, and I want to help."

Leopold sipped his water and nodded understanding. His head turned as Michael walked into the room, two knights in tow. They all carried black plastic containers which they set on the table. Michael went about opening each of them and gently removing their contents. The first was an African mask, brightly colored and fashioned from wood. The next, a bust in stone. It appeared yellowed from age, but depicted a man with a short haircut and determined expression. A knight came forward and removed an ornate dagger from his container, jeweled in the pommel and along its metal sheath. The whole of it appeared to be crafted from gold. After that, he placed an old leather medical bag on the desk. As the second knight reached into his container, Leopold stood up.

"It's that one," he said, pointing to the leather bag.

Cora looked at the bag. It's appearance was almost modern, with machine-shaped leather, made rigid with heat in the manufacturing process. Compared to the ancient and priceless treasures on the table, Leopold pointed to the most humble.

"Interesting," Julian said, stroking his chin. "That's the other artifact we got out of Buckingham Palace."

"You're certain?" Cora checked with Leopold.

"I feel...like I know it like my own family," he replied. His eyes glanced up at her for a brief moment, desperate and confused. "That doesn't even make any sense."

Gideon chimed in, "That would be consistent with some of the angles of attack Lucius was going with to find these artifact holders. He was tracing genealogy and lineage. Apparently, these artifacts often hold some ancient tie to their bloodline."

"You mean, I may be related to the person that once held this?" Leopold awed at the bag.

"It's possible," Gideon replied. "Though Julian, Michael, and Tesla are the only artifact holders we know of that claim a bloodline attachment to their artifact."

As if in a trance, Leopold's hand reached for the bag. Cora pressed her hand to his shoulder, stopping him.

"I should warn you," she said. "The result is almost immediate. You touch that with your bare hands, you will absorb the spirit."

Leopold turned to her, his eyes desperate. "I have to know."

Cora nodded and released him. She took a position to the side of him, prepared to catch him if he fell. All eyes in the room fixed to him to watch the event take place. Even Julian's knights were frozen in suspense. Leopold reached out with a trembling hand and set his palm on the leather handles at the top of the bag.

For a second, there was nothing. Then, his back arched. Eyes rolled to the back of his head, his muscles locked in place. His eyes slammed shut, flitting back and forth under his lids as though dreaming. As fast as it began, it ended with a gasp. Leopold opened his eyes, stepped back, and slumped back into his chair. He stared at the ceiling without a word.

"Are you alright?" Cora asked.

He nodded and reached for his cup. "I could use some more water, if it's not a bother."

"Of course."

Crowley jumped on him like wounded prey. "What are you feeling right now, in this moment?"

"It's hard to put to words," Leopold replied, his voice cracking. He shook his head. "Indifference? After all this waiting, this time, these dreams - I don't understand what the fuss was about."

"What?" Cora did a double-take, spilling water from the dispenser on the floor. "Who was he? Or is it a she?"

"It's a he," Leopold replied. "His name was Bernard Lincoln.

He was a doctor, born in 1851. Though, now that I know this...I'm sorry, Cora. I can't imagine how I'd be of any help to you."

Cora handed the glass to him, along with a perplexed look. "What do you mean? Of course you can help. You're one of us."

Leopold shrugged. "I'm truly sorry, but that's not the case. His knowledge of medicine is not only barbaric and outdated, but the very memories of it makes me nauseous if I dwell on it. The blood, the amputations...the gore of these memories is too much."

Crowley leaned forward from his seat. "Leopold? Are you feeling traumatized by these events? The numb feeling of indifference may be shock from facing so many grotesque images of your fears, lad."

"It isn't that," he replied. "I'm not numb. He was used to it, and I'm terrified by it. Right now, we're meeting in the middle. All I know is that he has nothing to offer that I would want, and you have no use for a biology teacher. I don't feel anything like what you described, Cora."

"Well, maybe if we gave you some time to process-"

"That isn't what I want, Cora," Leopold said, firm and stern.

Cora's eyes narrowed. "What are you trying to say, Leopold?"

"I'm saying that if it's all the same to you, I'd like to return to my life now."

COURSE OF ACTION

The recording stopped. Cora stood up and let out a deep breath. George turned to her, a confused expression on his face.

"Wait, that's it? He risked his life to get his artifact and then left?"

Cora let her arms fall limp at her sides. "That's it. I tried to convince him otherwise, but within ten minutes of this video ending, we put him on the transport and sent him back to London. I had to twist his arm just to take his artifact with him. He didn't even want it."

George crossed his arms and tipped his chair back, until the front legs came off the ground. "Have you ever seen something like that?"

Cora leaned her bottom against the computer desk. "Truth be told, you're the first person we planned on delivering an artifact to, and bringing into our fold. Professor Crowley had performed a psych evaluation based on what limited information we could find about you. Leopold was an anomaly, a chance encounter."

"And he's our missing man?" George asked, pointing at the screen.

Cora propped herself up and walked around the computer desk. Moving to the front of the room, she stood beside Gideon's unconscious body in the chair. She brought up her Arcadia screen and swiped it to one of the large monitors. The interior of a living room appeared. The layout and furniture looked like it was lifted from a stock photo. Every piece of furniture, from the couch to the coffee table, matched the decor of the room and the gray paint on the walls. At the center of the room, a lamp lay broken on the hardwood floor, the only disruption in an otherwise spotless area.

"This is Leopold's flat," Cora said. "I went to check on him three days ago. Instead, I found his lady friend from the college banging on his door. She said he missed their date night and knew something was wrong. I went in, and the place was empty."

George stood up and walked closer, examining the photo.

"I took these with my Arcadia," Cora said. "It's low-resolution 3D, best I could do."

George pointed to the lamp. "Signs of a struggle?"

"Yes," Cora nodded. Her head dropped. She swiped to the next image, her heart heavy. The picture on the screen changed to a closeup of the hardwood floor. At the center, a small, shining disc rested in a pool of dried, brown blood. "In the next room, I found this under the dining room table. Leopold's IdentChip had been cut out of his wrist."

George grumbled, the breath from his flared nostrils wiggled the hairs of his handlebar mustache. "Anything else missing? Money? Clothes?"

Cora shook her head. The memories still fresh in her mind tortured her. "No. His luggage was in the upstairs closet, no missing clothes. Gideon checked his accounts. No charges, no strange activity, and nothing at all since he went missing."

"And his artifact?"

"I never found it," Cora replied. "There are other elements that do lead me to think the disappearance isn't random."

"You mean in the two other missing persons?" George asked.

Cora nodded. "I only knew of one, so this is where Gideon comes in. I'll be getting this information for the first time, same as you."

Silence filled the room. George looked up to the ceiling, waiting for the disembodied voice to start speaking. Cora rolled her eyes.

"Gideon?"

"Yes, sorry," he replied. "I'm juggling a lot of balls at the moment, between these three cases and the trident."

George's brow furrowed as he looked to Cora for an answer. "Trident?"

Cora waved her hand dismissively. She did not want to get into that conversation and confuse him. "It's a separate matter. Another artifact we're looking for." She craned her neck back to the ceiling, even as she was aware Gideon was right next to her. "Alright, let's get into it. Bring us up to speed on the other two."

"Eyes forward to the monitors," Gideon replied. "What I have isn't much, but I'm going to cover it fast so we can move on the intel."

On the central monitors, two houses appeared in satellite view. Alongside them, a photo and biography listed for the residents, the top one a strawberry blonde with an easy smile. The bottom was an elven woman with lavender hair, her pointed ears peeking from her flowing locks. Her bright smile and sultry makeup made her exceed the already high standards of beauty for elves.

"The first woman is Olivia Orwell, of Newark Street, reported missing Tuesday when she didn't show up for work," Gideon said. "Now, comparing what little information we have on the two cases, there were no serology tests ordered at the first site."

Cora cleared her throat to stop him. "Serology?"

"Bodily fluids," George said, looking over his shoulder. "Blood, saliva...and otherwise."

"Got it," Cora shuddered.

"Right," Gideon continued. "This may mean this case isn't related at all. Blood was found at the second location and Cora found blood at Leopold's house. However, there are some similarities that also give me pause."

The lower screen grew larger to encompass both screens. "This new situation sticks out like a sore thumb. Elea Nguyen of Ashfield Street, about two blocks south of Leopold's house. She was reported missing Thursday, at least a day after we think

Leopold was taken."

George raised an eyebrow. "Don't see many elves in London?"

Cora shook her head. "They're a small percentage of the British population. Almost no one there converted to elf during The Awakening."

"Well, you're right on that one," Gideon replied. "She's in London on a work visa. She's studying cosmetology at one of the more chic boutiques in the city."

The screen cleared and was replaced by two ledgers, side by side. Gideon said, "Now, this is where things get real interesting. I flagged something odd with the Orwell woman when this first happened. Her bank account had a number of recent deposits that far exceed the pay rate for her job. When I checked it against our latest missing person, turns out Miss Nguyen has those same deposits, too."

George shuffled his feet and crossed his arms. "Did Leopold also have these deposits?"

"No," Gideon replied. "However, Miss Nguyen did have serology tests ordered, which means there was a struggle and some blood, like in the case of Leopold."

George turned to Cora. "Have you reported Leopold's disappearance to London police?"

"Not a chance," Cora replied, shaking her head. "I swore to Andrea I'd find Leopold."

"Andrea?" George's eyes narrowed.

"His love interest," Cora replied. "The woman that was looking for him when I got there. I convinced her not to call the police, to let me handle it. He's one of us, and if I put him in any danger by letting him leave, I'm damn sure going to get him back."

George shook his head. "The police could have combed the place with forensic tech. They may not even know they're looking at a pattern yet without this missing piece of the puzzle."

"There's a lot they wouldn't know," Gideon replied over the speakers. "We can't exactly explain Project Phoenix or the artifacts to them."

Cora exchanged a puzzled look with George before turning her head to the ceiling. "Gideon? Why would Project Phoenix even enter into this?"

"I'm still working on that," he replied. "The financial transfers for both women came from NextGen Holdings, but that's a shell company registered in the Cayman Islands. Digging up that dirt is going to be hard. What I can confirm is that Leopold has not received any payments from NextGen. There is one other thing, though. I'm not sure if it's worth mentioning or not."

"Spit it out, Gideon," Cora huffed, rolling her eyes.

"Aside from the confirmed data we've recovered from Project Phoenix, there are partials," Gideon said. "That is, data so badly damaged, we only got a piece of it. There is an elven woman with the last name Nguyen on the list of partials."

Cora's eyes flared wide. "Wait, what? Are you saying there's a possibility all three are artifact holders?"

"Well, no," Gideon replied, his voice urging her to calm down. "We don't have anything about an Orwell, partial or otherwise. All I'm saying is that they may not be random disappearances."

Cora stepped forward and put her hand on her hip. Her jaw clenched, her blood started to boil. Somehow, Lucius was involved. She could feel it in her bones. Even if he wasn't directing traffic, he was always the puppet master, pulling the strings.

"What's our next play?" Cora looked to George.

Before he could speak, another person walked into the room. Dressed in a Royal British Army uniform with a typical high-and-tight haircut, the most distinguishing feature about him was the ornate wooden bow hanging from his back.

"I hope I'm not interrupting," he said.

Cora moved her head back and forth. "Well, yeah, kinda. What's going on, Michael?"

"Julian wanted me to check on our new guest...and he wants a sitrep from you."

Cora rolled her eyes. She'd spent days avoiding Julian. Now didn't feel like any better a time to change her mind on that course of action. She motioned to George.

"This is George Earp, our sheriff from Texas," she said. She motioned to Michael. "George, this is Michael Robinson, Julian's number one guy, Chief of Operations for Atlantis, and the owner of Robin Hood's bow."

George snickered. "Robin Hood? Well, I'll be."

Michael stepped quickly to the front of the room and shook his hand. "Pleasure." ·

"Likewise," George replied. He stared at the ceiling. "Quite a marvel you have here."

Michael smiled with pride, as if he owned the damned base. "Atlantis is a hell of place, right?"

Cora held up a finger. "Michael, stick around for a second. George and I were just wrapping up."

"Sure, of course."

Turning her attention back to the sheriff, her eyes pleaded with him. She needed a direction, or a course of action. "How do we move forward?"

George traced down his mustache with a thumb and forefinger. "I'd like access to the second woman's house. If there was blood found there, we need to familiarize ourselves with the scene, look for patterns that match Leopold's house. Also, the money trail. If those two women had these strange deposits, we need to know who was giving them this money. It's a common thread between them."

Cora nodded. The answer seemed simple enough, but that was a job for the disembodied voice in the room. She looked to the ceiling. "Gideon? Can we make that happen?"

"I mean...yes?" Gideon replied, his tinny robotic voice approximated a sigh. "I can track the shell company to where they're located in the Cayman Islands, but actually digging up that intel might require you visit personally."

"We can do that," Cora replied.

"The other idea, that's actually the hard part," Gideon continued. "Getting you guys permission to enter the crime scene means I'd need to get you jurisdiction above London police. That means I need to hack into Interpol and set you guys up as consultants or something. That could take days."

Cora shook her head. "We don't have days, Gideon. We need to act on the intel as fast as we can."

"I get it, I do," Gideon said. "I'm on it. No matter what, both of these are going to take time."

"I figured as much," Cora replied, blowing out a long, exhausted breath. She turned to Michael. She didn't have any excuses left to dodge Julian. "Michael, can you give George a quick tour on the way to his quarters? I woke the poor guy up in the middle of the night and he hasn't slept since."

"Neither have you," Michael replied with his charming British accent, concern on his face. "The dark circles under your eyes, love-"

"I'll rest soon enough," Cora stopped him, raising a hand. "For now, I'll get over to Julian. Get this man whatever he needs - food, a place to rest, anything."

Michael nodded. "Aye."

Cora turned to George, as he walked back to the desk. He took up his duster and draped it over his forearm, then put his cowboy hat back on. He tipped the brim to her.

"I'll help you get your people back, ma'am," he said. "Count on that."

"Thank you," Cora replied with a bow of her head. He couldn't possibly know how much that gesture meant to her. He couldn't know how much she'd suffered over the past few days, juggling loss, guilt, and fear. Fully sober thanks to her stupid regeneration ability, hearing his words brought tears to her eyes. She was grateful Michael walked him out of the room before he could see, to know how vulnerable she was.

This was the first time she felt out of her element since this war with Lucius began. Breaking into places, gathering intelligence, dispatching enemies on the battlefield, that was all part of her training. A string of possible allies vanished from their daily lives, with no threat or ransom, that was all new to her. It brought with it the same helplessness that losing a loved one had, a grief with no reprieve. Facing Julian would only bring that feeling to a head. Still, she couldn't hide any longer, and made her way out of the computer room and down the corridor to his office.

IN MOURNING

The temperature of the base changed as Cora crossed the threshold to Julian's office. The largest office in Atlantis, holovid monitors lined one wall, keeping tabs on every detail of the base, two brown couches, a desk, and a holovid projection table. Despite all the furniture, Cora had to cross a wide, empty space to his desk.

His blue eyes watched her approach with an expectant expression. The past week had not been kind to him. She could see the sunken, dark eyes and days of unshaven stubble from the other side of the room. Behind him, Excalibur was mounted on the wall in all its gleaming, legendary glory. It was a beacon of light in an otherwise darkened room.

Beside his computer rig, an ancient book rested on his desk. At over a foot long and several inches thick, every page was written by Merlin's hand. It detailed his every encounter with Julian's bloodline, all the way back to King Arthur. Cora paused when she noticed it.

Julian's eyes shifted from her to where she was looking. Defensively, he rested an elbow on the book and met her gaze. She winced and psyched herself up to endure his lordly, often condescending British accent.

"It...it's good to see you, Cora," he said.

Cora raised an eyebrow. He was never pleasant with her. "It is?"

"Of course. I'm not upset with you, despite all things," he replied, rubbing the stubble at the back of his head.

"That's because you got your way," she replied. She wasn't about to mince words with him. "I heard you have Gideon on a wild goose chase for the trident now."

Julian raised his hands in surrender before she could continue. "Please, Cora. I didn't ask you here to fight again."

Cora put her hands on her hips. "Then what did you ask me here for? You want a sitrep? I went to Texas. Got drunk. Brought back a cowboy. He's going to help us find Leopold. The end."

"What about you?" Julian asked, his eyes red and glassy. "Are you okay?"

Cora felt her eyes flooding with tears. She clenched her jaw, struggling against herself to fight back the emotions bubbling to the surface. She turned the pain outward, staring daggers at Julian, accusing him.

"Why?"

"Because I'm not, that's why," Julian replied, his chin quivering.

Her facade cracked. Cora turned her head away as the tears came, forcing her eyes closed. Only a week ago, she was wheeling Merlin's decrepit, sixteen-hundred year-old behind around the base, playing chess, and talking about life in other eras. She knew his health rapidly declined after they arrived in Atlantis. Even as he warned her that the end neared, she always believed she had more time.

"He loved you, you know," Julian said, choking on his own words. He stifled back tears and struggled to maintain his composure. Hearing it only made Cora weep harder, until a drill bored between her eyebrows.

Cora shook her head. Loss was always a private thing for her. When her father was assassinated, her mother and uncle fought like wild dogs, leaving a ten year-old girl crying in a corner for her hero. Every loss since had been a private matter, either because she couldn't associate with anyone over it, or she was the only one left that cared for them.

"I didn't want to come here to fight," Cora sniffled back. "But I didn't want to do this, either."

Julian walked around his desk and put his arms around her. She startled with his embrace. They might have exchanged a handshake once, but a hug was out of the question. She couldn't find warmth or relief in his touch. Instead, she looked right past him to The Pendragon Codex on his desk, and her blood boiled again.

"You know his last words to me..."

Julian stepped back and held her by the shoulders. Solemn, he nodded back, "Find the trident. I know. But we don't know what it is or where to start looking. It isn't in the Phoenix database that we've salvaged, so we're flying blind. That's why I brought Gideon in on it."

"You know damn well the answer could be in there," Cora snapped, pointing to the book. "He could have drawn a sketch, or maybe written about it. I don't understand the magical script he wrote it in, but I'm one of the only two magic-users on this base powerful enough to try."

Julian sighed and walked back to his desk. Eyes weary, he looked too tired to fight her with the same fervor he had in days past.

"Cora, that's exactly why I can't let you look at it," he repeated. "I can't have you poking around in that book."

She shook her head and threw her arms up. "That doesn't make any sense! What is it you're so afraid of me finding in there?"

"Nothing!" Julian raised his voice. He leaned forward, resting his knuckles on his desk to prop himself up. "I've never read the book. I don't know what's in it. I have nothing to hide from you. More importantly, I don't answer to you."

"Then tell me why you're saying no! It's so damn arbitrary! That 'because I said so' bullshit might fly with your lackeys, but I deserve an explanation!" Cora yelled, her pain replaced with anger.

"Because Merlin insisted on it!" Julian shouted back.

Cora flinched. The answer had caught her so completely off guard, she didn't know what to say. Had she misjudged her relationship with Merlin? She couldn't imagine why he wouldn't trust her with his secrets, even after death. Julian had seen less of him in the past two months than Cora had.

Julian sighed, letting out his frustrations. His words came out more collected. "I told you how he felt about you, love. You were like a daughter to him, even with how short a time you were with us before he passed. Those last two months...I wasn't there. I knew the end was coming, and I buried myself in the work. I didn't want to face it. But you, you were there."

Cora felt the tears coming back, robbing her of all her well-placed rage. She fought against the tide turning, even as her heart broke with his every word. She wanted to tell him to stop, but she wanted to keep going. Hearing how he felt about her from someone else made it seem more real, like he was still there, speaking through Julian.

"You were there when I was not," Julian said with trembling breath. "That meant everything to him...and to me. Which is why when he told me to call you back here, I knew what was coming. I dreaded it. I almost didn't call you."

Cora reeled her head back. "What? Why?"

Julian sat back down behind his desk and shrugged. "Because...once you came, it would be the end. He was holding on for you...to say goodbye to you."

She walked to the couch and folded her head into her hands. She needed a good cry, and she wasn't going to let him see her do it.

"Before you arrived, he told me something," Julian said, shaking his head. He stared across the room, lost as he recalled the memory. "He said his last wish was that I don't let you look at The Pendragon Codex until I saw a sign."

"A sign? What sign? Why?" Cora rattled off questions as fast as they popped in her head. Nothing he said made sense.

Julian gripped the bridge of his nose. "I don't know what sign. He said I'd know when I saw it. But that's it, the whole reason. I'm not trying to drive a wedge between us. I'm honoring Merlin's final wish to me."

Cora lifted her head from her hands, showing her puffy eyes to Julian. Her throat was sore and her voice came out raspy and hoarse. "Why? He didn't trust me or something?"

"No! No, Cora!" Julian shook his head and strode to her side. He knelt beside her and put a hand on her shoulder. It was the most compassion she'd ever seen from him. She wasn't sure how to take it. "Look, we know you're going to meet Merlin again at some point, right? He told us that much before we went after Crowley. If I had to guess, he doesn't want you reading the book because it contains information of what you did in the past...will do? What you will do in the past? That is so confusing."

Cora scoffed, eyes wide, staring at him as though it were the understatement of the year. "I'm fated to travel back in time to meet a wizard, but no, you're right. The semantics are what's confusing."

Julian snickered. The smile on his face was infectious. Cora laughed, even if it was at her own sarcasm. With a heavy breath, Julian stood up and stared at the holovid monitors. Cora followed his eyes to the screen, showing GNN without audio. As usual, the news station couldn't go an hour without some puff piece about Lucius. Onscreen, he was glad-handing some foreign dignitary adorned in gold and silk, Lucius wearing one of his opulent British suits. His glowing amber eyes shined at the camera like a pair of setting suns.

"If Excalibur injured him, he does a damn fine job hiding it," Julian said with a huff.

Cora dropped her head. The dragon's attempt to incinerate her and Julian on that rooftop in Paris left her with no choice. If she hadn't stabbed him, they'd be dead. Still, she didn't want to do it, perhaps even regretted it. Her thoughts on the issue moved back and forth, more than once questioning whether she would have gone for the kill if he hadn't fled. Looking back on it, she was grateful he did. She broke free of that train of thought and opted to change the subject.

"Why did you bring Gideon into the trident business? I thought we agreed to keep it between us," she asked.

Julian turned to her and crossed his arms. "He's the best researcher we have, and my hacker is still in Madrid. Besides that, I'm about ninety percent certain Gideon isn't the mole."

Cora rolled her eyes. "You can take that up to a hundred. If Gideon was the mole, we'd all be dead right now. He can send communications without us knowing it, he's already proven he can break the security systems you've installed in this base, and he knows where we are. I don't even know where we are, Julian. He could literally lock us in Atlantis, give up our position, and have Bauer Securities come in here and cut us down like dogs."

How powerful Gideon was in the situation couldn't be understated. She already knew he wasn't the mole, though she believed that of everyone she spilled blood with during the Project Phoenix fiasco. Johnny, Giovanna, and Gideon could have cut their losses and let her take the fall. When Lucius kidnapped her during the UNS standoff at Heaven's Crest, they rescued her. Johnny took a bullet for her. It wasn't any of them.

"It's a fair point," Julian replied. "Tridents aren't known to be in great supply around the world, in museums or otherwise. I'm sure Gideon will help us locate it. How's the situation with our new guest?"

Cora stood up and walked around the room. "He's a good man, and I think he can help. He took to his artifact pretty well - just a coughing fit, nothing too traumatic."

Julian's brow furrowed. "And this was...who? Some American cowboy?"

"Not the one we thought it was, but yes," Cora replied. She walked to an intimate distance with Julian and wiped her eyes. "We're both a bit shaken. This couldn't have happened at a worse time, and it burns like hell. I can only imagine what you're going through. I have Gideon pulling data for these missing people, and he's working the search for the trident artifact."

"You think his plate is too full?" Julian said, surprise on his face.

Cora shook her head. "No, Gideon can handle it. I'm more concerned about us. We're both the types to dive into our work. So, you stay on the trident, and I'll stay on the investigation, okay? This way, we're not stepping on each other's toes, and we're not spreading ourselves too thin."

"Tip-top," he replied. He always said that when he disagreed with her and didn't want to rock the boat. It was a return to form, back to the Julian that annoyed her.

Cora turned away and moved for the door. She wasn't about to get dragged into another argument. She was much too tired and emotionally drained for that. "As soon as Gideon gives me a location, I'm gone. So, I'm going to get some rest while I can."

"Very good, then," Julian replied behind her.

"You should consider it for yourself, too," Cora added, stopping at the door. She looked over her shoulder. "At least get a shave, you look like you just came off a mountain."

"Thank you, mother, that will be all," Julian ribbed.

Cora left his office behind and slogged through the corridors, back to the crew barracks. A hot shower and a bed were on the agenda, with a fair amount of Jack somewhere in between.

THE INFORMANT

Balmy winds couldn't save Cora from humidity that turned the air into a milkshake. She couldn't have asked for a nicer view, though. From the patio of La Esperanza, she could throw a stone across the sands and hit crystal clear ocean. Even with shades on, the water was so clear and blue, with the salty scent of the sea in her nose, it took everything not to strip down to nothing and dive into the waters. Instead, she nursed her rum and watched for anyone approaching her table.

"He's late," George said, shifting uncomfortably in his chair. Coming from Atlantis without a change of clothes, the poor man was grossly overdressed for the weather. As it was, she had to tie Richard's bomber jacket around her hips. If nothing else, it hid her pistol well.

Cora clicked her tongue and tapped the comm button on her earpiece. "Control, confirm 2 p.m. local time for the meet."

"Confirmed, Echo-1," Gideon replied. "He could be running late, but he's coming. It's only ten-after. Enjoy the view."

She took another glance to the ocean, but only to steal a peek. Anymore than that, and she was likely to hop the fence beside her. The shining midday sun reflected like diamonds off the surface of the water.

"Caw," Vincent said from the banister. It was his first time in a tropical climate. He wanted to explore, too.

"Easy, buddy," she said, stroking his head with a finger. "We're working at the moment."

George laughed. "I'd swear, you'd think that thing talks to you."

Cora raised an eyebrow. "He's not a thing, he's Vincent. And he does, in a way. I can feel his emotions like I feel my own. Sometimes, it paints enough of a picture that I know what he's thinking."

"The bird's emotions, your own thoughts, and a dead Indian chief rattling around in your head. I don't know how you manage to juggle all that," George replied with a bow of his head. He sat back and sucked down the last of his cold beer. "As it is, I'm getting annoyed with this compulsion to look at everyone's teeth when I talk to them."

"That is a weird one," Cora replied with a laugh. "I don't know how I juggle it, either. But I'm alive. Now, going over this one more time - if we go sideways..."

The sheriff raised his hand. "I remember. Make physical contact with you, call Control with the keyword 'expat,' and we're out of here."

"The physical contact part is the important bit. I don't want you leaving me here. It takes Tesla around five minutes to replace that coil." Cora said, wagging her finger.

George's head spun on a swivel toward the entrance. "We've got company."

The man approaching their table wasn't what she expected. When she thought of secret underground informants, she pictured mousy, pathetic fellows that shifted allegiances with the wind. What she got instead was a wide man in a white muscle shirt, his bulging biceps and chest made more distracting by the sheer volume of tattoos on display there. From neck to wrist, the caramel-skinned man was adorned with tribal art and symbols with more meaning to him than she could ever understand. His face was clean of artwork and stubble, and his black hair was cropped close to the scalp. He wore black denim shorts and expensive basketball sneakers.

"Katie?" he said, pointing at her with a smile as he approached the table. His accent was vaguely Mexican, only adding to how sexy he was. If he wasn't a lowlife piece of shit, she would have been all kinds of interested.

"Guilty as charged," Cora said with a smile. She stood up and offered her hand. "Kathleen O'Malley. And you must be Tototl."

"Hey, you got the pronunciation right," he laughed, helping himself to a seat at her table. "No one ever gets that."

Cora took her seat and gave a dismissive wave. "I got lucky. My father couldn't even teach me Lakota," she said, trying modesty on for size. She spoke every important language there was to know in the 2080's, including Elven. Some gang-banger adopting a name from a dead language wasn't about to throw her. "Let's do some business, shall we?"

"Of course, of course!" he said, nodding his head. He shrugged his shoulders and pointed up to George, almost a foot taller than him. "I gotta ask, though - what's with the bird and who's the bean stalk?"

"That's Vincent. This is Doc. They're my bodyguards," Cora replied. "They don't talk much. But I'm much more interested in what you have to say."

Tototl slouched in his chair and got comfortable. He took an aloof posture, to assert his power in the conversation. It was cute, even if it was ineffectual. "You've got my digits?"

Cora reached up and tapped the comm button. "Control, my very handsome contact would like you to 'make it rain.' I believe that's the term."

"Confirm, transfer in process...and complete, Echo-1," Gideon replied in her ear.

Without moving an inch, a square of white light appeared in Tototl's left eye. His eyes began to move and twitch, along with subtle, jerking movements of his head. Cora looked away. The newest release of the Optics 4.0 firmware for Tetriarch eye implants allowed users to have creepy, hands-free access to their Arcadia via a pop-up display in their eye, controlled by what they focused on. Gideon had gone on and on about how great it was, but Cora tuned him out. She wasn't about to conjure up any images of scalpels and eyes in her head then, and certainly not now.

Tototl nodded to himself and smiled. "Alright, I see five k in credits."

"Half upfront, half on delivery, as agreed," Cora affirmed, crossing her legs.

"I think we can do better than that," he replied with a grin.

Cora sat up straight, feigning getting up to leave. "If you're going to change the terms..."

Tototl threw up his hands in defense. "Hey, hey, easy! Look, I know you're the contact for Xero. He's huge on UnderNet. I want to impress him, you know what I'm saying?"

Cora leaned back. Gideon's avatar on UnderNet, Xero, was well-known in information circles before he hacked the UNS Pentagon. It seemed for all his muscles, Tototl had a case of hero worship for the tall, lanky hacker back at Atlantis.

"What do you have in mind?" Cora asked.

Holding his hands out to his sides, Tototl smiled and cocked his head. "I'm going to do you one better than give you info, pretty lady, so you can just transfer them funds right now. No one does business that doesn't want to be known unless it goes through mi familia. Conquistadors."

George sat up with a start, eyes wide. Tototl flinched. Cora snapped her head to him.

"What? You got beef with Conquistadors?" Tototl asked.

George stared for a second, then shook his head, cooling off. "No. Don't suppose I do."

Cora raised a finger to Tototl and leaned in close to George. She whispered, "What is it?"

"Aztecs. They lost their PMC charter a few years back. They're basically a crime cartel now. Savages," George whispered back.

Cora nodded and smiled, even as the news shook her. This was supposed to be a simple fact-finding mission, but nothing was ever simple. Now, she had to deal with Native Central American mafia to broker information. She turned back to Tototl.

"He's worried about me giving up the other half before you deliver me anything," she said.

"No worries, big man," Tototl smiled. He tapped George on the shoulder and stood up. "I'm gonna take you to see my cousin. C'mon. I got my Jeep parked out front. The drive is only a couple minutes from here."

Cora kept a hard stare on the Aztec, trying to read him. If Vincent had concerns, she didn't feel it. He didn't seem smart enough to be bluffing. Tototl was no major player, he was a guy who knew a guy. He probably wandered around on UnderNet, found Gideon looking for intel, and figured it was easy money and a road to the big leagues. Hopefully, his stupidity wouldn't get her killed. She tapped the comm button on her ear.

"Control, let's get the man the rest of his money," she said.

"Confirmed, Echo-1. Do you have the intel?"

"Negative," she replied, her face soured as she got up from her seat. "We're going on a field trip."

"Understood," Gideon said. Unlike Julian, he knew better than to question her. "Comms are open."

Cora rested her forearm against the banister, and Vincent hopped to her. Drawing her arm close to her lips, she whispered, "Eyes in the sky."

"Caw," Vincent croaked. He worried about her, but he was always worried about something. She was convinced she got a spirit animal with an anxiety disorder. With a mighty beat of his wings, he took off to the blue skies and vanished in the sunlight.

"Damn, you got him trained and everything?" Tototl asked, waving her to follow him.

George exchanged a quick glance with her. She knew he didn't like it, but time was of the essence. The names kept turning in her head - Leopold, Olivia, Elea. Every second they weren't home, the likelihood they ever would be diminished. The risks were necessary.

Tototl drove southwest, for the southern tip of Cayman Brac, one of the small sister islands of Grand Cayman Island. One thing

Tototl could do was talk. Like Gideon, she imagined he didn't get out much, always plugged into NeuralNet, fancying himself a gangster in UnderNet. She nodded and smiled at the appropriate times, but didn't hear a word he said. She stayed focused on the route, keeping her bearings, and committing everything to memory. She would have killed to enjoy the palm trees, the sun on her skin, or just the oiled-up Caribbean men on the beach. Instead, she memorized driving directions like she was a damn GPS.

When the Jeep slowed down, they were at the southern tip of the island. Down a driveway shaded by palm trees, they came to a stop in front of a black metal fence. Two tatted-up Aztecs stood guard, hiding some serious firepower on their hips and strapped across their shoulder. These men didn't strike her as aloof, young gangbangers at all, though. Their posture rigid and their movements purposeful, they had some military training and age to them. If George was right and they were all former PMC soldiers, they might very well have fought in the Mexican Revolution back in '67.

Tototl made a loud, obnoxious greeting to them and smiled from ear to ear. They approached the vehicle on both sides. From the driver's side, the guard took a stern look at Cora, then back to Tototl.

"Have them step out," he said.

Tototl laughed and rolled his eyes. "No need for that mess. We're here to do business with Eztli."

"You searched them already?"

"Yeah, of course I did," Tototl laughed. He turned to Cora and George, getting them in on the joke. "Hey guys, you bring any weapons I didn't find?"

Cora laughed it off and shook her head. What a silly question. Of course she wouldn't bring weapons to meet with a stranger. There wasn't an Apex Predator with fifteen in the clip at her back that very second. Nothing to worry about at all.

The two guards shook their head and walked back, opening the gate without a word. The Jeep pressed on, further down the driveway, toward three of the tallest buildings on the island. Each building a different color, they were coral red, amber, and green, like a traffic light. As Cora kept her head moving. She counted three men patrolling the interior perimeter of the fence, and two more guards ahead at the red building. What she assumed was her destination, two more guards flanked an important-looking man in white dress pants. The matching white dress shirt hid the same tribal tattoos as Tototl, peeking from his cuffs.

The man looked to be in his late thirties, with a thick, black mustache partially balded by a nasty facial scar from nostril to chin. His hands were on his hips, and he did not look happy to see any of them, least of all his cousin. The Jeep came to a stop a few feet before the man. It was only once the engine was turned off that Cora realized how quiet the area was. Without the din of insects or any wildlife, she could have heard a pin drop. Even the wandering guards didn't seem to make a sound as they walked.

"Hey, cuz!" Tototl waved.

Cora and George followed suit as he got out of the Jeep, staying a respectful distance behind Tototl until they were introduced.

"These are the people I wanted you to meet," he said, motioning over his shoulder. "Ten large for some info on a business on Grand Cayman. Could be our in with one of the biggest hackers on UnderNet."

Without moving an inch, angry eyes shifted from Tototl to Cora and George. The scene changed so fast from resort town to crime compound, she didn't have the chance to borrow Vincent's sight to get an overview. She was regretting that now.

"Who's the cula?" the angry boss asked, staring at Cora.

Before Tototl could speak, she cleared her throat. "Excuse me? I might not know that term, but I know an insult when I hear one. I'm not a cula, I'm a Cora. I'm Sioux, from the Native Free Lands."

His lip curled in disgust looking at her. Tototl turned around and faced her with his big, dumb smile.

"He doesn't mean nothin' by it," Tototl said, stepping toward her. "This is my cousin, Eztli. He runs this island."

Three muted shots rang out. Cora jumped out of her skin. It wasn't apparent right away where the shots came from, nor where they went. The big, dumb smile on Tototl was replaced with a blank, vacant stare. Pools of red expanded in a circle from two spots on his white shirt. Blood poured from his mouth like a sieve. He dropped to his knees, then flat on the ground.

George grabbed Cora by the wrist before the body hit the ground. He tapped the comm behind his ear and shouted, "Expat!"

There was nothing. Only terrible, tense silence, and the gaze of Eztli and his two guards with pistols drawn. All of their weapons had silencers. On an island so small, it would be hard to enforce rules and hide bodies if they were constantly being searched for noise complaints.

"Tsk, tsk," Eztli said, staring at George. "You trying to call someone? Call for help?"

He took a step toward George and leveled the pistol at him. His eyes flared wide, his heavy accent made his words all the more menacing.

"This is my island. My house. You don't have a comm signal out of here unless I say so. You want help? You ask *me* for it."

"Hey," Cora said, raising a defensive hand. "It doesn't have to be like this. I mean, wasn't he your cousin?"

Eztli spared a glance down at the body. Blood pooled out from the corpse onto the concrete walkway. He met Cora's eyes, brow furrowed. She couldn't see a pang of regret.

"Every Aztec on this island is my cousin," he replied. "But I don't need worthless, incompetent fucks like this one bringing strangers to my house to ask me questions."

Cora nodded. "That's fair. Let's do business, then. You and I. What's the price for wasting your time today?"

He laughed back, a bitter mockery of enjoyment. "I don't want your money, cula. I want to know what you came to ask about. Then I'm going to ask you why you want to know. You're going to lie. So I'm going to start carving into one of you until the other talks."

Sitting Bull screamed at Cora in her mind. He might not have known much about the late 21st century, but he knew a war chief when he saw one. Peace wasn't on the table. Trade wasn't on the table. Blood was the only language he spoke in. She reigned him back to the corner of her mind and gritted her teeth. She needed answers.

"NextGen Holdings," Cora said. "They're a shell company on Grand Cayman. I wanted to know what they do, who owns it, and why they're sniffing around Wyoming."

Eztli took another step toward Cora, over Tototl's leg. He smiled with a mouthful of crooked teeth. Even his smile held sinister intent.

"NextGen doesn't have any interest in Wyoming," he said, his voice low. "I told you. You would lie."

George set one foot back slightly and bent at his knees the slightest bit. The posture change was enough to make Eztli notice. He waved the gun back to the sheriff's direction.

"You look like you want to fight, Mister Lawman," he said. His smile beamed with genuine joy. "Look around you. You aren't going anywhere. I've got you."

In terror of what happened next, Cora turned her head to George, to find him staring right back at Etzli. Something in his eyes was different. His posture, the look on his face, it was almost like she was meeting him for the first time all over again.

"You're a daisy if you do," George replied, the corners of his mouth turned up in a grin.

Eztli's brow furrowed, his face a mask of confusion. He cocked his head to the side. "What?"

Like the roar of a cannon, three deafening shots blasted Cora's ears in rapid succession. Her heart leaped out of her chest. She looked over George. He seemed fine. Her head snapped to Eztli. Him and his guards stood motionless, shock etched into their faces, a bullet hole between each of their eyes. Blood trickled down their noses. They fell in heaps to the ground. Cora struggled to process what she was seeing. Her eyes back on George, his artifact pistol was fired from hip level so fast and accurate, she hadn't even seen him draw the weapon.

"That thing works?" Cora yelled in astonishment over the ringing in her ear.

Yelling came from all around them. Men scurried in the distance, scrambling to draw weapons and take aim. George grabbed Cora by the arm and spun around, yanking her to him as though she were a child in his grip. He went low for cover behind Tototl's Jeep. He kept his back to it, eyes ahead for anyone that could get the drop on them. Once Cora was at his side, he let her go. She didn't hesitate to grab her Predator and jacked a round into the chamber. The magnetically propelled bullets could leave fist-sized holes in men with better body armor than muscle shirts. Her head swung back to George.

"You ready?" she asked, psyching herself up.

He pulled out a handful of bullets that looked older than she was. She didn't even know where he got them from. Michael must have brought him to the armory before they left. At least one of them anticipated this meeting turning into a bullet festival. George bowed his head back to her.

"Ooh, yes, ma'am," he said in a southern drawl he didn't have before. "I'll see you on the other side of this scrap."

"Oh, shit," Cora whispered to herself, eyebrows raised. It may have been his body, but that wasn't George in the driver's seat.

SPIRITS UNBOUND

Bullets clanged and pierced the opposite side of the Jeep as patrols closed in from the entrance. Before long, guards in the buildings ahead would empty out with a clear line of sight to her. Their numbers were unknown, her communications were down, and she was a party to the death of an Aztec crime lord. The only thing more frightening than the unknown ahead of her was the one on her right.

Twice during the Heaven's Crest standoff, Sitting Bull had taken her over, turning into an out-of-body experience. The spirit within her broke free of the space he occupied in her mind and took control. The first time, she gave in to the spirit, and he delivered a rousing speech to unite her people and prepare for war. The second time, Sitting Bull jumped in to protect her by threatening Lucius. Cora was too drugged out on Trillozine to stop him, and too mad at Lucius to try. She'd never seen it happen to anyone else before.

"Alternate!" Cora shouted. "Eyes on the building, cover me!"

Cora steadied her Predator across the hood of the Jeep. The first man to present himself was an Aztec with a shaved head and a silenced MPB-18 assault rifle. By the time he realized he was closing distance with a pistol aimed on him, Cora double-tapped the trigger. The space in his chest cavity where his heart should have been became a window. She spun and slid down, eyes ahead to the buildings. No movement yet.

George took her lead and wheeled around. Two rounds in rapid succession. A gurgling groan somewhere in the distance. Cora popped out from cover as George ducked down. A guard got wise and took a pot shot from behind a coconut tree. A quick survey of the treetop showed it was wonderfully ripe. She aimed high and fired off a round. Falling coconuts caused the guard to dive out of harm's way, into the sights of her Predator. But before she could fire off another shot, she heard a shot from her flank. Searing, burning pain radiated off her shoulder. With how much of her was behind cover, it was the work of someone very skilled or incredibly lucky.

She slumped back to cover in a heap, clutching at the wound. George took one look at her and gasped. He leaned in, analyzing her wound.

"My dear, I see that you are hit," he said, still speaking as another person. His eyes were wild, as though drunk on adrenaline.

"I just need a few moments," Cora sucked air through her teeth.

George bowed his head and pulled his sheriff's service pistol from the holster at his hip. He held up a weapon in each hand and smiled.

"Then I will kick up a row and buy you that moment," he replied.

Instead of firing from over the rear of the Jeep, George dove away from it, into the grassy area beside the driveway. Shots rang out from everywhere. They were going to cut him down out there. She couldn't have it. Not another loss. Not again. Her weapon arm temporarily crippled, she shut her eyes and felt for the warmth at the center of her being. Flipping it to the cold, dark side, her eyes filled in black from corner to corner. She pushed her Spirit Sight beyond herself, across the blue tether of energy that bound her to Vincent. In doing so, she opened her eyes to a view high above the compound.

Fenced in on all sides, it looked like any other resort it was sandwiched between. As Vincent swooped down, she was relieved to see George still standing, moving from cover to cover, drawing fire away from the Jeep. In a bizarre turn of events, she saw her own body, slumped against the vehicle. It was surreal and disorienting, enough that she had to look away. Two guards at the entrance remained, weapons trained inward, hesitant to leave their post. Two men laid down fire as they closed in toward George. A third one used the fire to try and flank him, but Cora saw the play.

Vincent gathered up glowing orange dust in his talons, pulled across their link from Cora. It coalesced into a ball. Tucking his wings back and leaning forward, he dove at the ground, aimed for the guard trying to flank George. At the last possible moment before striking the ground at his feet, Vincent pulled up. His talons released. The glowing orange ball exploded on contact with the ground. The guard lifted off the ground from the initial vacuum of air created, but the resulting shockwave threw him backwards a dozen feet.

"Caw," Vincent warned, an eerie sensation as she heard the raven through her own ears and from his at the same time.

Without warning, he severed their connection. The rug pulled out from under her, Cora fell from the sky, her vision reeling back into her own eyes. She started up with a gasp. Two men came down a flight of stairs along the side of the red building ahead. On shaky muscles, her head lolled as she examined the shoulder wound. It hadn't fully closed, but it would have to do. She grabbed up her Predator from the ground beside her and fired off three rounds. Her shaky aim let the bullets fly wild, tearing holes in the wood-covered stairway. The men scrambled and jumped the rest of the way down, diving into a somersault to get cover.

She didn't know how many were coming, but she knew she couldn't stay where she was. Taking to her feet, she ran for the back of the Jeep, bursting out of cover to support George and clear the front lawn. George had dispatched her coconut man, leaving only one, a hard target clear across the lawn.

"Cover me!" Cora yelled, racing for the tree George hid behind.

She pulled from the magic within her in a pulse, throwing energy to her feet and fingertips. As she reached the tree, her stride remained unbroken. The first step slammed her boot into the trunk, providing enough momentum to throw her other leg forward, another step vertically. Each step was harder than the last, gravity putting up a hell of a fight to stop what she was doing. Her thighs burned as she got five, seven, then ten feet off the ground. It was high enough to get a view of her target, hidden behind a shack near the entrance on the far side of the driveway.

Cora grabbed with her left arm, a firm grip on the tree, and spun around it like some pole dancer. With a clear view, she summoned another pull of magical energy and sent it to her arm, steadying her pistol grip. She let off two taps on the trigger, but he was down after the first.

Unable to wait any longer, the two guards at the front gate leaped over and made a run for them. From her elevated view, the two men from the red building came up from behind, about to draw them into an attack on two sides. Cora pulled another draw of magic, this time to her knees and legs. She kicked off into a flip, holding onto the backs of her knees as she tumbled through the air. She landed on one knee, the magic absorbing the shock, and took aim at the front entrance.

"Behind me!" Cora shouted.

George spun out from cover, a pistol in each hand. Now back to back, Cora fired two shots in rhythm with George. One Conquistador went down mid-stride. Sensing George's movement, Cora spun on her knee as he wheeled around above her. She turned back toward the Jeep and a head popped out from behind it. Predator at the ready, she let off another two rounds. The first shot hit the corner of the Jeep and tore right through it. The guard dodged at awkward angle, exposing him to the second shot that put him down for good.

The quiet returned, fast and unsettling. From the looks of the place, their compound had been converted from a resort. There was no way there were only ten men here. There had to be more, she just wasn't that lucky.

She craned up her neck to see George. His head went left, right, then back again. He took a careful step forward. Cora stalked like a cat, still squatted down, moving on all fours. From her lower vantage point, she could see up past the canopy of trees over the driveway more easily. It was as George stepped back onto the driveway that she noticed three men atop the roof of the red building, rifles aimed down.

She grabbed George by the sleeve of his duster and pulled with everything, yanking him back toward the Jeep as a hail of silenced bullets struck the driveway. Cora got pegged by flying shards of concrete. A few struck her face, opening a tiny gash that closed almost as fast as it opened. Silence returned. Hiding behind the Jeep again, she turned her ear toward the buildings.

Voices. Low and direct, whatever number of men were hidden in the buildings behind her coordinated their attack. She shut her eyes and shook her throbbing head. Reaching to her back, she pulled out a fresh clip and reloaded.

"What are they doing?" George asked, sounding more himself.

"Three shooters on the roof," Cora said, wincing as she checked her shoulder. "We try to break for the entrance, they cut us down. While we're pinned down, some number of guys who know this place better are going to come at us from multiple angles and rip us to pieces sometime in the next minute or so."

George reloaded both pistols and nodded. "So, what's our move?"

Richard trained her for moments like these. The best plan was to make other guy throw their plan out the window. She needed to go on the offensive, make them have to improvise in the heat of the moment. She needed numbers for that. She let out a heavy breath.

"I swore I'd never use this again," she grumbled to herself. Meeting eyes with George, she said, "We're going to make a break for the stairs. We have to get those snipers down. So, if you see someone that already looks dead...they're on our side."

"Wait, what?"

Cora closed her eyes and flipped the warm ball of magic to the cold flipside. Even with Crowley's training for the past two months, she still feared the darkest magic in her. It offered greater power than she'd ever known before, if only she'd let it spread through her like a virus. Containing it took everything she had. As her eyes opened again, George startled at the inky blackness staring back at him.

The washed-out, muted colors of the Spirit World were given light by the tethers of life all around her. Like tendrils made of white and blue energy, the strands crisscrossed all around her like a spider's web. She let the icy magical energy flow down her arm until four tendrils of her own appeared in her hand. They dangled from her grip like a fistful of ropes. She leaned out from cover, looking down the side of the Jeep to the front.

Tototl, Eztli, and his two guards lay in pools of blood. Her eyes fixed to their bodies, she threw out the tendrils without aim. Her will was enough for each of the four strands to find their home, wrapped around the neck of each corpse. She wound the ribbons around her wrists, the frigid cold of its current burning into her forearm. Clenching her jaw, she tugged back on the tendrils like a leash.

It only took a matter of seconds before Eztli's fingers twitched. Then his hand. A dead guard pulled himself to his knees. Tototl stumbled to his feet. The four of them stood erect, a low, hissing sound coming from garbled approximations of breath. The magic was so cruel, so detestable, Cora regretted it the second she had done it. She shook her head and looked at the horror she had made. She shut her eyes to it.

"Get them," she whispered, her word the only command they needed.

Hissing, chomping, gurgling noises were joined with screeches as the four corpses ran beyond the red building. With a thought, Cora shunted the Spirit Sight, returning her eyes to normal.

"Let's move!" she shouted, running out from cover. George ran up behind her.

She raced for the stairs at the side of the red building. A hail of bullets rained down behind her, too hard a target for them to hit. George kept pace the whole way. She was moving so fast she had to slam into the side of the building in front of the stairs to slow her momentum. Her shoulder took the brunt of the hit while she pushed off and scrambled up the winding steps. Bullets struck above her, but she knew those silenced rifles didn't have the muzzle velocity to punch through the dense wood and strike her.

Somewhere in the distance, the screams began. She tried not to dwell on it.

Three short flights of steps had brought her to the last corner that would provide her cover from above. Once she popped out, three snipers already waiting for her would unload as she struggled to climb the last flight. She needed to even the odds, even if all the magical consumption was draining her. She looked back to George and raised a finger to wait.

"Now, baby," she whispered, feeding as much magic as Vincent needed across their tether.

"Caw," he replied from the skies above.

A blast of sound and woosh of air marked the raven's impression of a dive bomber. Cora made the break for it, running out with her aim held to the sky. Of the three snipers, only one took aim, unfazed by her Stunbomb. She was fast, but he was waiting. A quick, haphazard shot clipped her chest, just above her left breast. She tipped back, resolved to return fire before her lights went out. She only knew she was hit and it was bad, no concept of the repercussions. She fixed her sights on the stocky, angry Aztec and pulled off two shots. Blood splattered and rained down on her from above. She didn't even want to know where she hit. Her free hand clamped to her chest, the corner where the banister met the building was the only thing keeping her up now.

"Hold on, now!" George yelled.

She pointed up the stairs, choking out the only words she had air left to say. "Five seconds."

He moved past her as she tried to steady herself. The sheriff raced up the stairs with abandon, shots fired even before he disappeared from her view. Cora fell forward, onto all fours. The world was spinning. She tried to breathe, but a lump filled her throat. It tickled her lungs, and she hacked out blood. Along with the cough, there was the distinctive sound of heavy metal striking the wooden landing. She looked down at the spent bullet. Her body took a lot less time to eject that one than it did in Paris. She supposed that was a good sign, but she also supposed that train of thought was a result of shock.

Crawling on her hands and knees, Cora climbed up the stairs, white-knuckling her Predator. Gunfire roared out above. Once she reached the top of the stairs, it ceased. George stood at the center of the roof against a backdrop of blue skies. The remaining two snipers lay motionless on opposite ends of the roof. She crawled a few more steps forward, trying to speak, but nothing would come out except hacking, bloody coughs.

The sheriff ran to her, taking a knee beside her and cradling her into his arms.

"Stay awake, ma'am," he said. His voice was back to normal, gone with the southern drawl. "You can heal through this?"

Cora looked up at his face, but she was seeing spots. She replied with a meek nod, knowing she'd only need to wait it out. In a way, it was terrifying. She got to experience a mortal wound, and the horror that comes with the end of life for a matter of moments before returning to a world where she couldn't seem to die. Her thoughts were broken by the screams below. She'd tried to tune them out, but in the absence of her ears filled with the sound of her pounding heart, cries and pleas were all that was left.

George noticed it, too, his head set in the direction of the sounds. She could only imagine his horror and disgust. It certainly couldn't match her own with the dark power, but whether he'd still want to associate with her after seeing those abominations was another story.

Another ball formed in her throat, this one coming with more urgency. She rolled away from George's grip, coughing out a thick wad of blood mixed with discarded lung tissue. It was vile and gory, turning her stomach instantly, but she could breathe again, deep and refreshing. She took heaving breaths in ragged, exhausted fashion.

The cries of men moved further away from her, then stopped altogether. Her dizzy head awash from asphyxiation, she couldn't focus enough to access her magic. The frigid cord tethering the undead to her will burned into her right arm, even as she couldn't see it there. Another glance at the wound in her chest, and she was just in time to watch the skin close around it. As she struggled to get to her feet, George put his hands into her armpits and pulled her up.

"Are you...you again?" Cora asked.

"I am," George replied, getting her to her feet. "I would hope you can explain how that happened to me later."

"I'll give it shot," she replied, though anything she said would be a guess.

She walked on trembling, unsteady legs to the edge of the roof. George joined at her side and gasped. From up here, there was a clear view of the interior of the compound. Tototl screeched and howled over a corpse on the deck one building over. The savage, mindless monster beat down with both fists against the chest of a man that had clearly been long dead for some time. Cora shook her head and blinked, summoning the dark vision back.

"I'm sorry you had to see this," she said. Dropping her head, she stared at the glowing blue cord wound around her wrist all the way to her elbow. She spun her arm in a circle, as if unbinding it from her. As it slid from her arm and pulled away, it disintegrated to sparkling blue dust. Like puppets with their strings cut, Tototl and the rest, wherever they were, crumpled into piles.

"What did I just see?" George asked.

Cora turned to face him, knowing her eyes were still black from corner to corner. She wanted him to see all of her ugly, the power she was both ashamed of and feared more than any monster.

"Necromancy," she replied. "Death magic. I don't know why this power is within me, but every time I use it, it goes too far.

Tries to take me over. It allowed me to make those...things."

George turned his head and looked out across the coast. Flashing lights moved toward them from far down the main road. He turned back to Cora. "C'mon, we don't have much time."

He made way for the stairs with a fast step. Cora followed behind, filled with confusion.

"That's it? I use that power and you aren't running for the hills?"

"Oh, I assure you, ma'am, that was a terrible sight I won't soon forget," he replied, racing down the stairs. "But I've seen what monsters look like. You aren't one of them. We came here for information. Let's hope there's someone alive to give it to us."

By the time they'd hit the bottom of the stairs, there were sirens in the distance, drawing closer. George split off, checking every last body for a pulse. Moving from the red building to the amber one, there were many that weren't worth checking. Blood and gore, from wounds no man could survive, marked the trail of death Cora's abominations had left in their wake. She sighed, nauseated by her handiwork.

"We don't have time to check for people hiding inside the buildings," George shook his head.

Desperate for an answer, Cora pulled from the darkness and granted Spirit Sight. If any wayward spirit remained, she could try and question them in the scant time remaining. At the scene of a car wreck, even in an empty forest, Cora could find spirits holding on for something to give them peace. As she checked one body after another, surveying the compound as far as her eyes could see in every direction, there was nothing to be found.

"That's impossible," Cora whispered to herself. "Every one of these men accepted their death?"

"What does that mean?" George asked.

Cora shook her head. "There aren't any spirits here. Not a single one. It's like they all were fine with it. No unfinished business, no last words, nothing keeping them here at all."

"And that's strange?" George asked, looking over his shoulder to the sirens growing louder.

"It is," Cora replied, stunned. She took one last look around and choked up. "But if we didn't get any information...all of these men died for nothing."

George put a hand on her shoulder. "That's how I know you're not a monster, Cora. You have a heart. C'mon, there's nothing we can do here. We have to get out of range of whatever is jamming our comms before the police get here."

Cora ran for the entrance, guilt stabbing her with each body she passed. Without any new lead to go on, those three people in London remained missing. She couldn't lose Leopold, not like this. Jumping over the fence, Cora and George only needed to make it another dozen feet before a bolt of lightning brought them back to Atlantis.

A DIFFERENT APPROACH

Gideon stood in front of the transport platform as Cora opened her eyes. On his left arm, a massive holographic Arcadia screen displayed between silver bands at his wrist and elbow. She leaned forward and rested her hands on bent knees. George stepped down, wobbly, but much better than he handled the first few transports. He offered a hand to Gideon.

"Nice to meet you in the flesh, so to speak," George said.

The two of them standing side by side, Cora realized she'd almost forgotten how tall Gideon was, always seeing his unconscious body in the computer room. George still had an inch or so on him, even without the hat and heeled boots. Either way, they both towered a foot over Cora.

"Likewise," Gideon replied, shaking his hand. He winced at the sight of Cora. "Oh, geez, is that blood?"

Cora looked down. The hole and the pool on her chest was all her, but the splatter on her awesome rock tee belonged to someone else.

"Yeah," she let out a heavy breath. "Turns out, our informant was connected to Aztec crime cartel. You might want to drop an anonymous tip to Cayman police. Blame it on a Sim deal gone bad or something. The crime boss was jamming signals, so I doubt there was any surveillance there."

"Were they involved in NextGen? Did you learn anything?" Gideon asked.

Cora balled her fists and stared at the ground. George set a hand on her shoulder and spoke for her.

"No. They seemed to know of the company, perhaps even went in on it, but the situation went life or death pretty quick," George sighed. "We didn't have time to look for survivors before the local PD showed up."

"Got it," Gideon nodded. "Geez. Do you guys need rest?"

"No!" Cora snapped back. "No. Have you got something for me?"

"PIECE OF SHIT!" Tesla yelled behind Gideon, banging his fists down on his computer. Over his shoulder, Madeline sprayed a fire extinguisher into the floor-to-ceiling metal box as it churned black smoke.

Cora looked around Gideon, then the whole of the lab. Three knights worked at various points in the room. Tesla stood behind his desk, arms crossed.

"Readings are wrong," Tesla shouted. "You not give power distribution as I specify!"

"Sorry," Gideon said to Cora. He turned over his shoulder. "What are your readings? Throw it at my head."

Filled with crazed Russian anger, Tesla picked up a tablet from his desk and whipped it like a throwing knife. With inhuman speed and his back turned, Gideon snatched it from the air and took a look at the screen. George reeled back.

"Woah! How'd you do that?"

Cora pointed at the hacker and took a seat on the platform. "This guy calls himself an 'enthusiast' of implants. He has as much tech in him as Madeline does."

"More," Madeline shouted from the other side of the room.

"See? More," Cora replied. "Wired-up central nervous system, eyes, arms, legs, the whole nine."

"Still less than Giovanna," Gideon said, his eyes glued to the screen. He nodded to himself and walked the tablet back to Tesla's desk. "You're right, sorry. I'm correcting it now. Get the coil ready for another jump."

Cora looked around the room as Gideon returned. "Brought in some engineers?"

Tesla shook his head. "No. Men here run electric grid. I install upgrades, test them with you."

Cora's eyes widened, brows raised. "Oh, how exciting. I've always wanted to be a human guinea pig. What kind of test, exactly?"

"We try new method of power distribution," Tesla replied with a dismissive wave. "Stupid American in my head have idea, maybe coil not burn out. No danger to you. Mostly."

Cora turned, alarmed. "Mostly?"

Tesla shrugged. "Worst case, machine explode, kill me, and you two have to swim back here."

The three knights in the room paused and turned to him. His eyes told them to get back to work.

"Is that all?" Cora said under her breath, walking to the far end of the room. She turned back to Gideon. "Where am I going?"

Gideon reached into the pocket of his tan khakis and pulled out two old-style identification wallets. Cora got excited. She loved acting.

"Kathleen O'Malley is now an attaché to Interpol," he said, handing one wallet to her, then the other to George. "And John Holliday is a consultant, investigating the possible connection with a known fugitive from the Free State of Texas."

"Thank you, sir," George bowed his head. "These can get us into the crime scenes in London?"

"They can and will," Gideon replied. "I've gone ahead and coordinated with local police. They have a Detective Constable Thomas that's going to give you a grand tour of Elea Nguyen's apartment."

"Oh, wow," Cora said, impressed with his work. "Guess I better run and change."

Gideon nodded back. "It's nighttime in London, and I need to help Tesla with the power distribution. Come back in about twenty minutes, I should be able to have the meet set up and iron everything out by then."

Cora nudged George with her elbow. "Alright, let's go. I think you could use more than beer for lunch."

She took the sheriff out of the lab, past the two knights on guard. Their stares told her what an alarming, bloody mess she was. She dismissed their expressions and moved on. It seemed silly to her, to have guards on any room in a base miles below the rest of humanity, but then she recalled the mole. One person on the station put the entire station and two hundred lives at risk. She looked at the featureless corridors and their hideous shade of green, knights every twenty yards, recycled air, and the horrid din of electricity. She hated this place, but she hated the idea of losing it even more.

"Ma'am," George said, his voice solemn.

Cora snapped from her thoughts, perking her head up as though she just discovered he was there.

"What the hell happened to me back there?" George asked.

She sighed. "I've experienced it twice. The first time, I all but asked for help from the spirit inside me. The second time, it took over to protect me. I was kidnapped, dosed with drugs to keep my magic suppressed, and drinking myself to death. That time, I didn't ask for it, but I couldn't stop it."

"That's what it felt like," George replied. "My spirit in life was a frail man, due to his health. Being in a stronger body, I could feel him want to take over. I remember...my blood started to boil when I saw that guy threaten you. I got so hot, and I just...lifted out of my body? I don't know how else to describe it."

"That's pretty apt," Cora shrugged. "The spirits aren't malevolent, but they are a different person. When we have some downtime, you might want to talk to Professor Crowley. He's a shrink, yes, but he's also studied dozens of the world's religions. He can teach you some techniques for controlling yourself."

"Shrinks?" he repeated with a curled lip.

Cora raised her hands. "I know, I feel the same way. But I would not have been able to control my necromantic powers over the past couple of months without him."

She came to a stop before a set of double doors and gestured to it.

"Where are we?"

"Mess hall," Cora replied with a smile. "The chef is an artifact holder. I haven't had a bad meal yet."

George's brow furrowed. "What? Chef? How are we even getting food down here?"

"Trade secret. I'll be back here in fifteen to pick you up?"

He tipped the brim of his hat to her. "Ma'am."

Cora lingered a moment longer. George cocked his head, stopping himself from opening the door.

"I want you to know," she started, pausing to take a breath. "I know you're tired. And maybe you've seen things out of me that might have given you concern. But you're still here. That means a lot to me."

George nodded and tipped his hat again before walking inside. He didn't need to reply. She knew he was a good man from the second she met him. Something about him told her that he was one of them right away. As she made her way to her quarters, back the way she came and west into E-Block, she found Giovanna coming from the opposite end of the hall. Cora smiled at the Italian supermodel shapeshifter. She would have known it was her from a mile away. There weren't any other people on the station that could be found walking around in a black Versace dress.

They met up at the door to Cora's quarters. Giovanna looked her up and down with a raised eyebrow.

"How much of that is yours, patatina?" she asked.

Cora punched in her door code, and it slid open with a hiss. Looking down at her shirt, her face soured. "At least half, maybe more. Most of it, actually. What were you up to?"

"I was looking for you," she replied, letting herself into the room behind Cora. She sniffed the room as she came in.

Cora didn't have time for judgment, playful or otherwise. She loved Giovanna like an older sister, even if they did look the same age. Once she heard the door close, she peeled off her shirt and bra, throwing them into a pile on the floor. There was hardly a point in modesty around a woman who was both flawless on the outside, and a horribly deformed burn victim under the facade. The nanites in her skin cells had even taken Cora's form at one point.

She left the bathroom door open and turned on the shower stall. As the water heated up, she emerged and went for the suitcase beside her bed. She rummaged around until she found the only dress blouse and skirt she owned.

"How long has it been since you slept?" Giovanna asked. Her Italian accent grew thick and high-pitched when she was upset.

Cora took off her biker boots and scooted out of her jeans. "I had a few hours between Texas and the Cayman Islands."

"Did you sleep?" Giovanna pressed, hands on her hips.

"No. What did you come here for, to lecture me? Leopold is still out there somewhere."

She walked stark naked past Giovanna and stepped under the shower. Giovanna followed, standing in the doorway.

"I'm saying this isn't your fault," Giovanna pressed. She shook her head. "You can't go from one tragedy to another, trying to put out fires like a chicken with your head cut off."

Cora soaped the blood from her skin until the water in the drain ran clear. "You taught me to endure, remember? Torture training, sleep deprivation...you and Richard made sure I could handle this."

"I also taught you to separate yourself from the work," Giovanna replied. She walked into the bathroom, inches from the water stream. She pressed her hand to Cora's collar, above her left breast. She shook her head, but Cora wasn't sure if it was disappointment or sadness. "I can see the new skin. The scar tissue that grew with it. I've been in combat with you, before you were a superhero, back when this would have killed you. You didn't get this being safe, did you?"

Cora pulled her shoulder away and grabbed for her shampoo. "I have the power, may as well use it."

Giovanna pulled her back around to face her and gave a gentle

84

slap on the cheek. It wasn't meant to hurt, only enough to sting. Still, it caught Cora off-guard, leaving her mouth hanging open.

"No! Your power is not an excuse to be reckless!" Giovanna raised her voice. Her eyes glassed over with tears. She made a gun with her hand and put it to Cora's temple. "One of these times, they're going to get you in the head. What then? You going to regrow a goddamn brain, or start using the one you have?"

"Okay, okay," Cora replied, raising her hand in surrender. "You're right, okay? I'm exhausted, and yeah, I'm probably getting reckless."

Giovanna shook her head and returned her hands to her hips. "I know you cared for the old man, patatina. I would do anything to take that pain away from you. But right now, it's clouding your judgment. You know you can't use all this technology to be everywhere in the world at once, use all of your powers and never sleep. You're going back out again, aren't you?"

Gideon. That lanky bastard was worried about her and ratted her out to Giovanna. He probably knew Johnny would admire Cora's gumption, so he told the hot-blooded Italian instead. Whether it was sweet or well-intentioned, right now it was another obstacle to overcome, even if Giovanna was right. Her conniptions could be rather convincing, but it wasn't like Cora could stop now. She robotically washed her hair, unable to enjoy the sanctity of the hot water relaxing her sore muscles.

"I have to," she replied. "This other victim is all we have left. I fucked up. I completely burned that lead in the Caymans. I'm running out of time."

"Let me go," Giovanna replied. "I'll take your recruit with me and we'll go. I'll even go as you if it would make him feel better. Just stay here and rest."

"Do you really think I'd sleep for half a second?"

"I can do anything you can do...we're talking to a bunch of cops," Giovanna replied with a dismissive wave of her hand. She shrugged. "It's not like you need to be out there, casting spells or talking to ghosts."

"Har-har," Cora replied.

"I'm serious," Giovanna insisted.

"So am I. I gave Leopold that artifact and turned him loose. I made him a target. And now he's gone," Cora said.

Giovanna stared at the ceiling. Next would come the part where she compared Cora to a mule and described talking to a wall. Cora braced herself.

"What was the alternative? Force him to stay? He wanted to leave!"

"He didn't understand the risks!" Cora raised her voice.

Giovanna raised an eyebrow, her lips turned down. She said everything with that look. Cora was being stubborn, trying to blame herself for things she had no control over. It didn't matter. No one was looking for Leopold. Cora kept his girlfriend from calling the cops. Cora swore she'd find him.

"What good are these abilities if I can't use them to save anyone?" Cora said, her emotions running too close to the surface for her liking. She couldn't afford to break down, not now.

Cora turned off the water and toweled off. Giovanna stayed silent. There wasn't a good answer to her question, there never was. Whether it was her father, Pops, Living Wind, or Merlin, they all left her with a void in her heart. Maybe if she could just save somebody, for once, she could sleep without nightmares and regret.

She sighed and moved past Giovanna, back to the bed. Cora got dressed into her presentable outfit. A glance up at the Italian wasn't even necessary. She could feel the eyes on her, face crinkled up at her fashion sense.

"Spit it out," Cora said. "You hate the outfit? It's the only dress clothes I own at the moment. The rest of my clothes are still sitting in a storage unit in Washington."

"What are you going as?" Giovanna asked, wincing as though she were bracing herself.

Cora rolled her eyes. "It's not Halloween! Well, yeah it is like that, I guess...an Interpol agent."

"In that outfit?"

"What's wrong with it? You picked it out!" Cora shouted,

throwing her hands up in defeat.

"I did?" Giovanna gasped, putting her hand to her chest, horrified.

"You did," Cora replied, sliding on pantyhose. "After we fled Berlin, we landed in Washington, and I needed to debrief at the Pentagon. This was the outfit you picked out."

Giovanna walked over to her with that obnoxious, sultry sway of her hips that was both hypnotic and distracting. Cora was convinced she didn't even know she was doing it anymore. She stopped in front of her and examined the cream-colored blouse and black skirt as if she had to fetch a diamond ring from a garbage can.

"We were in an airport mall, patatina," she said. "You work with what you have. I can get you another outfit."

"No time," Cora replied and shook her head. She grabbed her Predator and unclipped the holster from her jeans on the floor. Digging through her suitcase, she pulled out the few fresh clips she had left, leaving the clips with illegal Rhino rounds in the case. "I have to get George and get to the lab."

Giovanna waited until Cora stood up and moved into her path. Her rushing around the room came to an abrupt halt. Giovanna hooked one nail under her chin and forced her to meet her gaze. Cora huffed.

"For me, patatina," she pleaded. "Delegate. Don't push yourself too hard. You're not alone. Rest, soon."

"I promise, I will," Cora nodded. "For now, I've got George."

Giovanna kissed her on both cheeks and followed her out of the room. Back in the ugly green corridors, the pair walked side-by-side for the mess hall. Cora's tension kept her silent. She should have known better. Silence was like a blank canvas to an Italian woman. It yearned to be filled.

"So, is he cute?"

PROOF OF LIFE

Of course it was raining. That's all London ever did, every single time she'd been there. She should have been coming around the corner from the alley and meeting with the detective constable. Instead, she was standing in the rain, waiting for George to finish emptying his lunch into the gutter.

"I'm sorry, ma'am," he grunted, bracing his hand against the brick wall. "I didn't shut my eyes fast enough."

"It's okay, George," she said, patting his back. "It took me a while to get used to it, myself. Johnny still gets nauseous to this day."

Pushing off the wall, George righted himself and wiped his mouth with the sleeve of his duster. After a deep breath and a quick nod, he lead her out from the alley behind a three-floor terraced house on Ashfield Street. The black sky hid away the moon, leaving the wet streets with an orange glow from the holographic lights further into the city. They crossed the street and approached the location. A middle-aged man stood under an umbrella outside another terraced house. It was brick for the most part, painted white across the first floor with a bright yellow door.

Cora approached the pasty, rotund man with an expressionless, stone stare. Kathleen O'Malley was a joyless, cold woman. She was good at her job, but it had hardened her, so she could often come off curt, or even rude. She pulled out her wallet identification for the detective's inspection.

"Agent O'Malley, Interpol," she said.

"Good Irish name for an...Indian woman?" he replied.

"Native, actually," Cora replied with a tone that invited no further questions of her ethnicity.

"Picked a hell of a night to go out without an umbrella, eh? Detective Constable Thomas," he replied, squinting as he pretended to read her credentials. Cora snapped the wallet closed before he could really get a look. "Who's the big man, then?"

Cora motioned to George with her head. "John Holliday. We're working with the Americans on this one."

"Texans," George corrected.

The detective smiled with a spiteful glee. "All Americans to us, am I right?" He let out a belly laugh at his own joke. Cora kept her face stone. Realizing what kind of night he was about to have, the detective abandoned the humor and waved them toward the yellow door. "Follow me."

He shook out his umbrella and closed it, stepping inside a small foyer. They followed him up a flight of stairs. The path was narrow, but as long as she was out of the rain, Cora didn't care. The out-of-shape detective, however, wheezed with each step. By the time they were at the landing for the first flight, he was out of breath. He pushed forward, either unaware of how labored he sounded, or too bothered with impressing the agents to care. He took them down the first hall, to a row of doors.

"Spared no expense for your little visit," Thomas said, looking over his shoulder to Cora. "A forensic team was here about an hour ago. They set up holographic emitters so you could see what we saw."

Cora's brow furrowed. "Is this being treated as a homicide?"

"Not yet, no," he shook his head, stopping at a door. "But there were enough reasons to be concerned."

Police tape blocked off the door. Thomas punched in a code on the lock panel beside the door and opened it up. Standing to the side, he waved them in. Cora crossed the threshold, into a place

Gideon's hacking could not penetrate. The crime scene could give her insight to the connection between this woman and Leopold. What she wouldn't see with her own eyes, the detective could field questions and fill in the blanks.

The flat was a cramped one-bedroom. A faded, brown leather couch on the far end of the room sat in front of a holovid screen. Beside her, the tiny kitchen walkway was enough for only one person. The counter, sink, and stove were compressed so close together, she couldn't imagine preparing anything fancy in that space. Small black boxes were positioned strategically throughout the living area, projecting holographic images of any objects already collected as evidence.

Cora stepped past the entrance with George in tow, waiting for the detective to enter. He came in with a shrug.

"Only a few things to see, really," he said, his breathing heavy. "These apartments are pretty small. Mostly university kids in the area."

Cora made her way to the living room, surveying everything. Like Leopold's flat, there were a few things out of place in an otherwise well-kept home. A pillow and lamp rested on the floor in the center of the room. The throw-rug was crumpled, more signs of a struggle that took place here. She shut her eyes and recalled the scene at Leopold's house.

"In the kitchen, was there blood?" she asked.

"A few droplets, yes, and-"

"Her IdentChip," Cora interjected, shaking her head. Leopold's chip was under the dining room table, carved out of the implantation deep in the wrist.

George wandered on his own, past Cora and into the bedroom. Thomas cocked his head.

"What are we talking about here that concerns Interpol, if I may?" he asked. "Human trafficking? A killer?"

"Unclear at this time," Cora replied without looking at him. "There are distinct similarities between some of what was going on in Texas and what popped up in two cases here."

"Two?" Thomas repeated, puzzled.

"Olivia Orwell," Cora said, returning to the entrance area. She examined the blood splatter, and a holographic image of where the IdentChip was found.

Thomas shook his head. "My mate is working Orwell. We already had a sit-down about it, decided they were unrelated. No blood, no struggle, no bloody IdentChip. Girl is just gone."

George's heavy footfalls drew closer as he came back from the bedroom and moved to the bathroom. Squatted down, Cora snapped a few pictures with her Arcadia.

"Have you checked their communication and bank records?"

Thomas hesitated on the answer. "We put in the order, but we have not received them yet."

Cora stood up and put her hands on her hips. She sighed. There wasn't much here to investigate.

"NextGen Holdings," she said. "Does that company name mean anything to you?"

Thomas' brow furrowed. "No. Should it?"

George stepped halfway out of the bathroom, across from the counter. His face showed concern, his tone came out grim. "Agent, you need to see this."

Cora walked around the counter, but Thomas stood in her way. He looked concerned and uncomfortable, tensing his muscles as he leaned in to speak.

"Understand, what you're going to see is not proof of homicide," he warned.

Her blood started to boil. What had he kept from her, and why? He knew she was going to search the scene. Whatever George found, Cora would have found it herself, eventually. She blew past him, angry and fearful.

The bathroom theme was pink everything - towels, shower curtain, and throw rug. So much pink.

A single emitter rested on the towel rack, pointed at the sink. Cora's eyes followed to the mirror. Dried brown liquid traced out words in blood.

Stop looking.

Cora took a step closer. The blood was real. It hadn't been

washed away yet. Cora turned her head back, looking at the emitter, following it back to the sink. As she looked at the sink counter, a hazel eye stared back at her. She reeled back in terror. A single eyeball rested in a soap dish in a puddle of blood. Still in shock and disbelief, her gaze turned to George. His lips were turned down, hands on his hips. The detective appeared in the doorway.

"It's not our missing girl," Thomas said.

George shook his head in disgust. "We know. Miss Nguyen had green eyes," he huffed, walking out of the room.

Cora froze. Her heart skipped a beat. Leopold had hazel eyes. She raised a finger, pointing at the eyeball, but she choked on the words. She didn't want to ask. She didn't want to know. That message on the mirror wasn't for the cops. It was for her.

"You did a DNA analysis of the eye?" Cora said, her voice scant above a whisper. She couldn't look away from the horror staring back at her.

Thomas' head followed George as he left the bathroom. "We did. The blood on the mirror matches the blood in the kitchen. The eyeball didn't."

In a daze, head spinning, Cora swiped out the screen to her Arcadia. Her eyes couldn't focus on the screen. Her ears were on fire. Fear and confusion gripped her. With a few sloppy gestures, she set up a channel to receive data, which would stream right to Gideon. "Give me the DNA profile, please."

"Are you going to tell me if you have a match?"

"No," Cora said, her gaze as cold as her voice. "Do it anyway."

The detective sighed and grumbled something to himself. He moved through his Arcadia and swiped a screen in her direction. The file transfer started, Cora restrained herself from yelling a stream of questions at the detective.

"Can we start with why you didn't mention this until we found it?"

"Must've slipped my mind, then," Thomas replied. He leaned against the door frame. "But I figure now that you found it, you Interpol folks are probably going to want to take over the investigation?"

Cora groaned and stared at the ceiling. She couldn't explicitly state she was pretending to be an international agent, but she wasn't in any mood to play jurisdictional games. "Look, I have a case of my own to deal with, I don't need or want yours. If I promise to leave the case in your jurisdiction, could you just be open with me about your investigation?"

Detective Thomas' brow furrowed. He stood up straight and nodded, his neck fat jiggling. Cora took his surprise as leverage.

"Tell me everything about...this," she waved in the direction of the sink.

He shrugged. "Not much to tell. Other than knowing it isn't our girl, what you see is what we know. Her more expensive personal effects are still in her bedroom. No one has called her family for a ransom."

Cora couldn't focus. The eye was staring at her. The message was taunting her. She didn't want the eye to belong to Leopold, but she already knew it did. The soft-spoken biology professor was hidden away somewhere, being tortured and crying for help, and she wasn't there. She gave him his artifact and let him walk away from the protection of Atlantis. She shook her head and moved past the detective, out of the bathroom and into Elea's tiny bedroom.

George was already there, standing in the corner of the room with his hands on his hips. He was squinting as he examined the room, as if he were focused on committing every inch to memory. The room smelled like incense, a floral bouquet that was sickly sweet. The girl's bed was made with precision. Her dresser gleamed like a beacon, with light reflecting off the diamonds in her watch.

It struck Cora as odd to see it. She walked to the dresser and lifted it. She turned it over and shook her head.

"What is it?" George asked, his voice low.

Cora whispered back, showing him the watch. "This is a Cartier. Giovanna has one of these. They're like over ten thousand credits for low-end models."

She looked over her shoulder and raised her voice to the detective. "You mentioned calling her parents for a ransom. Are they rich?"

"Dad works in Elven Affairs in Tokyo," he replied. "It's a government job, so he's pretty comfortable. I talked to him, but he said that he and Miss Nguyen had a falling out. He did not want her to leave, threatened to cut her off, so she called his bluff. Turns out, Dad wasn't playing around."

Cora huffed, returning to her lower voice, intended only for George. "This isn't adding up. She's a glorified intern at a high-end salon, trying to stick it to her dad, but doesn't pawn the watch? The kidnapper leaves it here..."

George continued staring ahead to the room, fixated on something. Cora wanted a dive into his head, wondering how the scene looked through his eyes.

"No," George said. "Nothing about this is adding up."

He turned around and faced Thomas, thumbing the room behind him. "Why does the bedroom not look like it was turned?"

"Poked around a bit," Thomas said, shaking his head. His lip curled, dismissing the notion. "All the struggle you got right here, in the living room, and that disaster in the bathroom. Doesn't look like the bedroom was involved at all. Bed still made and everything."

George balled his fists and shut his eyes. It looked like he was suppressing a tide of rage. His face got flush and he shook his head. He turned back around and walked to the bed. Pulling the covers away, he ran his hand along the pink, silken sheets. His fingers traced along the pillows, the mattress, then stopped under the pillow. He took a breath, bracing himself. Grabbing up the corner of the sheets in a tight fist, he pulled the sheets away. A brown, terrycloth bath towel spread from the headboard lengthwise down the bed.

"Dammit," George sighed. He stepped to the side, pulling the corner of the towel away.

With his massive frame out of the way, three large brown stains blotted the mattress. One was where the bed met the pillow.

Another was at the left side, with a final one in the middle. Cora covered her mouth and gasped.

"What the bleedin' hell?" Thomas guffawed, stepping into the doorway.

George knelt down beside the bed, where the left stain carried all the way to the edge of the mattress. He held out both his hands as though he were cradling a pipe in his hands. His eyes cast down to the floor, following the position of his hands. He turned on the projector light from his Arcadia and checked the rug, moving his fingers slowly to brush it aside.

"This is where it happened," George said, his tone grim.

"No," Cora said, shaking her head. She felt like she knew his every word that would come next. Information to work from whittled away and now hope was making its way out the door.

"He knelt here, and he took the chip out," George said. He stood up and pointed at the stain by the pillow. "She was already dead by then. He had cut her throat. He didn't take the chip so we wouldn't find her, he doesn't want us finding where he hid her body."

The dark tone of the sheriff turned to anger as he looked back at the Detective Constable. "You did a real disservice to this girl not being thorough. Maybe now you'll do your job if you start treating it as a goddamn homicide!"

With that, George stormed right at Thomas, standing in the doorway. The fat man had to move fast to clear out of his way. It didn't appear George was going to slow down. As Cora listened, she heard the front door open and slam shut again.

Cora looked away from the bed, her heart breaking. Thomas appeared dumbfounded, but he deserved no sympathy. Cora didn't have any left to give any damn way. She shook her head at him and headed for the door.

"Shite, wait!" Thomas said, following her.

Cora turned at the door, one hand on the handle. "What?"

"Can't you tell me anything? Who are we even looking for?"

"Start digging into NextGen Holdings. Get with your friend working the Orwell case. Assume she's more than just a missing person," Cora asked, her eyes narrowed.

The detective shook his head. "So, you're under the impression these are both homicides done by the same person?"

Cora rolled her eyes and huffed. Her fear and guilt bubbling at the surface, it took everything in her to keep the tears from her eyes. She gnashed her teeth. "You're absolutely useless to me. Tell you what, you have our office number. If you manage to figure something out, you be sure to pass it along. If you do that, I might just keep this bumbling, half-assed investigation out of my reports."

"I will, Agent O'Malley," Thomas nodded like a scolded child. "You'll be the first to hear."

Cora didn't say another word. She couldn't if she wanted to. Slamming the door behind her, she weaved under the police tape and made her way downstairs. Tapping the comm button on her ear, there was only one question that mattered now. She didn't want the answer, but she had to hear it.

"Call Gideon," she said, trotting down the stairs. He picked up on the first ring. "Are you comparing what I sent you against the blood sample Doctor Daly got from Leopold in sickbay?"

"I am working on it, although I should warn you, I've never used an app for DNA matching before," Gideon replied. "It looks like it's going to take a few minutes...Do you have a suspicion it is?"

Cora stopped halfway down the stairs and shut her eyes. She couldn't hold it anymore. Leaning against the wall, the tears rolled down her cheek. Her voice cracked as she tried to answer.

"It was an eyeball, Gideon," she cried out.

"Oh, Christ," he replied.

Dead air filled the space between them. Gideon didn't know what else to say. Cora choked on the words as she continued. "Whoever did this left a message. It said, 'stop looking' in blood. Elea Nguyen's blood. But...it isn't her eye. The color...it's Leopold's eye color."

"Cora, come home," Gideon replied. His robotic, tinny voice made an impression of compassion. "If the worst is true and it's his, then we know he's gone. If not, then we keep hope alive, but it's going to take time to dig into these leads. NextGen is a proxy of a proxy. They do not want people knowing who or where they are."

"I swear to you, Gideon, even if he is gone, I'm going to find the guy that did this," Cora said. Anger and hatred coursed through her veins thinking about the monster. "I'm going to find him, and when I do...I'm going to take my time with him, Gideon."

ROCK BOTTOM

Cora stared at the cherry-stained oak of the bar. The crowd inside Dottie's Diner was background noise that she could tune out as long as she admired the grain, the shine, or how clean Dottie kept it. Her eyes moved back to the bottle of whiskey in front of her. The black label and white text blended into this blurry soup she couldn't quite read, and that was right at the level of intoxicated she wanted to be.

"So, it matched?" Still River said.

Cora took a pull from the bottle. "Of course it did. I knew it was Leopold's eye before we ever got the results. There, now you know."

"It took almost a week of moping and hiding in the forest before I could get it out of you?" her father said, adjusting his seat on the stool next to her. "Cora, this wasn't your fault. You can't shut down."

"Hey!" she said, pointing at him. She tried to focus on his face, but all she could make out was long black hair and a tanned face. She turned to the bar crowd. She couldn't see them either, but she imagined they were all staring at them. "Look around, Dad. Know why all these people are looking at us? You're a goddamn ghost, and you're telling me how to live, that's why."

Still River looked around the room before coming back to her.

"No one is looking. Well, maybe a few, but that's probably because they've never seen anyone drink that much and not die."

Cora stood and threw her hands up. Her words slurred together as she stumbled to keep her balance. "You know what? You wanted to know. Now you know."

She staggered past him and out the front door. It was much darker out than when she started her binge-drinking. She stopped and marveled at the full moon, hanging low in the sky and so bright. In a daze, she wandered into the parking lot. Her boots scraped along the ground with each step, kicking up gravel and making a racket. Patting herself down from Richard's jacket to her jeans, she hunted for the fob to her Harley. She'd only need to figure out where it was in the parking lot. Her memory on that was a bit fuzzy.

The bike had red trim on black, she remembered that much. Walking a straight line from the door, or as straight as she thought it was, she startled as she looked up. Still River rested ahead of her, leaned against her bike.

"Do not do that shit!" she yelled. Just because he could manifest himself seemingly anywhere in Heaven's Crest did not mean it was okay to sneak up on a girl like that.

He motioned with his head to the bike. "If you think I'm letting you drive like this, you're out of your mind."

"Who cares? It doesn't matter," Cora tripped over her words. "Nothing matters. If I die, the war ends. But we know I'm not gonna die, right, Dad? Fate has already spelled it all out for me. Leopold was supposed to die. I go out driving after two bottles of Jack and I get to live, no matter what."

Still River stood up with a start. Her vision too blurred to make out any details, it wasn't until he was almost on top of her that she saw the anger in his eyes. He raised a hand glowing with soft, pink light and pressed it to her chest. The energy from his touch hit like a punch, first in her chest, sucking her air away. The energy moved through her. She couldn't breathe. She stumbled backwards, away from him. With sudden force, the power wrapped around her throat. Her stomach twisted in knots. She clutched at her throat with both hands, gasping for air.

As she dropped to all fours, she felt the sear of pain as the tiny gravel shredded her knees through the holes in her jeans. The inside of her mouth filled with thin, warm saliva. She shut her eyes. She'd been fall-down drunk enough times to know what came next, though she couldn't remember the last time she'd gotten to this point before her regeneration put a stop to it. She threw up her entire stomach to the ground in repeated bouts of heaving. By the time she was through, cold droplets of sweat trickled down her brow. She opened her eyes to a world with so much clarity, it threatened to overload her senses.

"What...did you do to me?" she asked, her speech clear and precise. Any effect the alcohol had on her was gone.

"I will *not* sit back and watch you fill yourself with poison every time something doesn't go your way," Still River replied, his tone stern. "Like it or not, the war is between the dragon and you. You are human. You will make mistakes. People will die. You're going to have to accept the consequences of that, but you will not place that as a burden on your soul."

He reached down and lifted her up. She kept her head down, tears streaming down her cheeks. She was nine again and getting a lecture for being bad. A year ago, she'd have given anything to have this back. The reality made her feel small. He put his hand under her chin and met her gaze.

"Of the 687 souls that support you in this war, every single one will accept they had a choice," he continued.

Cora's voice warbled out, "Leopold didn't ask for this."

"He made a choice to walk away," Still River said. Gone was the blurry, angry look, replaced with the chiseled, leathery features of his strong Native face and flowing black hair. His eyes were full of compassion. "Perhaps Lucius' men did this, perhaps it was random. But you didn't do it, Cora. If you can't learn that lesson by now - after Living Wind, Pops...me..."

Cora fell into his arms and let herself go. She heaved and sobbed into his chest and he wrapped his arms around her. His corporeal form was frigid to the touch and completely unnatural, but there wasn't anywhere else she wanted to be. The numbness of thought brought on by drinking was gone. She felt stripped down, naked in a crowded room, her emotions out on display for the whole world. She envied drunk Cora from a few moments ago. This level of vulnerability was too much.

"I wanted to save him, Dad...I just wanted to save someone," she wept.

"I know, baby," he replied, patting her back.

She continued until her head throbbed and her eyes swelled. All the while, her father kept her close. She sniffled and caught her breath.

"Now, can you take us home on this two-wheeled death trap of yours?" Still River joked.

Cora stepped back from his embrace. "I could use the fresh air on my face. Go materialize at the house or whatever the hell it is that you do. I'll be there soon."

"Cora..."

She shook her head. "Really, it's okay. I've been here sulking, and George has had to get used to Atlantis by himself. Gideon is still looking into the shell company. I'm just feeling a little guilty."

Her father wagged a finger at her. "You knew you needed to step away, for the good of everyone. They're capable, exceptional people. They can prove that to you even when you're not there."

"I know," Cora nodded, brushing the tears away with her sleeve. "I do. That doesn't mean I don't feel like shit for not helping. I'll see you back at the house."

"As you wish," he said. Still River stepped back from her and dissipated into tiny balls of light and faded from view.

Cora dragged herself to the bike and threw a leg over the seat. The ride to Sitting Bear's cabin atop Heaven's Crest wasn't far, but she craved the solitude. The wind and the trees, the sun and the moon, she'd missed so much in Atlantis that connected her with nature. As the desire to ride intensified, so did the secondary feeling of anxiety. The feeling wasn't her own. She looked up and around Dottie's and found Vincent on the roof above the door.

"I'm fine," she said. She rolled her eyes and mumbled to

herself. "Now I'm consoling a spirit bird that worries too much. Yeah, my life is totally normal."

"Caw," Vincent said. He wanted to join her.

"On my shoulder or in the sky? Whichever you want, it's fine," she replied, getting her helmet on.

The raven knew her pretty well by now, she assumed. As she sped off, he kept to the skies above, invisible in the dark, yet he was always near. Sure, he had his own secrets he kept. The hairless, hammer-wielding beast of a man that joined the battle in Paris called him Munnin. A basic search on NeuralNet brought up all kinds of mythological references to that name. Who or what that raven was remained a mystery. She wanted to ask him. Of course, her Native name was Speaks With Ravens, though she was given the name without any of the little bastards talking back.

She arrived at the long, uphill driveway and parked next to Sitting Bear's beat-up old truck. The porch light was on for her, though she'd stumbled in from the forest in the dead of night so many times she could have found her way blindfolded by now. Taking one last refreshing breath of the night air through her nose, she pushed through the front door with Vincent in tow. He took to the upper beams right away. It was his favorite spot in the house to perch, lording over the whole house.

Across the living room, at the dining room table, the massive tank of a man that was her uncle sat at the head. His long, gray braids draped over both shoulders. In his hand, he fanned out a stack of black playing cards. Beside him, with his back to her, was Still River. Across from him sat Rhonda, a hippie woman from over a hundred years ago that was so connected to these lands, her spirit never left. She wore a bright red bandana across her forehead, and hid her eyes with large, round sunglasses.

"It's nine at night," Cora said, motioning to her. "How can you even see with those on?"

Rhonda smiled and tapped on the side of her shades. "I gotta keep a poker face. These two keep guessing all my cards."

"You have an expressive face," Sitting Bear replied with a grin.

Cora laughed and took her jacket off, laying it on the couch.

The holovid was on, but the volume was muted. A three-dimensional image of a bridge in China rotated on the screen. The vivid, oversaturated colors of the Vista Channel made it look more idyllic than it was. Cora had been there a few years back with Richard.

"Come on, Cora, I need help over here," Rhonda said.

Her eyes turned away from the mesmerizing display on the holovid and back to the table. "What are you guys playing?"

"New World," Still River replied, holding up a game tile. "You should jump in, we're just getting started."

She held up her hands in surrender. "Oh, no. I could never understand the rules, but I know the game always ends with someone flipping the table over."

"What? Not us!" Sitting Bear replied, mocking offense.

Cora joined them in a round of laughter. It was the first genuine laugh she had since she arrived. Her Arcadia buzzed on her wrist. She still wasn't ready. The smile wiped from her face. Whoever it was would need to call later. She raised up her arm to dismiss the call, but her silver bracelet was lit up red. It was an emergency call. Her heart fluttered. She dug into her pocket and fished out her earpiece. She tapped the comm button.

"What's going on? Is everything okay?"

"I need you to relax," Gideon replied in his robot voice. He was never out of NeuralNet anymore. "What I'm going to tell you could be something, but it could be nothing, too."

"Spit it out," she replied, turning away from her family.

"I can't break the security on the Cayman Islands bank, so I did the next best thing," he said. "I found a weak point in their communications routing and set up a listening post for outgoing wire transfers from that NextGen account both girls were getting deposits from. I just got a hit in London."

Cora's eyes flared wide. She ran for the guest room and piled all of her possessions into her bag in the dark. "Prep the transport. As soon as you get me back, I need Tesla swapping the coil. Is George aware of the situation?"

"Actually, I thought you might ask, so I notified him first,"

Gideon replied with a sigh. "He'll be waiting for you in Tesla's lab when you get here."

"Two minutes," Cora said, her voice frantic. "I'll give you the signal."

"Line is open," Gideon replied.

Before zipping her bag, Cora dug through it in the dark. It wasn't hard to find her holster and the fully loaded Predator inside. She withdrew it and clipped it to the back of her jeans. She closed up her bag and stepped sure into the living room, making sure to put Richard's jacket back on. She felt the tension all around her in the room, the eyes of everyone on her. They knew what she'd say, that she had to go again. They'd understand. Knowing that didn't bring her any comfort. She wanted them to twist her arm into playing their game and forgetting life for a while. Those weren't the cards she'd be getting dealt tonight.

Her father stood up, saving her the trouble. "I want you to be careful. Reckless doesn't suit you."

"I can't promise that," Cora replied, setting her bag on the floor. "Although, you are not the first person to say that to me lately. Maybe I should start listening."

Sitting Bear and Rhonda stood up and came around from their seats. They formed a line for Cora to say her goodbyes. Tears came to her eyes. She hated this part. This was the only place she wanted to be, and she was tired of leaving it behind. She hugged Rhonda and her uncle, pecking him on the cheek. Saving her father for last, she awaited another last-minute lecture. Nothing came. He held her until she was done and not a second more. She forgot how well he knew her for someone that missed the last half of her childhood.

"I love you guys," she sniffled. "I'll be back as soon as I can."

"We'll be here...waiting," Still River replied.

She walked out the front door, onto the covered porch. Cora shut her eyes. "Vincent."

The raven fluttered down from the ceiling, passed through the door and landed on her shoulder. She tapped the comm button on her earpiece. "Gideon, go for transport."

After the blast of light, she waited for the world to stop spinning. The din of electricity, the pulse of energy passing through the lights, the shitty recycled air, it assaulted her senses on every front. Her eyes opened to George, with a fair bit more stubble than she'd left him with. He stood waiting for her, arms crossed. His brown hat and duster remained, but he got rid of his uniform in exchange for jeans and a button-down black shirt.

"Overload at 19 milliseconds and coil is fractured," Madeline said on the other side of the room. She retrieved a reading from a panel on the floor-to-ceiling metal box. It erupted in plumes of black smoke around an upper access panel. The girl shook her head and swept her hair to one side, exposing the shaved, scarred side.

Tesla pounded a fist on his desk. "Of course it break. That's what coil do. It work, then it break, because it is PIECE OF SHIT!"

Cora threw her arms out to her sides and struck a pose. "Hey, Cora, welcome back!"

"Ma'am," George said, tipping the brim of his hat to her.

She sighed and took a seat on the platform. Once Tesla's tantrum was over and Madeline replaced the coil with a fresh one off the racks that lined the back wall, she'd be gone again. She looked up to the sheriff. She wanted to apologize, but she didn't even know how to begin.

"Are you okay?" she asked.

"Right as rain," he replied with a smile, relaxing his posture. He wrapped his thumbs around the belt loops of his jeans. "I've spent time with about every member of the senior staff this week. Went to the shooting range with Johnny a few times, lunch with Julian and Michael, and I worked with Gideon on hunting down this bastard. Everyone has made me feel at home."

"Are you, though? Home, I mean?" Cora said. She was terrified of the answer.

George squatted down to her level. "Ma'am, I know why you left. But now you're back, and we're going to make this right. We're going to track him down, and he's gonna pay. You don't need to worry about me."

105

A faint click in Cora's ear made her wince. George responded in kind at the same moment.

"Sorry for barging in, guys," Gideon said through her earpiece. "We're light on time, so I switched us all over to a secure comm channel."

"Echo-1 is online, Control," Cora replied.

"Echo-2, responding," George said.

"Alright, great," Gideon said with a sigh. "The full read is on your Arcadias now. The wire transfer was initiated approximately twenty-two minutes ago. The recipient is Carla Glass."

Cora swiped open her Arcadia screen. She paged through the info, following along as Gideon spoke. The girl was a young, beautiful brunette whose social media profile burst with bikini photos and making silly faces with her girlfriends.

"She lives on Christian Street in a fifth-floor flat," Gideon continued. "Again, another early-twenties woman with a dead-end job, putting herself through school. This deposit is four-thousand credits."

Cora tapped her foot. Patience was wearing thin as Madeline and Tesla loaded the coil. She wanted to move now, act fast.

"What if she's not home?" George said, standing back up. "She could be out somewhere, making this money from our mysterious benefactor."

"I...hadn't actually thought of that," Gideon replied. "I just assumed since all of our people were taken from their homes, that was...the M.O.? Is that the right term?"

"It may be, but I don't think these girls are being paid to get killed," George replied.

Cora stood up, shaking her head. "What do you mean, George? What are you thinking?"

"I'm thinking our killer and NextGen aren't related," George replied. He stroked his handlebar mustache thoughtfully. "Only two of our three missing people have these deposits. That money hasn't been touched. The killer is taking nothing of value. But those Aztecs on the island were willing to kill to keep their business a secret. They want to make money, not waste it. It doesn't add up."

Cora snapped her head to the old man. "Tesla, ETA?"

"A DAMN MINUTE!" he shouted back with anger and vigor.

"Control, we're just going to have to take our chances," George replied, tapping the comm embedded behind his ear. "It's the only lead we've got."

"If nothing else, maybe the girl can tell us what the hell NextGen is," Gideon said. "I'll take anything at this point."

"Same," Cora replied, getting back up on the transport platform. She spun around and looked across the room. Madeline sealed the upper access panel and fiddled with an old-style touch-screen panel. Tesla swiped through holographic screens on his monitor, checking read-outs. George stepped up and joined at her side.

"Caw," Vincent said. He was rather concerned.

"Be quiet, ya big baby," Cora replied, stroking the back of his head with a finger.

"Ready?" Tesla asked.

She grabbed George's hand and held tight. "Go."

FREE FALL

The swirl was more intense with this transport. It may have been the cost of doing it again so soon, but Cora didn't have time for it. She opened her eyes slowly, but the world blurred and turned all around her. Her hand blindly reached out and grabbed hold of something to brace herself on. It was cool, thin metal, like a banister. As her eyes crept open again, she was looking out over the heart of the city, far in the distance. Holograms dotted the late-night sky. Beneath her, a plunge of five stories to the ground.

The walkway was wide cement, an outdoor hallway that went past one door after another. Using the banister to stand up straight, she walked forward, turning to a jog as the nausea passed. George was right beside her, less affected than she was. They checked one door after another, until they reached 5E. The sheriff spun to one side of the frame, quiet as a man his size could be.

He motioned to Cora for a knock, but she shook her head. The stakes were too high. She needed information or her killer, and the element of surprise was all she had. Worst-case scenario, she'd scare the daylights out of the girl and get the intel. George nodded his understanding and counted down with his fingers. Three, two, one.

George pushed off the wall and faced the door, throwing out a kick that could have shaken the pillars. The door blasted open, and Cora ran through, Predator drawn. She moved low and fast, her gun following her eyesight. Secure the corners, check for hostiles, all the basics. She went from the kitchen to the living room in seconds, broke right around the corner and headed for the bedrooms. She froze.

The bedroom directly ahead was open to her. The brunette from the photo laid on her bed, hands folded on her chest. Her eyes were closed, but she wasn't sleeping. Even from the distance, in the dark of night, she saw the gleam of light bouncing off the liquid surrounding her neck. Standing above her was a man with a bandaged face and a brimmed hat. A long, black trench coat flowed behind him. Cybernetic eyes glowed green in the darkness. They were staring right at Cora. She didn't hesitate. Questions could come later. Right now, she just wanted to pull the trigger.

The moment's hesitation allowed the man to weave out of view of the doorway as her shot rang out. An explosion of breaking glass followed. George was right behind Cora as she ran into the bedroom. She stopped at the window beside the bed. On the outside walkway, the bandaged man went straight to the edge. He put a gloved hand on the banister and hopped over.

Cora gnashed her teeth and shook her head. George raised his hand.

"Wait, Cora, no!"

Don't be reckless.

Maybe some other time. She jumped over the window frame, sprinted three steps and vaulted over the banister. As she fell, the magic pumped hot in her guts, and she sent all she could to her legs. Below, the bandaged man hit the ground so hard with his feet that a halo of dust kicked up where he cratered the asphalt.

She spun her arms in circles, guiding the free fall. He was already running again by the time she hit the ground. The magic in her legs absorbed the impact as it had before, but gravity still worked against her. Pulled into a kneeling position, she had to climb back to her feet before she could give chase.

The solid impact of his feet on the ground caused echoes. He was running on cybernetic legs with a full prosthesis. He raced with the trained precision of a track star. She fed more magic into her legs to burst her speed or she was never going to keep up. She looked ahead of her prey, to the path he was going to take. She tried to anticipate and looked for shortcuts, any advantage she could get. Without stopping, he leaped over a car as if it were a hurdle. He blew through the parking lot and hit a fork - the street ahead, or the construction barricade off to his right. He leaped over the barricade wall, Cora right at his tail.

A sudden pulse of energy exploded into her legs. She jumped, five, ten, fifteen feet into the air, much higher than he had. The overhead view served her well. It was an empty, muddy lot with a large metal shipping container and little else. No witnesses, no bystanders, and no cops. She hit the ground inches from his back. He was just out of reach, but point blank for a shot. She steadied the Predator. The bandaged man froze.

He spun around with impossible speed. His gloved hand struck her wrist with such force that her arm flew out to the side, throwing her Predator across the lot. His other hand thrust forward, a palm strike that sent her flying backwards through the air. Her back struck muddy dirt and rocks almost a dozen feet away from him.

She grunted and tried to tell herself to get up. Breathing was a spike in the center of her chest, a possible fractured sternum. Instead of taking advantage and fleeing, the bandaged man marauded toward her. Each heavy step, servos turned and whirred in his legs. As he drew closer, the dim light illuminated the eyes hidden beneath his hat. They glowed a faint green as miniature gears turned within.

"I warned you," he said in a low, cockney accent. His voice was deep and hoarse, with the unnatural modulation of a machine. "Now, I'll send him back to you in pieces."

Even as he reached down and grabbed her by her bomber jacket, Cora's mind was on his words. Her eyes flared wide. She gasped, knowing he was about to strike her again, but only one thought was on her mind.

"He's...alive?"

The bandaged man pulled her to her feet as if she were a ragdoll. No sooner had Cora hit her feet, he threw a body shot. The crack of breaking ribs rang out through the empty lot. Her eyes tried to roll in the back of her head from shock. Dizzy and unable to focus her vision, she shut her eyes and cupped a hand at her side. Orange, glowing energy gathered into a ball. He put a hand on her shoulder to keep her in place. With his other hand, he cocked back a gloved fist. Cora let the ball slip from her fingers.

The Stunbomb shattered like glass on the ground between them. A burst of concussive energy threw them both backward in opposite directions. Once again, she slammed into the hard, rocky mud on her back. She struggled to breathe, but the smallest expansion of her lungs was a knife in her chest. She pulled more from the magic, sending it to her wounds. It wouldn't speed up her regeneration, but it made the pain lessen.

It took everything to get on all fours. Across the distance, the bandaged man was getting to his feet much faster. Her powers were barely a match if he closed the distance, but she was already too hurt to move as fast as he could. She double-tapped the comm button on her ear, grateful it was still there.

"Arcadia...record...mode," she whispered, every syllable a struggle.

She crawled in the direction of her gun, a shining light over a dozen feet away. It taunted her, a weapon that might equalize the fight. She could see it, but she'd never reach it in time. No sooner had the thought popped in her head than he was on her, moving with the kind of speed she'd never seen before. Even the most adept and gifted users of cybernetics, like Madeline and Gideon, never moved like this. A metal shin swung out and caught her in the mouth. Her lower jaw shifted unnaturally to the side. Another bone broken, taking her speech with it.

Desperate, she wrapped her arms around the metal leg. She pulled magic to her hands, though she had no plan for what to do with it. She called out to Vincent, a silent plea for help across their tether. She felt the drain on her powers as Vincent siphoned off her.

The bandaged man used his free leg to press down on the back of her head. She gasped and sucked in air, even as it hurt, knowing what he was about to do. Unable to resist the cybernetic strength he possessed, he mashed her face into the mud. With enough pressure to push her several inches into the dirt, she couldn't turn her head sideways to find a pocket of air anywhere.

With a blast of energy and the wind at her back, the pressure was released. She yanked her face from the dirt. Trying to pull in breath was like sucking through a straw. The bandaged man reeled backward from Vincent's Stunbomb, trying to find his footing as Cora held fast to his other leg. With the magic still pulsing through her hands, she pulled up from the mud and flung her arms with everything she had. Taking his foot out from under him, she managed enough force to flip him through the air before he smashed the ground on his back.

For someone who could heal a simple cut within seconds, her regeneration could not work fast enough to repair the damage dealt by single blows from this guy. The amount of tech she'd seen in him was more than any human she'd ever heard of, save for Giovanna. Cora crawled backwards, eyes over her shoulder. The metal shipping container was behind her and she scrambled for it. The pain from every breath and the radiating ache of her jaw destroyed her focus. She tried to figure out how to use the terrain to her advantage, but the agony robbed her of clear thought.

The bandaged man was back up. She pulled magic to her palms as fast as it would come. The Stunbombs she created were barely-formed as she let them fly, releasing little more than twinkling balls of light. They burst before hitting his chest, striking some kind of energy shield and throwing out his trench coat behind him. He slowed his approach, but never ceased the advance. Her magic was more an inconvenience to him than an offense.

He grunted and charged after her. With everything she had

left, she pushed up to her feet and took a fighting stance, back to the shipping container. He closed the distance and threw a hook. Cora weaved under it. By then, he'd cocked a second shot with the other hand, a body blow. She leaned left, and the punch struck the container with a sound like thunder. Standing tall, she pulled back a fist for a shot. His superhuman speed already had a third punch on the way, a right cross. Cora weaved right. His punch struck with full force, denting the crate with a boom so loud it deafened her. She shook it off and threw a punch with everything she had.

The force would have been enough to cold-cock any man alive. The shot was perfectly placed to ring his bell, a hook at the side of his upper cheek and temple. Instead, it felt like she'd hit a wall. Bones crunched and popped in her fist. Every part of his bandaged face felt as if there was nothing but metal underneath. She cried out, pain and horror blending together. He pulled his fist back again.

Two shots rang out above her. Both struck the bandaged man's chest, staggering him backwards. He didn't react to the hits as much as he seemed bothered by them. His head turned up, and another shot blew the hat right off his head. He turned and ran. Three more shots blasted as he fled, but he moved so fast they only struck at his heels.

Cora dropped to her knees, on the edge of consciousness. Somewhere in the distance, there were sirens. The bandaged man was already on the other end of the lot, and jumped an eight-foot wall without breaking his stride. Her head lolled side to side, trying to pick where to collapse. She fought against it, but it was a losing battle. As the last of her strength faded, it was George that appeared at her side. Between her choice of the mud or the burly cowboy, she opted to let her lights go out in his arms.

GLIMMER OF HOPE

Doctor Daly was the last thing she wanted to wake up to. The grouchy, bearded Irishman had the bedside manner of a monkey with a machine gun. Beside him, a much hotter nurse with dark hair and veiny biceps checked her vitals on the machine beside her bed. She opened her mouth. The whole right side of her face ached and her jaw throbbed like she'd had her wisdom teeth out all over again. Her chest felt sore, but she could breathe. Memories came back in waves. The poor girl. The bandaged man. Leopold was alive. She gasped and sat up with a start.

"Easy there, lass," Daly said. "Fractured damn near every bone from your neck to your waist."

Cora patted herself down. She moved her neck around. Everything hurt. "I'm healed. How long was I out?"

"Little over two hours," he replied. He lifted his arm and swiped out a long Arcadia screen. As he moved through screens, a projection of the inside of her body stood beside her bed. She studied it for a moment, but the wonder fast gave way to nausea. The sight of her interior muscle conjured all sorts of bad images. Daly motioned to the projection. "You're not fully healed. Some of these bones still have fractures that are knitting."

She looked around. The doctor and nurse were the only ones in sickbay. No one kept a vigil over her.

"Where is everyone?" Cora said, her voice rising.

Doctor Daly cocked an eyebrow. "Staff meeting."

Julian. She takes a couple-hour nap and he's already nosing in. She shook her head and checked her arms. She found the IV in her left arm, ripped the tape and slid out the needle. Daly was already in motion, coming with a vain attempt to stop her.

"What are ye doing? You've got broken bones! Internal bleeding!"

Cora turned away from him and finished her task. "I'll be healed up by the time I get to the meeting."

Doctor Daly set his hand on her shoulder. "Your regeneration doesn't work that fast when it has a volume of damage to repair like this, lass. This would have killed anyone else."

Her brow furrowed, her gaze snapping to him. She was tired of this conversation. "But it didn't kill me. So I have work to do."

She looked down at her clothes. She was wearing a thin hospital gown that left her back naked. Looking over her shoulder, she caught the eye of the male nurse.

"Hey, Beefcake, get me my shirt," she said.

Like a deer in headlights, the nurse looked to Daly, then back to her. For someone so physically strong, a short Native girl made him awful nervous. "We...we had to cut it off you."

Cora groaned and turned around. That was the fourth or fifth shirt she lost in the past few weeks. "That shirt had the single greatest alternative band of the late twentieth on it. It was my favorite shirt!"

"I'm sorry, miss," he said, eyes wide. His British accent and fear of her somehow made him sexier. "We couldn't risk taking it off of you with all the internal damage."

Shaking her head, she locked eyes with Doctor Daly. "Next time, just stick me on a slab until I'm done regenerating."

"You're still not finished regenerating, lass," Daly replied. He closed his Arcadia screen and put his hands behind his back. "That's alright, though. Don't mind my medical advice. You run along and go play. Come back and see me if you start coughing up blood or have an aneurysm."

Cora found her boots tucked under the bed. "You're a terrible doctor."

"You're a shite patient," Daly replied before walking away.

Cora got her boots on with a huff and walked out of sickbay. Her head went back and forth, looking down two ugly green corridors. The conference room was on the opposite end of the base from her quarters. Checking her wrist, her Arcadia was gone. There wasn't any time to waste. The team was just going to have to live with her rocking the latest medical fashions.

By the time she'd reached the conference room, at least three knights had asked her if she was alright. The truth was that she wasn't okay at all, and she knew better. If there was even a chance Leopold was still alive, she had to keep moving. She blew past the guards at the conference room door and let herself in.

Gideon was standing at the far end of the room, motioning to a holovid projection on the wall. He stopped mid-sentence and his jaw dropped. Every chair turned to her. Julian sat at the head of a long table, flanked on either side by Michael and George. Johnny, Giovanna, Crowley, even Madeline and Tesla were invited.

"Wow, looks like the gang's all here," Cora said in a huff.

Julian stood up, a shocked look on his face. "Bloody hell, Cora, what are you doing here? You belong in sickbay."

"Leopold is alive," Cora replied. The room became smaller as tension filled the empty space. "The man we're looking for said as much, that he'd be sending back Leopold to me in pieces."

"He survived having his eye removed?" George asked.

"Dear God," Julian said, his mouth hanging open.

Cora walked in, pulled out an empty leather chair, and sat down. The cold leather stung her naked back for a second. She sucked air through her teeth, the ache in her chest reminding her she was still injured. Folding her hands in her lap, she leaned back.

"Where were we?"

"Patatina, what are you doing?" Giovanna asked. Cora was growing tired of the worried looks on everyone's faces.

"Getting back to work," Cora replied. She pointed at the door behind her. "If you think some wired-up psycho is keeping me locked in there while Leopold might still be alive, you're nuts."

"Ma'am," George started.

Julian cut him off. "Cora, may I speak with you outside?"

She pounded her fist on the conference table. Her eyes went to each caring face at the table before settling on Julian. The pity made her angry. "This isn't up for discussion, or debate. I'm fine. If I'm not, I'm a hell of a lot closer to sickbay than I was two hours ago. Now, the clock is ticking. Where were we?"

Awkward silence fell over the room. Gideon was the one to break the tension.

"Alright. The biggest piece of the puzzle we're missing right now is this guy's selection criteria. If we can understand why he's selecting these victims, we can get closer to determining where he'll strike next."

"Any traction on NextGen Holdings?" Cora asked.

Gideon shook his head. "Other than tipping us off when it's too late, it's practically a dead lead. I can't get into the Cayman bank's systems, I can't turn up an owner...I don't even know who this company is a proxy for. I've got some feelers out in UnderNet, but the intel just isn't coming our way."

Johnny leaned forward and rested his arms on the table. He looked at Crowley. "Tell her your theory."

Cora turned to the Professor, eyebrows raised. "You have a theory?"

Crowley turned in his seat toward her. He moved his hand down his bushy salt-and-pepper beard. "I do. I think Leopold is a distraction."

"What?" Cora cocked her head to the side.

"If you take Leopold out of the equation, we have three young women that have received large sums of money from a shell company. Shortly thereafter, they met an untimely end at the hands of this cybernetic fellow," Crowley replied. He held out his hands. "He left a message warning you at the second scene, before we even knew what we were looking for. He was already preparing to use Leopold as leverage against you. I think Leopold is the distraction. The problem is you. He doesn't want you hunting after him."

Gideon took a deep breath. "Unfortunately, it looks like a more fruitful path. Taking Leopold out of the equation puts more in common with the three girls. Olivia Orwell is still missing, we haven't found a body for Elea Nguyen, and this latest one might have vanished, too, if not for you guys getting there so fast. But all of them share the deposits."

"What about the artifact connection? Could this be Lucius picking off our people?" Cora asked.

Another silence came over the room. Gideon turned to Julian, his mouth twisted.

"Tell her," Julian said.

"Tell me what?" Cora asked, fuming. She knew she wasn't going to like the answer.

Gideon's head turned toward the ground. "George knew chasing after you would likely leave the crime scene to the cops. He took Carla Glass' Arcadia off her body and kept it."

Cora looked at the sheriff. His lips were drawn down, his face grim. "What did you find?"

Gideon walked between Johnny and Giovanna to the table. Two Arcadia bracelets rested there. He fiddled with the screen on one of them and swiped it toward the wall. A projection appeared of a text message from an unknown contact. Cora looked it over.

You should leave.

Cora looked at the time stamp. It was fifteen minutes before Gideon called her in Heaven's Crest. Within the next half-hour, Carla Glass was dead. Cora's brow furrowed as she examined the phone number.

"...6485...why does that number sound familiar?"

Gideon placed his hand over the other wrist computer. "I had to go through your Arcadia, too. The number is in there. Lucius sent this message."

Cora's hands balled into fists. The dragon was involved in her losing someone. Again.

"Pity you've failed to mention our enemy is in your speed-dial," Michael said.

Cora's eyes went cold. She turned to Michael, staring daggers at him while he sat there with his rigid military posture and his passive-aggressive accusations. "My enemy. You're along for the ride."

Michael folded his hands on the table and smiled, the kind of pursed-lip grin that hid a seething rage. "Very good, then. I'll just sit here and mind my place."

Cora shut her eyes and huffed. Michael could be a bit of a jerk, but he had saved her life in Paris. She knew she may have crossed a line, maybe even been a bit of a bitch, but no one at the table would ever understand the bizarre relationship she shared with her would-be mortal enemy. It's not like she even understood it herself.

"Sorry, alright? Can we move on, please? Any clue why Lucius sent this message, or how he knew she was the target?"

Gideon shook his head. "If you didn't have this number in your phone, we'd be in the dark as to who even sent it. Everything we've learned tonight raises more questions than answers. There's more."

His hand still lingering on her Arcadia, Gideon looked uncomfortable. He'd probably been all through it. Like a purse, it was an invasion to touch a woman's Arcadia, but Cora didn't care. Other than late-night whiskey-fueled shopping for boots, everything on her Arcadia had been work related since Gideon gave her the damn thing during the events in Berlin. She raised her eyebrows and motioned to his hand.

"What did you find?" she asked.

He swiped out her screen and threw a projection onto the wall. It was a still frame of the bandaged man in low-quality 3D. The latest Arcadia had a great camera, but paled in comparison to holovid-quality video recorders. Gideon stepped back to the wall beside the projection. The video started to play, with the bandaged man taking a running start before kicking her in the face. Her damn jaw was still sore from that.

"You were moving around a lot, obviously, so I had to run the video through a stabilizer algorithm and do some major enhancements," he said. He peeked over at his computer screen. "Here's what we do know - he's about 6 feet, 2 inches, weighs approximately four hundred and twenty pounds."

"Wow, big boy," Johnny said. He lifted his shades to get a better look at the screen.

Cora's eyebrows raised. "How is that possible? I needed magic to keep up with how fast he ran."

"Well, Madeline might be able to back me up on this," Gideon said, pointing her out. "Spinal mesh grafts, or 'wired reflexes' as they're called, give a superhuman reaction time to existing bone and muscle groups, but I actually saw a performance increase once I had arm and leg implants."

Madeline nodded. "Oui. Machine to machine interface is always going to be faster than tissue."

"But the weight of all that tech," Cora guffawed.

"Here's where things get weird," Gideon announced. He froze the video as Cora readied herself to box him. The bandaged man's fist slammed into the storage container as she weaved out of the way. Gideon used his hands to gesture a zoom-in, closing in on the fist. "You had this look at his arm for a split-second. The gloves he's wearing and his coat cover over the enhancement obscured the model. But right here, where his arm is at full extension, the serial number peeks from his sleeve."

Gideon zoomed in further on the arm. It was black metal, bare rods, only resembling the skeletal shape of a forearm in the loosest sense. At this range, the 'Property of Tetriarch Industries' serial information could be read of a rod in the wrist. Gideon looked expectantly at everyone in the room.

"What is it I'm supposed to be seeing?" Julian asked, squinting his eyes at the projection.

"The serial number here," Gideon pointed out. "It starts with XLR. That's not for release at Tetriarch Cybernetic Medical Facilities. This model is a prototype. XLR means it's experimental. Only Tetriarch R&D would have access to this equipment."

Cora scoffed and shook her head. "So, this monster is a stooge for Lucius?"

"It certainly seems that way at this point," Gideon replied. He shrugged his shoulders, defeated. "But if there's an artifact holder connection between the four of them, I haven't found it yet. We only know Leopold for sure, and a possible on Elea Nguyen."

Cora gripped the arms of her chair tight and tried to pull herself back to her feet. Her body didn't want to do it, aching every inch of the way. She took a cleansing breath to work through the pain and turned to Julian.

"Any luck with the other thing you were looking for?"

Julian glanced at Gideon before answering. "Negative. Gideon has done some digging, but we've come up with bollocks. With the bloody mess this Lucius business is, maybe we should change gears, team up, and focus solely on solving this, then?"

"No," Cora shook her head. Julian shifted uncomfortably in his chair, but she raised a hand before he could protest. Her throat closed trying to speak. "They were Merlin's last words. Please, stay on it. I promise you, I've got this. If there's even a hope Leopold is alive, I'm going to find him."

Julian's head dropped. He rubbed the stubble on the back of his head. Without making eye contact, he nodded back. "Very well."

Cora turned to Tesla. "Can you prepare the machine and have it on standby? As soon as I have a lead, we're moving."

"Machine will be ready," Tesla replied, getting out of his chair. "All I ever want is to go to meeting and fix piece of shit machine in dead of night."

She restrained a laugh at the cantankerous old man as he left. She clapped her hands together. "George, please get some rest, I know you need it. Gideon, I'd say you, too, but I don't even know if you sleep anymore."

"Six or seven hours every couple of days," Gideon nodded and gave a thumbs up. "I'm good, don't worry."

Giovanna let out a loud, purposeful cough, clearing her throat and grabbing the attention of the group. "Everyone, clear the room please."

She was staring at Cora. Her eyes said she meant everyone but her. Johnny turned to her.

"Gia, you're really gonna lecture her again? She's busting her ass to save this guy."

Giovanna pointed a finger in his face. Her expression was fire. "I know damn well what you think."

Johnny threw his hands in the air and got out of his seat. Madeline got up with him. She walked around the table to Cora and placed a hand on her shoulder, drawing her close.

"If it were me out there, missing," she whispered into Cora's ear. "I'm glad to know you'd be doing the same for me, mon ami."

Cora nodded her head, with an expression as if the girl had asked the most ridiculous question. It wasn't even a thought as she replied, "Of course."

Michael got up without a word, and Julian with him. They were both angry or frustrated with Cora for different reasons, and neither was good at hiding it. They took their restrained emotions and their rigid posture and marched out of the room, whisper quiet. Crowley stood up from beside Cora and bowed his head to her.

"I'd tell you that you really need to come see me, but..."

"You know I can't," she replied. Cora enjoyed their talks, his magical training, and his wisdom, but she didn't need a shrink right now. He could be there to pick up the pieces of her mental state when this was all over. "For now, I need my head in the game. I can't have you tinkering with it."

Crowley hesitated, but responded with a nod. He patted her shoulder and made his way for the door. Once he was gone, the only person left in the room with them was Gideon, gathering up his computer rig. Cora reached for her Arcadia, her hand stopped short of grabbing it.

"Done with this?" she asked.

"Yeah," Gideon nodded. "All yours. I'll be in the computer room if you need me."

As unlikely as it seemed, Giovanna still made Gideon nervous. It was doubly-so when she was upset. Maybe it was her flawless, bombshell appearance that intimidated him, or the Italian passion and flair that went into everything she did. Whatever it was, he scrambled to gather up his things and left. As the door shut behind him, Cora crossed her arms to a chorus crinkling from the hospital gown. Giovanna hadn't moved from her seat. She was in vicious schoolteacher mode. Cora had seen that look too many times in training to mistake it for anything else.

"Is this going to get ugly?" she asked.

"You have no idea, patatina."

WAR ON TWO FRONTS

"Why are you trying so hard to save him?" Giovanna demanded, her tone stern. "I want to hear you say it."

Cora scoffed, cocking her hip out to the side and resting her hand on it. "That's a ridiculous question. What would Richard have done, if it was you or me?"

Giovanna jumped out of her chair with such a start, the seat fell to the ground behind her with a boom. She slammed her knuckles into the table and leaned forward. Even in a blood red evening dress, the intimidating soldier in her came through.

"Don't you dare even invoke his name!" she shouted, her Italian accent thick and fiery. "Leopold is not Richard."

Cora's face twisted in confusion. "I know that."

"He's not your father."

"Stop," Cora said, stepping back.

"He's not Dante. He's not Living Wind. He's not Pops. You knew Leopold for a day," Giovanna pressed.

Cora put her hands out to her sides. "He's one of us."

"Bullshit!" Giovanna seethed. She walked around the table, stalking toward Cora like a cat. Invading Cora's personal space, she stared her hard in the eye. Cora tried to look away, seeing the servos turning in her hazel eyes and that ring of light around her irises, but Giovanna wouldn't have it. She weaved with her, keeping their eyes locked. "He ran away. That's it, plain and simple. He was called to something greater, and he ran because he was weak."

Cora couldn't believe what she was hearing. She raised her voice to match. "What do you expect me to do, just let him die? Let this monster go on killing innocent people?"

Giovanna raised a finger. "I said nothing of the sort. We need to chase this down. We - us. Not you, not this two-man show with the cowboy. You're pushing yourself because you want to be the one to save him."

"I'm not looking for glory," Cora huffed, still trying to avert her gaze. "I have the magic, George has the police know-how."

"You need to save him for you," Giovanna wagged her finger in Cora's face. "After everyone you've lost in all this, you think you can balance the scales."

Cora's jaw clenched, a reflex to hold back tears. When Giovanna attacked, she cut to the bone.

"You can't," Giovanna said, shaking her head. "Richard was only the last in a long line of people I couldn't save. The ones you can don't make up for what you've lost. There's no catharsis at the end of the rainbow, patatina. There's only one less body weighing down your soul."

No matter how much her sore muscles tightened, Cora couldn't hold back a single tear from rolling down her cheek, betraying her. She tried to speak, but her voice only came out a whisper. "Please, stop."

Giovanna's expression softened, but she kept her perfectly manicured red nail pointed in Cora's face. "I warned you. If you sidelined me again, I would leave."

Cora's mouth fell open. Throwing up her hands in defense, she raised her voice, "I didn't sideline you!"

"I told you to let me take over. To help. Anything," Giovanna said. She stepped back and put both hands on her hips. "You need to heal. You need to back off on this. Let me step in and help while you recover. That *thing* almost killed you!"

Cora's head dropped with a sigh. She was in too much pain to put up much of a fight. Maybe Giovanna had a point. She had been so driven to save Leopold, but didn't know him well enough for this to mean so much to her. She let it get personal. Her father said it was her greatest strength. Lucius said it would be her downfall. She let her hands fall limp at her sides.

"Alright. Let's get a team together on this. You head it up. I'll take some time to recover," she said, raising a finger right back at her. "But I will be first in the chain with any breakthroughs, and I will be asking for a report twice a day."

Giovanna crossed her arms and cocked her head to the side. If she was pleased with the answer, she didn't let it show. "Now you're starting to sound like a leader and not like a lone wolf. About damn time."

Cora pointed her thumb to the door. "Now, if it's all the same to you, I'm going to go to my quarters and drink myself into a nap."

Giovanna sighed and shook her head, guiding Cora toward the door. "Look at you. You're still wearing a hospital gown. You have internal bleeding. I checked with Doctor Daly."

"Then the alcohol can sterilize the wounds, whatever," she replied, rolling her eyes. "I'm regenerating. I'll be fine, mom."

Giovanna slapped her on the butt, hard enough to sting. Cora jumped from the hit, startled as much by the smack as she was with the fact it happened at all. Her mouth fell open, staring at the Italian in shock. Giovanna shrugged back.

"Act like a petulant daughter, I'll spank you like one," she said, opening the door to the hall.

Cora stumbled into the ugly green corridor, still surprised. Giovanna stopped her with a hand on her shoulder and turned her around. Two knights were on either side of them, guarding the empty conference room. Giovanna stepped so close, they were shy of touching.

"I'm only looking out for you, patatina. You know I love you," she said.

Cora nodded, tears trying to glaze over her eyes again. She never heard the Italian say the words out loud, even if they both felt it. Bonds in blood, after the ordeals and trials they'd been through, were stronger than family.

"I love you, too," Cora replied, closing the distance and wrapping her arms around her.

After a warm embrace, they parted ways and headed in opposite directions. Cora headed for her quarters, stumbling every so often. The walk wasn't very long, but she underplayed her injuries more than she realized. She hadn't hurt like this in a long while, as far back as she could remember.

Once she was in her quarters, curiosity won the day. She reached behind her neck, sweeping her black hair off to one shoulder and untied the knot to her gown. She let it fall to the floor and walked to the mirror in the bathroom. Staring at her naked flesh, the smooth, caramel complexion was broken by blotches of purple, blue, and speckles of red. Her mottled left side was the worst of all, where the bandaged man got a body shot in. The damage radiated out in a swirl of color, down to her kidney and across to her stomach. She tried to lift her arm to get a better view, but a hot knife stabbed into her lung and told her to stop.

Washing medical tape and the day off of her, she came out of the shower without relief. She treated herself to her one pair of satin pajamas, but it was more a precaution to make sure there was no harsh rubbing against her skin. She settled into her bed and leaned her back against the wall, a fresh bottle of Jack at her side. With a thought, she called Vincent to her. He passed through the ceiling and landed beside her on the bed. She smiled and pet him.

"Hey, buddy, what have you been up to while I was out? More of your raven secrets?"

"Caw," Vincent replied. He was worried, as usual. His eyes darted up and down, looking her over.

"I'm fine. It hurts, but I'll recover," Cora said. She rubbed the back of his neck between her index finger and thumb. "Thanks for caring, though."

She lifted up her bottle and unscrewed the cap. "Just my bird and my booze for a while. Holovid on, turn on GNN."

The screen projected out on the other side of her room and formed a three-dimensional image. People marched down a city street, carrying signs in the Cyrillic alphabet. Cora always meant to learn Russian, she just never had the time.

"...amid rising inflation. President Sokolov said in a speech today that Russia's sovereignty will not be threatened by the International Credit System and will wait for the 2090 deadline."

The image switched to a savvy-looking representation of a news anchor with brown hair and shiny teeth. It was all a lie. GNN hadn't used live human anchors in years, everyone was CGI now.

"When we come back - are you getting the nutrition you need for your limb implants? One doctor says no, we'll talk with him about his new study. Also, the streets of Chicago are rife with crime, most of it related to Sim. But a troll gang called the Seventh Street Saints are taking the law into their own hands to clean up their city, and they're winning the people over. We'll have that and more when we return from this commercial break."

"Ugh," Cora said. She hated commercials, especially the breaks on GNN. They lasted forever, always pushing trendy tech, Tetriarch implants, and Arcadia games loaded with microtransactions.

She switched her focus to her Arcadia and sipped straight from her bottle. Swiping out the holographic screen, she went back to her photo gallery and found the video with Gideon's alterations. She played it back again, studying every move of the bandaged man. The sight of her hand crumpling unnaturally and breaking against his face was sickening. Wiggling her fingers on her right hand, she reminded herself it had healed, at least enough that she could use it. The top of her hand still ached like someone drove a car over it.

Cora drank some more and watched it again, this time at half speed. It wasn't that she was looking for something in particular, but anything she could learn might help. If there was a way to fight him one on one, she didn't see it. He was tall, augmented, he had greater reach, and he weighed almost as much as her Harley.

Despite that, he moved faster than any human she'd ever seen.

She continued on for some time, watching the video over and over on loop, pouring as much whiskey down her gullet as it would take. When the tingles came and her brain swam in the liquid, she finally felt relaxed enough to take a break. She swiped off the screen and dropped her Arcadia at her side. Her head tipped back, she shut her eyes and enjoyed the brief moment of bliss that came from forgetting life for a while.

"...but are they real? That's what deep-sea researchers are trying to uncover as they continue the hunt for mermaids."

"Oh, they're real," Cora laughed to herself. Her favorite place on the Atlantis station was a long, secluded hallway with floor-to-ceiling glass that stretched for a hundred feet. She visited that spot every morning that she could, to keep her in touch with nature. After the first few days on the station, she knew she was being watched right back. Day by day, the mermaid grew more brave, until Cora could see the skittish thing inches away from the glass. Her face and body only vaguely appeared human, with smooth features and scaly blue skin. The mermaid studied her for a few, fleeting seconds before getting scared and vanishing into the depths. "I call her Rebecca, and she's a curious one."

"Next week is an auspicious day in world history. Thursday marks the twenty-sixth anniversary of the dragon Lucius emerging from an inactive volcano in Edinburgh, Scotland. The first of his kind to awaken, he heralded a new age of dragons. The site where he emerged is now a tourist attraction seeing some twenty million visitors a year. Festivities are planned..."

Cora opened her eyes, her brow furrowed. As she set her gaze on the holovid, the bastard was looking right back at her. His long, flowing silver hair and glowing amber eyes of his human form deceived the world. If they saw what she saw in Paris, they'd fear him and they'd be right to do so. She ground her teeth looking at him, knowing everything he'd already cost her. His little war with her turned lives upside-down. It would have been fine if they were like her or Julian, government agents, fighters, or soldiers. But Leopold was innocent. These women were innocent.

With a heavy breath through her nose, fuming at the thought of him, she grabbed up her Arcadia. The words on the screen were a tad blurry, but she could find the contacts. With a few button presses, she grabbed up her ear piece from the night stand and put it in. The phone rang, then again. On the third ring, Lucius picked up.

"What do you want, Cora?" he said. She hadn't heard his voice in so long, she had forgotten his unnaturally deep baritone and the reverberation behind his voice, as if it came up from a deep pit.

"He's killing girls, Lucius!" Cora blurted. "Young, college-aged girls! It's not just my artifact holder. What the hell did you send after me?"

Lucius sighed. "You're drunk."

"Just enough to call you," Cora replied. She didn't realize until she said it how slurred her speech came out. She looked over at the bottle, still half-full. Her regeneration must have been too preoccupied fixing her to kill the buzz.

"After Paris, we don't have anything to discuss," Lucius said.

Cora's face crinkled. "What's that supposed to mean?"

"I need to spell this out for you? You tried to kill me."

She scoffed, incredulous. "You've got to be kidding me. You're mad at me for injuring you? You were breathing fire on me at the time, remember that part?"

"...Irrelevant."

"Is that why you sent this...thing after my people? To punish me?" Cora asked.

Lucius paused, long enough for Cora to check her Arcadia to make sure the call was still connected. "What are you talking about, Cora?"

Cora let out a loud, frustrated groan. "You're really going to make me play this game with you? The man with all the bandages. He's walking around, loaded with experimental Tetriarch parts, and he's murdering women. You texted one of the girls before she died."

"I have not sent anyone after you," Lucius said, keeping his answers short and curt. It wasn't the usual conversational gymnastics he employed, making her sift through the lies he slipped in amid the truth. "I am, however, aware of a break-in at one of our London research facilities. Some of our...sensitive projects were stolen."

Cora got out of bed and paced the floor of her room. "I don't suppose you'd be willing to let me see the security footage of this guy?"

"No."

"Lucius, he's killing these women," Cora pleaded. As cruel as he could be, he wasn't a monster like this. Not in any way she'd ever known him.

"Then I'll set up a charity in their name."

"Stop it!" Cora yelled. She stopped walking, on the verge of tears. "Punish me, alright? I fought your guy tonight. He almost killed me. Even regenerating, I had broken ribs, my right hand was shattered to pieces, dislocated my jaw...is that enough for you? Do you want more? Take it out on me, don't let him hurt these people!"

Lucius didn't reply right away. She couldn't be certain if he was choosing his words or didn't care at all.

"I had to talk to a shrink for weeks about Paris, okay?" Cora continued. If he wasn't going to speak, she would. "I was worried I hurt you. I didn't want to do it. I thought about calling you a hundred times, even after you tried to kill me. I was actually relieved when I saw you on GNN, walking around, looking fine. You want this war. I want nothing to do with it."

"I didn't order anything, Cora," Lucius replied. "This problem is yours alone. I had nothing to do with it."

"But you know something," Cora insisted. "How did you know to text Carla Glass? Please, tell me that much."

"The same way you did," Lucius replied, his voice cold. "I'm always aware of what you're up to, or have you forgotten?"

Cora let out a bitter laugh and shook her head. "No, that's never far from my mind."

"You want to know what I know? You already do. A pattern

has emerged. Find it, figure it out on your own, and stop trying to lay it at my feet. I didn't make this problem for you," Lucius replied, venom in his tone. "As for your pity, save it. I healed, stronger and more ready for you than you will ever be for me. No number of cursed undead and magic balls are going to stop me, Cora. You got a lucky shot in and got away with your man and your life. You won't be that lucky forever."

She started pacing again, her face hot with a fire that she could not find solace from. "I am so tired of this, Lucius! We eat breakfast together, then you try to incinerate me. We have a pleasant conversation, then you kidnap me and drug me for weeks. You go hot, then you're cold. I can't ever tell if you're trying to ingratiate yourself or find a new angle to murder me from, but I wish you'd pick a damn lane already."

"...Why don't you sleep this one off, Cora? As you said, you're injured," Lucius replied, dry as the desert.

"No!" Cora stomped her foot. "Answer me. Do you hate me?"

Again, silence. She always seemed to find new ways to make him uncomfortable.

"I do not hate you, Cora," he replied. "Does that answer satisfy you?"

"No. Help me bring this guy in, Lucius," Cora said, freezing in place. It was a gamble to ask for his help. God forbid he asked for anything in return.

"I told you already, Cora," Lucius said, clearing his throat. "You have the pieces in front of you. That's as much as I am willing to do. I wish you the best of luck. Monsters like these...they need to be put down. They don't deserve the life they've been given. I'll be keeping tabs, of course. I'm eager to see what you do."

Cora sat down on the bed. Everything hurt the whole way down. "I'd say thanks, but I know you're keeping things from me."

"We all have our secrets," he replied. His voice softened. "Before I go, I would offer my condolences."

Her brow furrowed, anger rising. "For what?"

"I understand you lost someone recently," Lucius replied. "No doubt, that's playing into this call and your current state."

"You don't have the right," Cora said through gritted teeth.

Lucius scoffed. He seemed amused by her position, only riling her more. "To be fair, I knew the wizard much longer than you. I have all the right in the world. For as much trouble as he caused me throughout the centuries, I know you're hurting. For that, you have my condolences."

He just had to twist the knife. Even when he made it sound like he cared, he still hurt her. He couldn't help himself. Cora held back her emotions, at least long enough to get through the conversation.

"Is that it?" she asked.

"You called me, Cora," Lucius replied. "You may hang up on me in frustration now."

"Good idea," she said, ending the call.

She fell to the side, throwing her face into her pillow. She screamed at the top of her lungs into it, until she exhausted her breath and succumbed to tears. She wailed and sobbed into the pillow, pounding her fist on the bed in a fit of rage. She'd have to spend the next several hours recounting his every word, sifting through what was said as though she were panning for gold. Before that could happen, she'd have to get over how his words shattered her. He always found the chink in her armor to pull her emotions right to the surface, exactly where she didn't want them to be.

"Caw," Vincent said, nudging her with his head. He didn't want her feeling like this.

Despite the pain, Cora rolled to her back and looked at the raven. Her eyes were puffy and sore. "I know, okay? He shouldn't get to me like that, but he does. I don't even know why."

Like this monster, her missing artifact holder, and these other girls, the way Lucius got to her and what came next was just another mystery to solve. Lucius could wait. For now, the dragon did claim one thing she could hold on to. She needed to find the pattern and put an end to the bandaged man.

A RAW NERVE

"Does it ever stop raining in this city?" Cora asked, shaking the drizzle off her raincoat. She kicked her legs, dangling three stories off the ground. The fine mist of rain soaked through her jeans in almost every conceivable place except her rear, which she kept firmly planted to the edge of the roof.

Even with the magic of Eagle's Sight powering her eyes, visibility was terrible. The holograms and neon lights of downtown were only a couple of miles away, the outer fringes still close enough to cause a gaudy sheen over the slick stone. Puddles reflected some fifty-foot woman in the distance hawking a new Prada boutique.

"Not really, Echo-1," Giovanna replied. Her tone turned sarcastic. "That's part of the charm."

"Echo-3, reporting," Johnny chimed in. His voice cold and calculating, he was in business mode. Without the benefit of cybernetic eyes or magic, his scouting was through the scope of a custom Barrett M115. "North quadrant is quiet. Weather sucks."

Wherever her view wasn't distracted by colored lights, sprawling flat complexes blocked her line of sight. Three stories was high enough to keep her eyes on the southern region of the victim map. She had a clear view of the streets, and if push came to shove, she knew her magic could handle a jump to ground level.

Cora tugged at the hood of her raincoat, drawing it closer to her brow. She rubbed the bridge of her nose. Three days bed rest had removed any trace of injury, save for headaches. It was a limit of her regenerative abilities - there was no cure for tension, nor its effect on the body. She tapped her comm button.

"Echo-4, how are you looking out there?" she asked.

George cleared his throat and spoke softly. "West quadrant is bustling. Too busy to keep track of."

"It won't be much longer," Gideon relayed in his robotic voice. "Twenty minutes to midnight, closing time at most of those establishments."

"Closing time at midnight? Wow, Control, London is full of party animals," Cora replied. Back in the UNS, during her college days, she avoided the lame bars that closed before four. She sighed, and her nose crinkled. The combined smell of ozone and the dumpsters in the alley below mixed with a chemical scent in the air. "Echo-1 reporting. South quadrant is quiet and smells weird."

It was the most conversation she'd had over the past hour. Given the choice between another night in bed, staring at GNN and Lucius' face every thirty minutes, or coming out on a stakeout, she'd still choose the rain and boredom. At least she wasn't breathing that recycled Atlantis air anymore. Still, she was getting antsy. A stakeout wasn't a direction, it was busy-work while Giovanna prayed for a lead. The locations of Leopold and the three girls was enough to throw a net around the immediate area. Not knowing what the bandaged man's criteria was for choosing his victims, though, made finding him in a city of fourteen million near impossible.

"Control, any lead on those phone calls?" Cora asked. Giovanna had uncovered a number of calls on Carla Glass' phone in the days leading up to her murder. In the intervening three days since, two of the numbers no longer worked.

"Negative, looks like we're slamming another wall on that," Gideon replied. He sighed. "Both phones were burner bands, probably bought at a gas station or a department store. Neither of them have been turned on since their last calls, which probably means they're in the bottom of a recycling bin somewhere."

"Echo-1, how are you holding up?" Giovanna asked.

"Echo-2, I'm fine, I swear," Cora replied, shaking her head. "More rested than I have been in six months."

Giovanna paused before replying. Cora expected her to try mothering her some more, if she hadn't already realized how much Cora didn't want it. "Affirmative," she replied, her tone defeated.

The comm line fell silent. Their next check-in wouldn't be for almost another half-hour, when closing time evacuated the streets and brought a semblance of peace to the city. Cora looked to her left. Vincent perched beside her, keeping a vigil over the city.

"You're a good guard bird," Cora smiled and leaned into him.

"Caw," he replied. She could tell from his determination that he was taking his job seriously. She found it adorable.

Ten minutes went by. For the part of town she was in, everyone seemed to be asleep for the night. She couldn't even remember the last time she'd seen a car pass by. The rain ensured no one would want to come out, either. She got up and walked along the edge of the roof. Even if it wouldn't give her a better vantage, at least she'd have new things to stare at.

A cry came out from the distance. Cora froze and listened close. She heard it again. It was a woman, and the sound couldn't be mistaken for a drunken partygoer. It was fear, pain, or some blend of the two. Magical energy flowed to her legs as though a reflex. She took off running. Vincent darted into the sky with a flutter of wings behind her.

She closed on the edge of the roof, assessing the street level and the next building across. She still couldn't see anyone. The next roof was better. She pushed harder, into a sprint at the last second and leaped across the street below, slamming down and continuing her stride on the next building. Another pained wail. She tapped her comm button.

"Echo-1, responding to a female's cries, heading north on

Sidney at Ashfield," she said.

"Echo-2 on the move, en route to your location," Giovanna replied.

Ahead, Vincent perched on the roof of the building adjacent. He opened his wings and croaked, letting her know he found her. Cora doubled her breakneck pace, sprinting to the edge of the roof. She only looked down long enough to make sure she wasn't falling on top of the girl, sailing right over the edge. The alley between the two buildings was narrow and littered with garbage. Cora dropped almost forty feet before hitting the ground. Her magic absorbing the shock, she pulled herself from her knees and took in the surroundings.

Before her, a grimy, poorly-dressed man in a soaking wet jacket held a woman by her chin with a tight grip. Pinned against a brick wall, the woman's face changed from fear to shock. Startled, the man turned around. His scrunched face and jagged, crooked teeth invited comparisons to a rat. Slick, sparse strands of hair atop his head struggled to hide baldness. He looked up at the rooftop, then back to Cora.

"What the bloody hell you supposed to be?" he spoke in a cockney accent.

Cora looked right past him to the girl. In her late twenties, she'd put more mileage on herself in that short time than she should have. Sunken, darkened eyes that had spent too much time hiding from the sun and using Sim stared back at her. Though the rain thinned it out, a trickle of red dropped from her nose. Her lip was starting to swell.

"Are you alright, miss?" Cora asked, stepping forward. It wasn't the bandaged man, but he'd do. She didn't have anything else going on tonight. She just needed an excuse.

"Bitch is fine," the man spat. "Best mind your business and run along, 'fore you get yourself hurt."

The woman was either too scared or too shocked to reply. Cora took another step closer. The guy was still holding her against the wall by her face. That was as good an excuse as any.

"You'd hurt me?" Cora asked, playing coy. She folded her

arms behind her back and stepped closer still. Smiling with dark intent, she asked, "Care to show me how?"

The man smiled, his mangled teeth doing everything except lining up correctly. As Cora hoped, he released the woman and turned his body completely around. "You mental? Come to start a fight? You her sister or something?"

"Not at all," Cora replied, shaking her head. She took a final step, within striking distance. Her brow furrowed. "I was in the neighborhood, and I couldn't help but think how much better it would be without a piece of shit like you in it."

He laughed, amused by the whole situation. He shrugged and gave a delayed nod. "Alright, love, if that's the way you want it."

All she needed was the excuse. One step forward. He twitched. Cora lunged forward. She completed the motion, dropping to a knee as she side-stepped him. He had almost walked right past her, if not for her left hook to the groin on her way down.

While he was still in the throes of anticipation, waiting for the full bloom of pain to wash over him, Cora spun on her knee. She was back to her feet a split-second later, behind him. She grabbed the collar of his jacket and tossed his back to the brick wall. Too weak to fight back, he went with it. He clutched at his manhood with both hands, a grimace of pain etched into his face. Cora wanted his attention. She took a step back, lifted a leg and fully extended it to his neck. The heel of her boot pressed against his throat, his wide eyes refocused on her.

"You get off on this?" Cora demanded, her temperature rising. "You like hurting girls?"

"It ain't even like that," he choked out, trying to get air past her boot. "She's a lost cause. Ain't worth your time saving."

Cora shook her head and guffawed. She spared a look at the girl. She was frightened, eyes vacant, huddled against the wall watching the scene unfold just inches away from her. She trembled, either from the rain or terror. Either way, she reminded Cora of an abused animal, too timid to run away and too used to the abuse to bother.

A pulse of magic swarmed from her center to her fist, coursing through her like wildfire. It happened so fast, Cora didn't spare a thought for how she did it. Once it gathered in her hand, it was an itch she had to satisfy. She released her boot from his throat. No sooner than he took his full first breath did Cora throw a punch with magical force behind it. So much power ran through her in that moment, she didn't feel the impact. She didn't notice her knuckles dragging across his face. All she knew was what she saw - a burst of light from her hand as the magic transferred from her fist to his face with concussive force. She watched his body collapse to a heap in the alley as if he had no control of his own movements.

The man got back to a sitting position as fast as he could, as though he were trying to prove to himself that he was alright. It was a reflex born out of shock. As he got to his feet, Cora couldn't see him for what he was, only the labels that suited him best. Abuser. Coward. Victimizer. She threw another punch while he was down, taking him off what little balance he'd gathered. Half his bleeding face landed in a rain puddle.

"You like hurting girls," Cora all but growled through gnashed teeth. "Maybe I like hurting you."

She kicked him in the face with her boot heel as he got up again. The woman beside Cora shrieked with that same wounded and helpless animal cry that brought Cora here. The man's eye rolled around in his skull, but he hadn't learned a thing. He'd probably had his bell rung by bigger and stronger men his whole life, that's why he needed to assert his dominance over women. It was time for a lesson.

Cora grabbed him by the jacket with both hands, forcing him back to his feet. The corner of his mouth dribbled rain-washed blood. She pulled harder, yanking him up. His head lolled around on his shoulders, as if something in his neck had come loose. His eyes wandered and danced in the sockets, but didn't know the tune. She gripped him underneath the chin, the same as she'd found him with the girl when she arrived.

Holding out an upturned palm, glowing orange illuminated the sheets of misty rain coming down around them. The woman beside her cried out again, sliding down the wall to her bottom and clutching her knees to her chest. The man was too out of it to notice Cora's light show or just didn't care. She cupped her hand, forming the ball. Bringing it closer, she used her other hand to keep a firm grip on his chin.

As the Stunbomb drew closer, he became aware of it. His eyes flared open, pressing his back firm to the wall.

"Open!" Cora yelled, digging her fingertips into his cheeks. Reluctantly, he obeyed, parting his lips the slightest bit.

Without hesitation or patience, Cora forced the Stunbomb into his open mouth. Now the size of a tennis ball, it was already too large to fit in his mouth all the way. Impatient, she shoved it farther, as far as she could push it without shattering. The moans and whimpers of protest were only matched in volume by the cries of the woman on the ground beside her. Cora waited until she saw the glimmer of realization in his eyes. Deep within, she flipped the magic inside her to the cold and brought it to her eyes. The man tried to scream at the sight of her, muffled by the magical grenade in his mouth.

"I let this ball explode, they'll be picking your teeth out of the wall behind you," she said, her voice like ice. She stared at him through blackened eyes.

Vincent croaked in the distance. She tuned it out. Tears fell from the corners of the man's eyes, silently begging for his life.

"Echo-1, stand down!" an Italian voice shouted from down the alley.

Cora turned her head. Giovanna was running toward her, but froze with a single look at her eyes. Behind her, George kept moving. He held up his hands in a disengaging manner.

"This isn't who you are," he said. "Don't do it like this."

"Is that even our man?" Giovanna asked him.

George shook his head without taking his eyes from Cora. "No. That isn't him. Echo-1, you need to let him go. Whatever he was doing, there are police here for that."

Cora returned her gaze to the man. Out of the moment, with fresh eyes, he was whimpering. He reeked from pissing himself. A pathetic coward, he wasn't worth another life on her soul. She opened her palm, the glowing orange ball burst into harmless twinkles of light and dust. She released his jaw and stepped back. His eyes moved from Cora to George and Giovanna, scared out of his mind.

"Run," George said.

Without hesitation, the man fled the alley and disappeared from view once he hit the street. Cora shook off the Spirit Sight and focused on the woman at her feet. She offered a hand.

"What did you do?" the woman said, slapping Cora's hand away. She sobbed, even as she got herself back on her feet.

Cora shook her head, perplexed. It was hard to think straight with the blinding amount of emotion and adrenaline still coursing through her. The reaction to being rescued wasn't at all what she expected.

"Don't worry," she said, pointing down the alley. "I scared him, if nothing else. He won't touch you again."

The woman put her hands on her hips. Her face twisted, angry and dark. The sunken, dark circles around her eyes fixed on Cora. "Yeah, I know! Now how am I supposed to get work around here?"

"What?"

George and Giovanna joined Cora at her side. The Italian weaved around the woman, examining her.

"Varicose veins around the back of her ear, dark eyes, shitty teeth and clothes, pasty skin...she's a Sim addict," Giovanna said. She pointed at the woman as if she were just an object. "She's as much a piece of shit as that guy was. Probably her pimp."

"Sod off, bitch!" the woman shot back, turning and redirecting her fury.

Giovanna pointed a thumb at George. "He warned your boyfriend. Now, I'm warning you. Run."

The woman scoffed at first, but as her eyes lingered on Giovanna, there was no mistaking how deadly serious she was. She took a few nervous steps backwards. "Oh, I don't need this. You bunch of freaks!" she shouted before she took off running.

Cora shook her head. She wasn't expecting a celebration, but she certainly didn't anticipate the woman would be mad for beating up her abuser. "Where will she go?"

"She'll probably go track down the pimp, beg him to take her back," George replied with a sigh. "More afraid of change and getting her next Sim than thinking about tomorrow. We don't have that garbage in Texas, really, but we have other stuff...it always ends the same."

With a deep, cleansing breath, Cora turned to Giovanna. The Italian was fuming, that much was obvious with a single glance.

"Look, I'm sorry you had to see that," she started.

"I want you off this. Now," Giovanna replied.

Cora's jaw dropped with a gasp. "What?"

The Italian stuck a finger in her face. "You almost killed that man. When I got here, you were taunting him. The whole side of his face was swollen. Did you do all that?"

"Well, yeah," Cora replied. Looking back on it, it felt so good to indulge the inner beast in the moment. To make him feel fear like he caused it. To make him hurt like he hurt others. "I saw him roughing her up."

"Call a cop," Giovanna said, motioning to the alley. "We didn't bring a holographic billboard to announce we're here. We need to blend in. This guy knows what you and George look like. That girl is going to tell everyone she knows about the three of us. If you can't hold on to your own emotions, get back to Atlantis."

Cora held up her hands in mock defense. "I'm sorry, alright? I got carried away, but-"

"Control," Johnny's voice came over the comm line. It grabbed the attention of the entire trio. "What's going on in north quadrant? We have a lot of activity at the police station."

"Checking," Gideon replied. "Oh, God..."

Cora tapped her comm button. "Control, what's going on?"

"There's a lot of chatter right now, but they're scrambling to cordon off roads. A body has been discovered. Reports of a bandaged man fleeing the scene."

"Address!" Cora shouted.

"Forwarded to your Arcadia," Gideon replied, breathless. "Go north two blocks and make a right on Adelina."

Cora blew between George and Giovanna and took off into a sprint. This was even worse than the last time. They got no warning, and would have even less time to investigate before London Police would be crawling all over. Part of her hoped she never made it there. If she could find the bandaged man fleeing, all the better. She'd much rather put a Stunbomb in his mouth. No amount of yelling or pleading from Giovanna would ever make her hesitate pulling the trigger on that one.

PARTING GIFT

"How did we miss this?" Cora yelled, racing down the street.

"There aren't any outbound transactions from NextGen. I don't understand," Gideon replied. He sounded flustered. "I'm only going to be able to dig deeper for a pattern when we know who the victim is. I'm on it. Apartment 5C in the Blocks. Be advised, the person that discovered the body will be waiting outside."

Rounding the corner, Cora made her way down the final street with no sight of the bandaged man. Instead, she found an old woman clutching an old-time smartphone with both hands. Her face as white as her hair, her tremble was obvious from a dozen feet away. Cora stopped in front of her, checking every direction.

"The bandaged man. Where did he go?" she asked, breathless.

The old woman pointed behind Cora. The face of the building behind her, a six-story apartment complex, was gouged with scars that scaled all the way to the roof.

"Hand to God, he jumped over the fence and ran up the side of the building," she replied.

"Dammit," Cora whispered to her side. She couldn't see Vincent, but she felt him close by. "Get eyes up there. Let me know if you see him."

"Caw," Vincent replied, perched behind her. His resolve was admirable.

With the way the bandaged man moved, he was either long gone, or watching from a safe distance. If he had some perverse need to view the scene like she'd heard about in true-crime holovids, Vincent would find him. Cora shook her head. She reached into the back pocket of her jeans and fished out her wallet. Flashing it for only a second, she nodded to the woman.

"Kathleen O'Malley, Interpol. Apartment 5C, yes?" she tapped the comm button to open her microphone. "Who is the tenant?"

The old woman teared up. "Heather Lowell. She...oh, God, it was so horrible."

Giovanna and George came up alongside Cora. She replied to the old woman, "The police should arrive soon. We need to get a look."

Cora exchanged a glance with Giovanna. The Italian replied with a quick nod and put her arm around the old woman.

"C'mon, love," she spoke in a British accent, leading her inside. "Let's have a cup of tea and calm our nerves."

Cora lead the way with George right at her heels. They made their way to the elevator and rode up to the fifth floor. The doors opened to thin, industrial gray carpeting lining a corridor with flat white walls. They jogged down the hall. Sirens wailed. They hadn't even found the room yet and they were running out of time.

"Heather Lowell," Gideon said in her ear. "Dropped out of Queen Mary University earlier this year. Twenty-one years old, parents divorced, neither of them living in the city. I'm going into her financials and social media, that's going to take a bit."

An open door signaled the end of their search. Cora paused before entering, but swallowed the terror all the same. The place was small, like the others, but very modern. Modular countertops that folded away to expand the living room area, a decent-sized holovid monitor, and plush couches rounded out the amenities. She walked past the signs of struggle in the living room, the fight for a life that ended in vain. Cora knew where she needed to go. The bedroom at the end of the hall was the only room without lights on.

Her first step into the bedroom, the rug squished. Cora shut her eyes. Feeling blind along the wall, she found the switch and flicked it on. She stepped back and screamed, slamming her back into George's chest.

"Oh, God," George whispered.

Blood on the green bedroom rug blotched the carpet in puddles that appeared black. The white walls were splattered, the furniture, even the ceiling was speckled in Heather Lowell's blood. As for the bed, it was impossible to determine the original color of the sheets, as they were soaked through completely. The girl's body, her clothes drenched in kind, was hacked to shreds. Beyond the obvious slash across her throat, dark red lines in her exposed flesh indicated innumerable stab wounds. Cora turned her head away, swiping at her Arcadia screen as she began to cry.

"Control, photos incoming...prepare yourself," she said. Moaning, she added, "He tore her apart."

"...Understood, Echo-1."

She held her arm steady as best she could. George's hands grasped both of her shoulders. He tried to comfort her, but she could feel the rage in his touch. Whatever the bandaged man was, he wanted to avenge these girls with a kind of fury no court would abide. Without looking back upon the girl, Cora moved into the room a small bit, careful to avoid the blood in the rug. It was bad enough she stepped in it once already. The last thing she needed was to taint the crime scene and have the police looking for a five-foot-two woman with biker boots. Once she had enough angles to make a decent three-dimensional model for them to study, she backed out of the room.

"Control, do we need to take her Arcadia?" Cora asked.

"Negative," Gideon replied. "I'm already piggybacking off your near-field connectivity and breaking into her wrist computer. How long do I have to copy it?"

The sirens were outside. They had arrived.

"We're out of time," Cora said with a sigh. She wiped away tears with her sleeve. "I can make the play that I was first on the scene, but if I ruffle too many feathers, they may start calling around, asking about me."

"I need at least two minutes," Gideon replied.

"I'll buy it," she said.

"Cora?"

She turned. George wasn't behind her anymore. He stood at the edge of the doorway adjacent to the bedroom. That dour, grim look on his face spoke volumes.

"No," she pleaded, her eyes raining tears.

Even as Cora's heart begged her not to follow, she stepped to the doorway. Peering in, a message was written in crimson on the mirror.

I warned you.

In the blood-soaked sink, a clear plastic bag rested over the drain. It was so drenched that it was impossible to make out the contents. George took a breath and pulled out a pair of rubber gloves from his pocket. He pulled them on, even as it looked like the last thing he wanted to do. Cora held her breath. Whatever horror he'd find, she knew she couldn't brace herself enough.

George grabbed the corner of the bag between his thumb and forefinger. As he pulled it up, the bathroom light struck it and cast the contents in silhouette. It was a hand, severed at the wrist. Cora covered her mouth with both hands, stifling a scream. All the sheriff could do was shake his head in disgust. There was commotion in the hall. The police were coming. Thinking fast, Cora stepped away from George.

"We need to get that to Doctor Daly," she said. "We can't afford to wait on the police report."

George cocked his head to the side. "Ma'am, you better be able to get us out of here." With that, he shoved the blood-soaked bag into the pocket of his duster. He rushed to remove the gloves and pocketed them along with the gore-filled bag.

She had to act fast. Footsteps charged down the hall. She tapped the comm button. "Gideon, do you have it?"

"Ten seconds, just give me ten more seconds," he replied.

Cora pulled out her wallet and raised both hands as she marched to the front door. Two uniformed officers appeared in the doorway with stun pistols drawn.

"Kathleen O'Malley, Interpol," she announced. "This is John Holliday, my consultant. We were first on the scene. Is Detective Constable Thomas on site?"

One of the policemen examined her badge as they both lowered their weapons. The lead officer nodded, taking a second to examine her face. There was no hiding the puffy, red eyes from crying. The officer's face softened, concerned. "He's on his way. What happened here?"

Cora pointed a thumb behind her. "One female in the bedroom, deceased. She's...pretty bad."

The faces of both men turned to disgust, lips curled. They wanted to know more even as they didn't want to ask.

"She's all over the walls. The ceiling," Cora added, her voice heavy with the words.

"Jesus," an officer replied.

Gideon spoke into her ear, "I have her Arcadia copied. Get the hell out of there."

"I'll let you secure the area," Cora said. Pointing past them to the hall, she was already planning her exit. "Thomas will be arriving shortly? I guess I better get downstairs to meet him."

"Right," the officer replied. Looking at his partner, he shook his head. "Bloody hell. Let's have a look, then."

Stepping to the side, she let the officers pass and moved into the hall. With a quick glance over her shoulder, she jogged back to the elevator and got in. George let out a breath he must have been holding since the police reached the door. He pressed a hand to his chest.

"What was that? You're going to have us meet with Thomas? How is that getting us out of here?" he said.

"We leave now, it looks suspicious," Cora replied, wiping her eyes. Part of infiltration was understanding psychology. She was trained to recognize when all else failed, blending in with people in a hostile environment required making it seem like she belonged there. "We stay on, converse, and by the time we leave, they'll be grateful to have us out of their hair."

Tapping her comm, she said, "Echo-2, status?"

"...such a nice girl. The man ran across the street, and hand to God, he jumped over the fence and climbed up the side of the building..."

George turned his head to Cora, puzzled. "What was that?"

Cora rolled her eyes. "Giovanna probably drugged the old woman to sleep and assumed her form. She opened her comm to let us know who she was while continuing with her statement downstairs. That means we can't get out of here until we regroup."

"That complicates this further. We have a plan for that?" he asked.

"We'll know when the window is open," Cora replied. The horrors in George's pocket, the fact she knew the hand belonged to Leopold, it would all have to wait. Put her emotions on a shelf and focus on the task at hand, as Richard would tell her. Besides, she had faith in Giovanna. "I worked alongside her for over a year. We have a sort of...connection. It's hard to explain. Just stay quiet as you can and let me handle it."

The elevator doors opened to more cops. One of them wasted no time approaching her, his hand raised to halt them.

"Ma'am, are you a tenant?"

Cora held up her wallet. "No. Kathleen O'Malley, Interpol. Where is Detective Constable Thomas?"

Surveying the area, she spotted Giovanna posing as the old woman on the far end of the lobby area, near the tenants' mailboxes. She was talking with another officer as he nodded and notated the information on an antiquated tablet device. Once the officer in front of her was done examining her credentials, he stepped back and tapped the comm button behind his ear.

"Detective Thomas, I have a Kathleen O'Malley at the scene, asking for you," he said. Pausing for a reply, he winced. The detective was shouting loud enough that Cora could hear the faint sound of yelling from the cochlear speaker. "She was already here. No, sir, I think she wants to talk."

He shook off the shouts that rattled his eardrums and turned to

Cora. He pointed back to the red front door. "He'll be arriving momentarily, out front."

"Thank you," Cora replied. Without another word, she walked out the door and into the night. The narrow street before her was flooded with blinding flashes of blue lights on the six police vehicles swarming the entrance. It was still pissing rain, the kind of thin, obnoxious drizzle that wasn't enjoyable for anyone. Another vehicle, all black with a blue flashing light on the dash, approached at the back of all the madness.

Cora stepped sure with George in tow. Thomas grunted as he pulled his heavy frame out of his car. He shook his head at the sight of her.

"How were you here so fast?"

"The two of us were staking out the area surrounding the victims," Cora replied. "I was just around the corner when I caught wind of the dispatch."

"Caught wind, did you? Of a police dispatch on a secure channel? Must have been a strong wind," Thomas replied. He offered a bitter smile with his sarcastic wit.

Cora rolled her eyes. "Look, I've already been up there, and I've already fought this bandaged man the old woman reported fleeing. What he did to that girl...he's an animal...with more tech in him than any sane doctor could legally put in."

Her head perked up. It wasn't until she said the words that she recalled a story Giovanna had told her during the Paris mission. She made a mental note before she forgot. The doctor outfitting the bandaged man could be a lead worth pursuing.

"So, you're saying he's our man? Did you get a good look at him? Anything we can work with?" Thomas asked.

"No. I don't have an identity, no face, nothing," she replied. She pointed her thumb back to George. "The sheriff here put two slugs in him and he shook them off. It was the only thing that saved my life. We're talking about a total body prosthetic."

The detective grinned and rested his arms on the roof and door of his car. "If that's true, there aren't many places he can hide. Walking around with that much tech is illegal, and everyone knows it. He wouldn't be able to go out in public anywhere."

George wagged a finger at the detective. "That might be it. Our way to flush him out."

Cora raised an eyebrow. "What are you thinking, Holliday?"

"We'd have to bring him up to speed on our other case," George warned her. She nodded, interested to see where he was going. "Detective, the case we're currently working involves another victim we haven't made you aware of yet."

"There's a fourth girl?" Thomas said, his mouth falling open.

"No. It's a man. Leopold Collins," George replied. He leaned against the hood of the car. "He's a Professor at the same school this latest victim disappeared from. We have reason to believe he's still alive. He's being used as leverage to keep Agent O'Malley off the case. These messages in the mirrors, they were directed at her."

Thomas did a double-take, eyebrows furrowed. He was furious. "You had a personal connection to this case and another victim, and didn't divulge this information sooner?"

"Due to the sensitive nature of this victim, I could not at the time," Cora said, holding up her hands in surrender. "That came from the top, I had no say over it."

The detective slammed his car door and put his hands on his hips. "So, this killer knows you?"

"He knows *of* me," Cora corrected. "I don't have a clue who he is."

"Unbelievable," he replied with a huff. He turned back to George. "How do you presume to flush him out, then?"

George folded his hands together. He was in his element. "We put a face to the crime. If you can call a press conference first thing in the morning, we'll put a bounty on his head. Get his girlfriend to talk about Leopold."

"His girlfriend?" Cora didn't like the sound of that. After the promise she made to the woman, going back and asking her for help would show they were desperate. Maybe it was time to admit that they were. There were only so many torture sessions Leopold could survive through, if the loss of a hand and eye hadn't killed him already.

"I'm telling you, the emotional angle works. It humanizes victims in the minds of their captors, something they absolutely do not want to do," George said. His confidence on the subject was amazing. "Right now, Leopold is an object. If he becomes a person with people who care about him, it becomes harder to objectify him."

Thomas nodded. "Right. Which may also lead to his murder, instead."

Cora took a deep breath. It was a risk, but if Leopold was still alive, he didn't have much longer. She turned to Thomas. "Can you get a press conference together with the local GNN outlet? We'd need this to go big."

The detective paced. He motioned to the apartment building. "What am I looking at when I get up there?"

"A woman painted on four walls and the ceiling," Cora scoffed. She hated being so blunt, but this shouldn't have been a negotiation. "You want to let this guy walk these streets another night?"

"We do the press conference," George followed her lead, hammering the detective. "Then you get every man you have in plain clothes walking these streets. You can't miss a four-hundred pound wired-up psychopath."

Thomas raised a finger. "One condition."

"Name it," Cora replied, her eyes narrowed.

"It's my show," he replied. "The victim is your guy. You get him back, great. But I want to nail this prick to the wall for these girls."

Cora nodded. "I can agree to that." She swiped out her Arcadia screen and brought up the detective's information. "I'm sending you a message. When you have a place and time for me, reach me at this line. For now, I need to get to the girlfriend's house and make sure I deliver."

"Very good, then," Thomas said, pushing his gut between Cora and George as he walked through them. "Now that you've held me up long enough, I need to get on this scene."

Cora waited until he disappeared into the apartment complex before she spoke. She turned to George, dumbfounded.

"I wouldn't have known any of that," she said. The relief he gave her with such ease, knowing a direction when she felt lost, astonished her. "I couldn't do any of this without you. Thank you."

He tipped the brim of his cowboy hat, replying only with, "Ma'am."

She tapped the comm button on her earpiece. "Echo-2 and Echo-3, we're clear for evac. Rendezvous at Position Gamma."

"Confirmed," Johnny said into the earpiece.

"...and thank God for you lads. If you'll excuse me a moment, I'm feeling light-headed. I'll be right back. I think I need to sit down and take one of my pills," Giovanna said in the old woman's voice.

Satisfied, Cora got walking, getting as much distance from the crime scene as she could. "Control, tell me you have something."

"The money issue is still a factor," Gideon replied. "Heather Lowell received a deposit of four thousand credits earlier today from Cove Investments Group. It's another damn shell company in the Caymans. I'm working on putting two and two together."

"Something occurred to me," Cora said. "This bandaged guy. He has to be local. Didn't you say full-body prosthetics are impossible to find doctors for?"

"Shit, you're right," Gideon replied. "I'll pull all available data for doctors in the area that have been suspected of illegal augmentation and I'll jump into UnderNet to see who's doing that kind of thing."

Cora sighed. Vincent was in the skies above her, feeling disappointed. Wherever this monster fled to, they were closing in on him now. For that to happen, she'd have to visit Andrea Toomes, and destroy the poor woman. Even if she got Leopold back, he'd never be the same. She could only hope there was a light at the end of all this darkness.

CRY FOR HELP

When Andrea Toomes opened the door, her hand clutched over her mouth. Tears filled her tired blue eyes. She pleaded without words. Maybe it was the expression on Cora's face, or the towering, grim lawman behind her. Cora hadn't given condolences for his death, but she may as well have. The poor thing assumed the worst.

Cora stepped forward and grabbed both her shoulders. "Hey, it's not that, okay? We haven't found him...yet."

"You didn't?" Andrea whined.

"No, I swear," Cora shook her head. "We need your help, though. Can we talk?"

Andrea stepped back and adjusted the sash of her black silk robe. She sniffled and wiped her tears with her palm. "Of course," she said, gathering herself. She turned and headed for the kitchen on the other end of her flat. "Come in out of the rain. I'll put on some tea."

Cora stepped in and held the door for George. Not wanting to drip through the woman's house, she took off her raincoat and set it outside the door. She stepped in, adjusting the sleeves of Richard's bomber jacket to her elbows. "I'm so sorry to come to you at such a late hour and give you a scare. I know how that must have looked."

"I've been on pins and needles, Miss O'Malley," Andrea said. She braced herself against the kitchen counter with both hands. Her chin quivered. "I just want him back."

"I know," Cora replied, shutting the door.

"For days, I went across the street, picking up his mail, pretending he was on vacation," Andrea said. She sighed. "As it turned into weeks, I didn't go anymore. I couldn't. Now, I just sit on my stoop and look at his flat. I guess I'm expecting the worst."

Cora walked across her living room and leaned against the counter opposite Andrea. She held out her hands and Andrea took them. "You have my word. I'm doing everything I can to find him."

"I know. I do," she replied, withdrawing her hands. She busied herself with making tea. "I'm sorry, you said you needed something?"

Cora motioned to George behind her. "I've brought in every person I thought could help. This is John, a sheriff from Texas. He's worked missing persons cases before. I have many others I've been working and consulting with. Tonight, I had to finally bring the police in on this."

Andrea paused. "What happened tonight?"

Cora waited until she had Andrea's full attention. She took a deep breath. "I need you to understand, this is going to be hard to hear."

"You...you said he was alive," Andrea replied, cocking her head to the side.

"I still believe he is," Cora said. She shut her eyes. "But the disappearances in the area, I believe they're all related. Leopold...he's been maimed."

Andrea gasped and dropped a spoon on the counter. "How? What happened?"

"I don't know how to put this delicately, I'm so sorry," Cora replied, her eyes welling with tears herself. "There was a...part of him that was left at a crime scene tonight...and that wasn't the first time it happened."

The poor woman screamed into her hands. She sobbed and

wailed. "No!" she shouted. She pointed at Cora. "No! You tell me right now, is he alive?"

George stepped forward and raised a hand. "Ma'am, for what we know right now, he's alive. This killer is using Professor Collins to try and pressure us off the investigation. That's why we brought in the police, and that's why we need you."

"What?" she cried. She shook her head, trying to think through weeping. "What can I do?"

"Right now, this man is using Leopold to try and keep Agent O'Malley and I off of this," he replied. He walked around the counter, into the kitchen, and bent his knees until he was at her height. "He's augmented...heavily augmented. With the police for numbers, we need you to put a face to Leopold. We're going to try to convene a press conference in the morning. I'd like you to speak about Leopold. Tell all of the UK what kind of man he is, and how you want him home."

She crumpled forward, falling into George's arms. She fell apart, heaving into his shoulder. "I do. I want him back so bad."

George held her in his arms and stroked her back.

A vibration in Cora's arm startled her from the moment. She looked down at her wrist. Gideon was calling. She tapped her comm button and walked back toward the front door.

"Go ahead."

"I've got something, but I don't know what I have," Gideon said.

Cora looked over her shoulder. George had a good handle on Andrea. She walked to the front window and looked out. "I'm listening."

"NextGen Holdings and Cove Investment Group both tie into a network of shell companies that have been handing out these checks all over London," Gideon explained, his tinny, robotic voice like a drill in Cora's ear. "Heather Lowell's Arcadia had the same number in it as Carla Glass. The company these girls were working for is an underground Sim network."

"Sim? These girls were all drug addicts?" Cora asked, her brow furrowed.

"No, Cora. I can probably confirm with autopsy reports, but I think these girls all have wet drives," Gideon replied. "They were getting into prostitution, but not the regular kind. They were recording the experiences for the user. These girls were making Sim with their clients."

Cora gasped, clamping her hand over her mouth. "That means this monster..."

"Yeah," Gideon said with a sigh. "He's been making them record their murders, instead. With that data, he can relive every feeling they had - pain, fear, helplessness. He can admire his own work from the other side."

The news hit Cora like a truck. It was beyond sick. Most Sim addicts wandered to places beyond their reach - a deserted island, conversing with lost loved ones, cheating on a spouse without repercussions. By living out the experiences of someone else, they didn't have to be who they were for a while. As the mind grew used to the stimulation, the direct input dulled their own natural senses, until the brain couldn't feel anything in the real world anymore. The technology proved so damaging, it was outlawed in almost every country within two years.

"Who is she talking to?" Andrea asked George.

"One of our analysts," George replied.

Their conversation continued. Cora shook her head and tuned them out. "I don't understand, though. Why Leopold, then? He has no tech, no wet drive. If this bandaged man hadn't taken him, I wouldn't even be after him."

"The only thing that makes sense to me is that he needed Professor Collins for something," Gideon replied. "I'm digging through every paper Professor Collins has ever published, trying to find something...anything that would be of use to an over-augmented Sim-addict serial killer. If I'm being honest, it's just another direction and I'm spreading myself pretty thin. I don't know enough about biology to really know what I'm looking at."

Shutting her eyes, she blew a breath out of her nose. Between this investigation and the search for the trident, Cora was pretty certain Gideon hadn't slept in days. While she could relate, guilt started to prey on her. He wouldn't ask for help or give up on her. It wasn't in him. He'd keep this pace up until he hurt himself in NeuralNet.

"Anything else? Doctor Daly got the hand?" Cora asked.

"Yeah, Giovanna got it to him. He's running tests now, but DNA results can take many hours," Gideon replied. He sighed. "I wish I had more, but we're in a holding pattern for test results, scans, backtraces on these shell companies. I'm sorry."

Cora stared hard out of the window. "Gideon, don't ever apologize. You work harder than anyone I know. I've been able..."

She stopped. Across the street, Leopold's flat stared back at her. The windows black as the night, it wasn't until Cora really looked at it that she realized how completely lifeless it was.

"Cora, are you there?"

"Gideon, I'm staring at Leopold's house and every single light is off. Absolutely everything," she said. She grabbed the handle for the front door and stepped outside. Walking across the lawn, she confirmed her suspicions. "Yeah, there isn't a porch light, automatic door light, nothing."

"Checking..." Gideon said.

Cora continued closer, crossing the street. As Andrea had mentioned, the mailbox was overstuffed. She hadn't been to the house in a while. A sour smell hit her nose, turning her stomach instantly. Carried on the wind, the scent was vile, even as it was faint.

"Oh, I'm such a cube," Gideon said into her ear. "He missed his electric bill. Services were turned off a few days ago. I should have just paid the bill for him. I'm sorry."

Against her own better judgment, Cora took another sniff. She winced at the scent. Crossing the lawn to the front door, the smell grew in intensity.

"Something reeks," Cora said. "Coming from the house."

"Yeah, everything in his fridge has probably turned," Gideon replied.

Cora fumbled with screens on her Arcadia until she turned on the flashlight. Even as it felt like paranoia, she reached to her back and pulled out her Predator. She tried the doorknob. It was locked. Without power, only a physical key would get in. As late as it was, she didn't want to start waking a long row of neighbors on both sides.

"Vincent," she whispered to the air.

He was never far away, even if she didn't know where he was. The raven flew to her shoulder and awaited his orders.

"See if you can unlock this from the other side," she said.

Vincent phased through the front door. "Caw," he cried out a muffled croak. He had no idea what he was doing.

"It was worth a shot," Cora sighed. She took a step back and aimed her Predator for the doorknob. It was the worst idea in the world, attracting attention like that, but the smell was starting to get to her. As she leveled her weapon at the door, a fluster of activity sounded on the opposite side. Flapping wings. Pecking. Then a click.

She tried the knob. The door opened up. The scent hit harder, but not as much as she expected. Vincent flew back to her shoulder, proud of himself.

"Well, you should be. I'm impressed," Cora said, distracted. Without lowering her weapon, she steadied her grip with both hands, leading with the flashlight from her Arcadia.

The room was the same as she left it - a crumpled corner of the living room rug with one of the lamps face down on it. She crossed the living room and went to the kitchen. The nauseating stench did not intensify any further. She stopped at the fridge and opened it.

"I have soy milk, a few bottles of wine, and some Thai takeout," Cora said. "It's all turned, but this isn't where the smell is coming from."

"Wait, you're in the house?" Gideon said. He sounded confused. "Your Arcadia is picking up a wireless signal that wasn't there a minute ago."

Cora cocked her head and looked around. No portable generators and no lights anywhere in the house were on. "How strong is this signal?"

"Full strength," Gideon replied. "I can't connect to it, though. It's encrypted."

Stalking up the stairs, Cora made her way to the second floor. She checked the bathroom - empty, as she had left it in the first search she performed. It was only a few weeks ago, but those weeks stretched into eternity. She couldn't recall a full night's sleep that wasn't a result of massive internal injuries. She couldn't imagine victims would have piled up like this. Moving on to the bedroom, the closet was left open. Cora had checked for missing clothing, luggage, anything that would indicate where Leopold went. The only thing that wasn't there was his artifact.

"How's the signal now?" Cora asked.

"Weaker," Gideon replied. "Did you move to the other end of the house?"

Cora raised an eyebrow. "No. Second floor. Does this place have a basement?"

"Checking. Yeah, looks like it. Satellite view of the house shows exterior access from the backyard," he said. "It looks like one of those slanted, trap-door kinds from way-back."

Cora jogged down the steps. "Checking it now."

"You think you found something?" Gideon asked.

"God, I hope not," Cora said. The words aloud made her terrified. In her head, visions of finding Leopold's body in the basement gripped her. If he was already gone, if he was under her feet the entire time she'd been looking for him, she didn't know how she could live with it. She dashed out the front door and around the house to the back. A gate blocked her path to a small backyard. She unlocked it and moved in.

"That wireless signal keeps going in and out," Gideon said.

"Ran around the house to the backyard," Cora said, approaching the basement doors. She bent down and checked the handles. Wrapped around them was a simple bike lock. She used to break locks like these blindfolded. It took only a few moments to crack the code by feel and take the chain off. Grabbing hold of both handles, she stood up and pulled. The doors opened right up, and what came with it was a concentration of the horrid, sour stench. It came so strong and took her so off-guard that she wheeled to a knee and threw up on the grass.

"Body," Cora choked out. "There's a body in the basement. That's the smell."

"Oh, no," Gideon replied. "Cora...you don't have to go down there. I can call George, or the police."

"No!" she said, forcing herself to stand. Tears filled her eyes, from a combination of heartbreak and sickness. She willed herself to breathe through her mouth and stop taking in the foul odor. "I have to know."

She pointed the flashlight to the blackness. Five steps took her to a cement floor. Her motorcycle boots clicked on the stone, echoing through what appeared to be a largely vacant room. It didn't look like Leopold used the extra space for much except a few boxes. On the back wall, a wine rack and bookcase lined one end, and on the opposite, a large freezer. Cora shook her head, eyes filled with tears. It was Leopold. He was in there, she knew it. Her heart skipped.

Every step she came closer to the end of her investigation. She'd have to cross the street and break Andrea's heart again. Tell her what she found. A tear rolled down her cheek. One corner of her mind said, 'no' on a loop, begging to be wrong. The freezer was a top-loading model, waist-high. She shut her eyes for a second, trying to brace for the heartache that would follow.

The lid pulled open without resistance. The air from it hit her face, though she dared not inhale. Inside, there wasn't one body, but two crumpled corpses. One stacked on top of the other. Covered in dried blood, their desiccated faces were so badly distended, she couldn't have made out a face if she wanted to. The bodies were curled into a fetal position to accommodate the small space. Both were clothed, but so stained in brown that she couldn't tell what color they used to be. The figure on the bottom was small, probably a woman. Cora shined her light at the face of the body on top.

"Cora? What did you find?" Gideon asked.

She couldn't reply. Breath was robbed away, along with any

words she had.

"Cora!" Gideon shouted.

On the other side of the room, a thud rang out, striking the steps. Cora heard it, but couldn't take her eyes off the freezer. The face on top was a woman, too. She had lavender hair and pointed elven ears. Another thud hit the stairs. The gears turned in her mind as she put everything together. The sound of that bandaged monster coming down the steps meant she figured it out too late.

"Leopold?" she called out, pointing her Predator at the stairs. Her Arcadia light illuminated black metal and carbon fiber legs. She moved up the form, to his black coat and bandaged face. His glowing green eyes stared back at her.

"He's been gone a long time," the bandaged man replied, his voice an unnatural, digital modulation. It was akin to Gideon's robotic NeuralNet voice, only much deeper and more frightening. A gloved hand raised a finger and tapped his temple. "He still rattles around, from time to time. Makes me keep an eye on the woman. Then you had to involve her."

"That's far enough," Cora cried, aiming her weapon. Her eyes were clouded by a fog of tears. Whether it was Leopold or not, another step and she'd empty the clip into him. "Who the fuck are you?"

"It's...it's me Cora," he replied. His voice changed, sounding terrified and confused. The cockney accent was replaced by the gentle, meek Irish accent of Leopold. He took another step forward. "Help me! I can't stop him!"

In that moment, she saw her search at an end. She saw Andrea's face when she answered the door. Her hand trembled. A split second later, he dashed another step forward with inhuman speed. Grabbing the barrel of her Predator, Cora was shaken out of her trepidation and double-tapped the trigger. She was too late. The slide locked in place by his grip, the weapon wouldn't fire. With a tug, he snatched it from her hands as if she were a toddler and tossed it away. It clanged on the floor somewhere in the darkness behind him.

His other hand came up, the antique leather medical bag in

his grip. Inches from her face, he reached to the side and set the bag on the corner of the open freezer. Snatching her by the throat, he laughed, a chortled, synthetic sound. It grated on her ears. Using Leopold's voice was a ploy, and she fell for it. He moved forward, backing her against the wall between the freezer and the bookcase. With both hands, Cora struggled against his grip. For all her strength, she didn't have enough to pull a single finger off of her.

"I've been...interrupted. Twice now," he said. The way he spoke was nothing like Leopold. His mouth curled into a smile beneath the bandages. Within, she could see a dozen reflections of her horrified face in chrome-finished teeth. "I'm going to take my time with you. Savor this, real proper."

Cora averted her eyes. For the first time, her Native instinct to despise the sight of technology was a burden to her. There was so much of it in him, that just to look upon him prompted everything short of a panic attack. His grip tight, she wasn't getting enough air. She needed a breath, to regroup and think clearly. All she could see in her mind was dental surgery to install a metal jaw.

"Ah, yes," he chuckled. It was a garbled, cruel sound played over static. "You don't like implants. It's funny. It was because of you I got the first one. Leopold held on so hard, believing in your words. With enough cybernetics, he thought he could poke holes in his paper cup of a soul. To purge me? My soul? He wanted so badly to be free of me. All it did was make me stronger, better at my work. Eventually, the old boy came around."

Cora shut her eyes and called out to Vincent. Opening herself to him, she let him pull magic from her like a well. Over the shoulder of the bandaged man, a ball of orange light grew, coalescing from twinkling dust that swirled in from nowhere. Vincent rushed forward, a Stunbomb gripped in his talons.

Without turning around, not even so much as a twitch, a gloved hand snapped backwards blind. He grabbed Vincent out of the air. The raven phased out of his grip as the bandaged man crushed his fist together. The orange ball fell to the ground at his feet, shattering like glass. The resulting explosion struck at an invisible wall of energy inches off the surface of his body. Cora's eyes flared open.

"A valiant effort," he nodded. "A bit more ready for you this time, Boss."

BOOM!

A crack like thunder echoed through the room, followed by another. Then again, each one as deafening as the first. The bandaged man's face changed from sinister glee to shock. His gripped released from her throat. She gasped and heaved air into her starved lungs. The bandaged man slumped, then fell to the side with a boom as loud as the gunshots. Over four hundred pounds of metal crashed to the floor in a heap. At the other end of the basement, George stood by the stairs, pistol in hand.

Cora fell to her bottom, hands clutched around her throat. The cybernetic hand's grip had been so tight, she still felt his fingers on her flesh. She tried to swallow, but her throat was too bruised to listen. Her eyes, filled with tears, tried to roll back in her head. She didn't recall seeing him move, but George was suddenly squatted by her side.

"Hey, stay with me," he said. "No sleeping on the job, ma'am."

In and out of consciousness, she struggled to listen. Her regeneration got to work. The fog over her mind lifted like a veil. The bandaged man was up on a knee, behind George. Her finger pointed up. She spoke, but no words came out. George met her eyes, and realized too late.

Trying to pivot around, the bandaged man was faster. He snatched the collar of George's duster. With an effortless pull, George flew across the room with such velocity, his back tore through the shelves of the bookcase. The top half broke apart. George bounced off and hit the ground on his face. A split-second later, the entire bookcase collapsed over top of him. Unsatisfied, the bandaged man got to his feet and took a step in George's direction.

She wasn't healed, but it would have to do. Cora pushed off the wall, back to her feet, and threw out a front kick. Knowing she'd only strike him in an arm made purely of metal on a frame like a wall, she braced herself. Her heel dashed out as he was mid-step. The strike was little but a nuisance, taking him momentarily off-balance. The play had the desired effect, though. His attention switched to her in a heartbeat. His hand once again lashed out, grabbing her by the throat.

In the distance, somewhere far from this chamber of horrors, a chorus of sirens blared. Gideon must have called them in. The bandaged man cocked his head, listening to it, judging the distance. He put her right back to the wall and lifted her off her feet.

"My work is being interrupted again," he said. He blew out a frustrated breath through his nose. "No matter. Perhaps if I fix you, I can continue my work in peace. Spend some proper time taking care of these harlots."

Kicking her legs and thrashing in his grip, both hands wrapped around his forearm. He didn't budge. Nothing she'd ever encountered in all of this war carried such inevitability. He was like death incarnate, a force of nature that could not be fought against or stopped. She could only watch in abject terror as his free hand reached into the medical bag. She gave Leopold that bag. The spirit within, whoever it was, had taken him over completely. There were no other artifact holders involved, no connection between Leopold and these women. Lucius didn't send him after her. This abomination was her creation.

The halo of light from her Arcadia glinted off the silver finish of a scalpel in his hand. She kicked with greater vigor. Vincent croaked and screeched, fluttering about his face. A few wild slashes with the scalpel caused the raven to dodge. Once he was in the right place, a quickly-timed backfist slammed into Vincent as he was still corporeal. She heard his tiny body hit the cement floor somewhere in the darkness. Cora wanted to scream as she felt her connection to him go numb.

Glowing green eyes focused back on her. The bandaged man bowed his head. He was saying goodbye. The silver blade moved past the black hair on her shoulders and dug into the soft flesh under the back of her jaw. The most terrifying part was that she could not feel it at all. Even as he dragged the scalpel across her throat, even as the hot blood poured onto her chest, the only thing she could feel were three words.

I deserve this.

THE VOID

Cora's eyes opened to a field of leaves and dirt. Instead of bright, brown hues, everything was washed in gray. The vibrancy of the world muted, it carried dread and familiarity all at once. She pulled herself up and grabbed at her throat. There was no wound. She felt fine. Her clothes appeared brand-new. Even Richard's well-worn bomber jacket had no blemishes.

All around her, the clearing gave way to trees. Tendrils of blue energy coursed through every living thing, pulsing like veins. The whole, dense forest was alive. The faint glow of auras surrounded the spirit animals that dwelt there, making them appear like fireflies. The brightest aura, the light at the center of her vision, came from a man approaching her from the distance. He glowed in white, with a web of tethers that connected him with all things in the forest.

Her brow furrowed. "Dad?"

****

"Ten milliliters adrenaline!" Doctor Daly barked in his thick Irish accent.

"That's double the recommended dosage! She could go into tachycardia!" another man shouted back. Cora couldn't recognize

167

the voice.

"We need to spike her regeneration! I can't have her body eat all of it!"

There was a pause. Daly continued, "Administering. Keep an eye on her heart rate."

****

She met Still River halfway, stepping through the forest and weaving around trees. Once clear, Cora ran and threw her arms around him. There was no chill of death, only the warm embrace of her father. He held her close, and safety came with it. He'd protect her from the nightmare she'd lived through. She cried on his shoulder, soaking the flannel shirt in tears.

"I know, baby," he said, his words so soothing. "I want so badly to take this away from you."

"Is it over now?" she begged.

He gripped her by the arms, firm but gentle. Holding her at arm's length, he met her gaze before he answered. His eyes were serious and offered no comfort.

"No! I've lost years. I've lost your mother. I won't lose you, too," he said.

Cora shook her head and dropped it in shame. "I don't want it anymore, Dad. I can't do this."

As if the words were magic itself, a shaft of light appeared on the forest floor, piercing through the lack of color. It was a glorious, beautiful spectacle. Cora's eyes followed it, back to the source. Above the canopy trees, well into the distance, she saw the peak of Heaven's Crest. At the summit, a door of light shone brighter than anything she'd ever seen, yet never hurt her eyes. The light was warm, hypnotic, and inviting. It beckoned her to come, a feeling from deep within, like an instinct. The light flashed at her eyes.

****

"Is there anything else you can do?" Julian asked.

"Even with the regeneration, I don't understand how the lass is still holding on," Daly replied. "She should be dead."

"Please," Giovanna said, her voice cracked. "Tell me she's going to make it."

Daly sighed. "I don't know. I'm sorry. I had her in surgery for nine hours. I've patched her together, closed the wounds as best I could. If it were anyone else, I'd be wasting my time. She'd have been gone already. I don't know if her regeneration can fix this damage fast enough."

"Do you need anything? Blood, plasma?" Julian asked.

"What I need is for her to heal faster," Daly replied.

"Use me," Giovanna said. She sniffled and cleared her throat. "The nanites in my skin cells are designed to close wounds and repair surrounding tissue. If you took a skin graft from me and used it as a mesh, that could speed it up, no?"

Images danced in Cora's head. Tiny little robots, like spiders, walked all over her flesh. They climbed inside her, laying eggs. She would have screamed, begged them not to listen to Giovanna.

"Doctor! Her heart rate is spiking!"

****

"You can't!" Still River shouted, shaking her free of her gaze at the door of light.

Snapping back, her brow furrowed. "Why? This is my fault! I turned Leopold into that monster!"

His hands moved up, soft and gentle, cupping her by the cheeks. He shook his head. "No, Cora. We make our choices. Our will is our own."

"Not Leopold," she cried. She stepped back from his embrace. The comfort and safety was tainted by the memory of what she saw. "His will wasn't as strong as...this spirit. It took him over completely."

"No!" Still River raised a finger, stopping her train of thought. "No man alive could make me harm you. No one could make me pollute these lands. If Leopold can't wrest control from the spirit, then he doesn't want to. That's what really upsets you about all of this."

Cora's face became a mask of confusion. That couldn't be right. "What?"

Still River stepped forward again, placing his hand on her shoulder. "You want to blame yourself for handing over this artifact, and setting free the spirit of a monster. You want to count Leopold as one of his victims. You don't want to accept that you had him with you for an entire day, that you grilled him in the interview, and you didn't see the darkness inside him."

"It wasn't like that," Cora replied, shrugging his hand off her. She stole a glimpse at the beautiful light. It still called to her, waiting patiently. It taunted her with peace and respite. "I was there, I asked him everything. We vetted his every account. I looked him in his eyes."

"And you didn't see it," Still River pressed.

She shut her eyes and gnashed her teeth. "What are you doing here, Dad? What am I doing here?"

"I didn't bring you here. You did. You came here to give up," he replied. He couldn't be right. All she wanted was rest. "I can't let you go, Cora."

****

"The graft is applied," Daly said. "Vitals?"

Cora couldn't feel a thing. She couldn't see anything, either, but that didn't stop fear from gripping her. Her mind was a fog, like the week spent in Lucius' compound, strung out on Trillozine. She couldn't feel Vincent's presence. Her heart broke all over again.

"Doctor, blood pressure 135 over 86," a man called out.

That's when the burning began. For all that she couldn't feel, the heat on her neck seared like a flame. She wanted to grab at it, claw at it, but her hands wouldn't move. She didn't even know if they were still attached to her at all.

"Adrenal levels rising! Heart rate climbing fast!"

"Goddamn it! Her body is rejecting the damn nanites!" Daly shouted. "We have to reverse the graft!"

****

"I'm tired of this war, I'm tired of fighting, I'm tired of losing people I care about! I'm just tired, Dad!" Cora shouted.

Still River crossed his arms, leaning his back against a tree. "We all need a rest, Cora. You deserve it more than anyone."

Cora paced the forest floor, kicking up leaves. The door of light's call nagged at her like an itch in her brain. She dared not look at it again. The power coming from it seduced her. It offered a way out from everything.

"I'm dying up there," she said. The words didn't carry any emotion at all. She wasn't sure what to feel. "They're trying everything to save me, and I'm still slipping away."

"That has more to do with what's going on here than you realize," Still River replied. He swept his long black hair off his shoulders and stepped toward her. "I'd beg you to stay, if that would help."

Cora dropped her head. Guilt came over her. "I can't do it, Dad. I want to be free of this."

****

"...she's just not regenerating fast enough," Daly said. "I had to go in and sweep out the nanites, which only aggravated the situation."

"Why aren't you putting her on life support?" Julian demanded.

Daly sighed. "We tried when she first got here. At the time, her body had so much to repair just to keep her alive, so it worked. Now, it's attacking anything I put inside her. It's barely tolerating the IV, Julian. Hooking her up to a respirator would probably kill her at this point."

"So, what are you saying?" Giovanna yelled, her Italian passion taking over. "We just let her lay here and waste away?"

"I'm saying that any measures I take may actually make it worse. Even if she somehow comes back from this, she wasn't getting oxygen for the first nine minutes," Daly explained. "We have no idea what kind of brain damage may have occurred. She could come out a different person. She could never wake up at all. What I'm saying, lass, is that anyone who wants to should come and say their goodbyes."

****

"Tell me you really believe this was all your fault, and I'll walk you up the mountain myself," Still River said.

"I gave him the artifact," Cora said. She took a seat on a nearby rock and folded her hands between her legs. "I didn't figure out who it belonged to, what the ramifications could be."

"Oh, so Leopold wasn't a person with complex thoughts and hidden desires. You handed off this artifact to a blank slate," Still River argued. He nodded, his sarcasm thick. "You're right, Cora, due diligence is where this went off the rails."

She stared up at a gray sky. Even in the brightest day, the sun didn't touch the Spirit World. "I have so much blood on my hands. If I go back there, it only gets worse."

****

Sniffles and tiny moans filled Cora's ear.

"Oh, patatina. I can't stay here and watch this. I can't watch you leave me," Giovanna cried. "You're more than family to me. I want you to know - no matter what happens, I will get him. I know how. The monster that did this does not get to go on breathing. I won't bear it."

There was a pause. She fell back to wailing at her bedside. "I can't do this, Johnny! I can't! Let's go."

****

"No, no, no!" Cora said, her eyes opening on the forest. Her father kept a distance, letting her have her space.

"What's wrong?" he asked.

"My people...they're going to go after that thing," she said.

Still River shrugged. "Who cares, though?"

Cora's brow furrowed. "What?"

"It's a win-win for you," he replied. He pointed to the sky behind her. "You climb up there and leave this behind. Soon enough, friends will join you there, or they won't. Maybe they'll succeed where you failed."

His words harsh, they hit like a punch in the stomach. That wasn't what this was about, though. She didn't want the path of least resistance.

"Lucius said fate put us in this war! I'm tired of having my future dictated to me! If that's the life some invisible force wants me to have, they can keep it!"

****

"I don't worry about you, love," Julian said. He was holding her hand, or someone else was. "You haven't gone back yet. You haven't seen Merlin. I know you'll come back to us. Take the time you need to heal."

"Great pep talk," Michael ribbed.

"I told you, it's rubbish," Julian replied. "I know she's coming back."

Footsteps carried Julian's voice away. Michael was still holding her hand.

"He's right, you know," he said. "Soon enough, you'll be up and doing your best not to pull rank and make Julian feel insignificant."

He leaned close, his breath on her ear. "I pulled your arse out of the fire in Paris, you know. Gave you time to heal from a bullet to the heart. This? This is nothing, love. We'll be seeing you soon, then."

****

"Stop it!" Still River shouted. "You can't have it both ways! You're either over there or you're here."

Cora shook her head. Drifting back and forth, splitting her consciousness, it wasn't something she did willingly. "I'm not doing it on purpose!"

"Like hell you're not," he replied. He walked over to her rock and squatted down to eye level. "Your heart is conflicted. You don't want the fight, but you don't want your friends to carry the torch."

She clicked her tongue and huffed. "I want to keep them safe!"

"Sometimes, you will," he nodded. He reached out and took her hands into his. Locking her gaze, he continued, "Sometimes, you won't be able to save everyone."

****

"This is hard to say," Madeline began. With her sweet, soft-spoken French accent, it was sometimes difficult to reconcile that this sixteen year-old girl was once dressed like a ninja and beating her ass all over the Louvre. "It is even harder because I have to say in English, since you couldn't bother to learn some French."

She let out a bitter laugh and collected herself.

"You are a warrior, mon ami. The bravest I've ever seen. Stronger men, even elven men, would have wilted before Lucius, but not you. You bloomed in the field of battle. You may not believe as I do, but you are a warrior of God. Like Saint Jeanne, you were meant to lead us to victory. I won't see you end like her, too."

Madeline got low, her voice now close to her bedside. She whispered to herself in French. Cora imagined the young girl, with her shaved, scarred head, her body likely riddled with the same, and she was praying at Cora's side. She couldn't feel much of anything, but she felt a tear stream down from the corner of her eye.

"Come back to us, mon ami."

****

"I want to, though," Cora said, eyes filling with tears. "I want to save everyone I love."

She turned around on her rock and looked up to the splendor atop Heaven's Crest. The light promised peace. It welcomed her.

"It's a way out, Cora," Still River said. She couldn't tell if he was coming to understand her feelings or if it was meant to stir something in her.

Whether he intended it or not, the seduction of the light faded. Her heart was tainted by its presence. She saw it for what it was.

"It's an escape," she whispered, a tear falling down her face. "It's how I leave those I love behind in exchange for what I've lost. I...I wouldn't even have you there."

"Not while there is so much work left to do, no," Still River replied.

She turned to her father and stifled back another tear. "I'm so afraid of what comes next."

"You should be," Still River nodded. "But don't let fear lead you around by the nose. Your heart and your mind will always guide you towards the truth."

Cora stood up and her father moved with her. Looking over her shoulder, the light on Heaven's Crest was gone. The door closed behind her, knowing she'd made up her mind. She stepped forward, her father in step with her. She could afford to linger a few moments more. Her hand reached out and clasped his. No words were exchanged. None were needed. She walked among the trees and held her father's hand, the only moment of peace and respite she'd find this day.

THE GAPS

"She's awake," a man said.

Cora opened her eyes. Her back was sweaty and ached. Her throat was dry and sore. The face before was Professor Crowley, sitting in a chair by her bedside. He still dressed like a college teacher despite sitting in a military sickbay keeping vigil. He leaned forward, the tips of salt-and-pepper beard danced along her forearm. Goosebumps came with the tickle.

"Can you hear me, Cora?" he asked.

She nodded, and it hurt like a pinch along her throat. Treating herself like glass, she was afraid to move too much, even though her body was sick of its current reclined position. As much as it hurt, she tried clearing her throat. Doctor Daly walked over from his desk and stood at the foot of her bed.

"I've had better beds in truck-stop motels," she said, her voice so raspy she barely recognized the sound.

"I've had better patients in prisons," Daly jabbed back. "You can talk. That's a good sign."

She lifted a hand and pointed at her neck. "How long am I going to sound like this?"

"How the hell should I know? The only person ye should be talking to right now, lass, is Saint Peter," he replied.

"Well," Cora shrugged. "Better get to work on my jazz career

176

before I lose this smoky voice."

"You're terribly funny," Daly replied. He walked to her bedside opposite Crowley, to a metal tray on wheels. He held up what looked like a spring. "Your regeneration is in overdrive. You've done this to five needles now. I don't even know if we can ever use medical equipment on you anymore."

"Explains why I'm so thirsty," she replied.

Daly sighed. "I'll get you some water. Not whiskey. Water."

He walked off. Cora turned her attention to Crowley. He smiled, his kind face and disengaging eyes trying to break down her personal defenses before he said a word.

"I didn't imagine you'd be the one keeping a vigil," she said.

"There were many reasons for that," he replied. "What do you remember?"

As her faculties returned, her mind flooded with a million questions. The time since the injury was a blur, coming back in fragments. She remembered the final words of her friends. She remembered time spent with her father in the Spirit World. The door of light. She felt for the magic within her. Warm, but weak, it felt as drained she was.

Her eyes opened wide. Machines beside her beeped and chirped. Panicked, she reached out for the tether and called out to Vincent. She held her breath, awaiting a response. Seconds went by, frightening and horrible moments stretched on forever. The raven phased through the ceiling in a dive, landing by her thigh. He pecked at her leg.

She smiled with eyes full of tears. She couldn't recall the last time she'd felt such relief.

"Caw," he said. He had been very worried about her.

"Me? I thought he killed you!"

Daly walked over, holding a cup with a straw. "Ah, I see you've already made yourself at home and turned my sickbay into a zoo. Lovely."

Cora swiped the cup from his hand. Her relationship with the doctor was so acidic, she wondered how much either of them were playing. She pet Vincent while keeping her eyes on the doctor. "If you want to leave him a present on his desk later, feel free."

Daly grumbled and walked off. Cora took a cleansing breath and turned to the Professor. "Okay. Hit me."

"That's not how we do this, Cora," he replied, bowing his head. "You've undergone a major injury, both physically and emotionally. Trauma-"

"Screw my feelings," she interjected. "Lay it all on me."

"We'll be going slow," Crowley replied. He stroked his beard and crossed his legs. "As we continue, I'll assess how much more I can give you. We can't jeopardize your recovery."

Cora fumed. She didn't like it, but that's probably why Julian appointed Crowley. It was hard to get mad at him, even when she tried. Trading sarcastic barbs like she did with Daly seemed cruel, given his kind disposition. She shook her head and asked the simplest question she could think of.

"How long?"

"You've been unconscious for five days," he replied. He leaned back in his chair and observed her reaction. She hated feeling like she was being judged.

She gripped Vincent by his body and lifted him to her lap. "What do we know? Have there been more victims?"

"One, that we are aware of," he replied. "I've been brought up to speed on the latest in the investigation. I promise, I will convey everything to you once I feel you're ready."

Cora clenched her jaw. One more life stained her soul. "What was her name?"

Crowley sighed and shifted in his seat. "Christine Pond. Please, don't ask anymore about that just yet."

She took a sip of water. Every muscle down her throat ached as it passed through. She winced. "Why isn't Gideon the one telling bringing me up to speed?"

"Mister Parker is...overwhelmed with feelings of guilt," Crowley replied. "I offered to counsel him, but he declined. In short, he blames himself for not putting the pieces together sooner."

"That's ridiculous," Cora scoffed, trying to sit up. The machine beside her started chirping again. "I didn't know until thirty seconds before the bastard cut my throat."

"When Julian, Michael, and I became involved, we noticed something on the map," Crowley said. "The pattern and location of the murders were similar to another one in British history. They were called the Whitechapel Murders. You might be more familiar with the name of the perpetrator, dubbed 'Jack the Ripper.'"

Cora shut her eyes. Her heart skipped a beat. She must have listened to a dozen true-crime holovid documentaries that mentioned that case. If she had let Julian or Michael in on the investigation, maybe they would have seen it sooner. Then she realized how Gideon must be feeling.

"Oh, God," she said, shaking her head with a heavy sigh.

"You can't fault yourself," Crowley said. "The fourth murder cemented the pattern. Overlaid on the map with the original murders, Julian believes, and I concur, that the locations, victim choice, and method all line up. What the artifact was doing in Buckingham Palace, we still have no idea."

"The tech? How did he get it installed so fast? There's usually weeks of physical therapy involved for a single arm...who put it in? How did he get a hold of it?" Cora asked questions as fast as they came to mind. The monitors were beeping again. She gave them a sour look.

Crowley raised a hand to stop her and offered a gentle smile. "I don't pretend to understand the technical side. Gideon would have to explain what he's found. From what I understand, there may be a controller installed in his brain...does that sound right? Something that's handling his movements while he adjusts to the implants. As for who put it there, Gideon is solidly convinced only doctors at Tetriarch could have done it."

Somehow, it always came back to Lucius. This time, the lies wrapped around his curt and abrupt deflections. Maybe the idiom was wrong - three-thousand year old dragons could be taught new tricks. She hated that he was still so good at lying to her.

Julian entered the sickbay with Michael in tow. He looked like shit. Dark circles under his eyes sunk into a face that hadn't shaved in days. He had reverted to the overworked mess he was when this whole thing started. Carrying a cloth bag at his side, he wasted no time making a line for her bed and looked her over.

"There she is," he said with a smile.

Michael bowed his head. "The Sergeant's unwavering faith is rewarded. Glad to see you up, Cora."

"News travels fast," Cora said, giving a side-eye to the doctor.

"Of course it does," Julian replied. "I was to be notified of the slightest change in your condition. How are you feeling?"

"Like I'm recovering from a serial killer slashing my throat?" she said. She grabbed a sip of her water and endured the pain as it went down.

Julian looked at Crowley. "Have you told her?"

Crowley sat straight with a start, slamming both of his palms on the arms of the chair. "Dammit, Julian!"

Cora had never seen the Professor mad, let alone furious. Of course, that meant there was something sensitive he didn't want her to know. She raised her hand from off Vincent to prevent a squabble with her trapped in the middle.

"I'm fine," she said, her voice husky. She rolled her eyes at the sound of it. "Alright, I will be fine. We can keep going."

Crowley leaned forward, shutting his eyes as if to will himself back to calm. "Cora, you were without oxygen for a very long time after the injury. You had three heart attacks on the operating table. We were lucky to have gotten you out when we did."

"George is dead," Cora said, her head dropped. "Isn't he?"

"What? No," Crowley replied, shaking his head. "He crawled on top of you and held your wounds shut. Issued the emergency transport order. Other than some bruises, Mister Earp is fine. He saved your life."

She let out a heavy breath. It was a mercy, but now she couldn't imagine what they were hiding. "Look, I came this far, to be awake. I'm not going to fall apart now. Just tell me."

Crowley's brow furrowed as he glared at Julian. She'd known about the Sergeant's distaste for Crowley and the sway he held over the Atlantis soldiers, but she had no idea the feeling was mutual. She didn't even imagine Crowley was capable of the venom she saw in his eyes.

"Very good, then," Julian said, breaking the tension. He turned from Crowley, focused completely on Cora. "Three days ago, when you were in much worse shape, Giovanna and Johnny came to me. They wanted my blessing on an op to bring in or bring down the bastard that did this to you. I approved it."

Cora sat up from the bed with a start. It wasn't until after she'd done it that a thousand prickles, pulled muscles, and aches caught up with her. Through a grunt, she shouted, "You what? What did you let them do?"

Michael held up both his hands in surrender. "Cora, you have to understand. Where we were three days ago, Madeline brought in the Chaplain to give you last rites. Everyone was shocked, hurt, angry...we all wanted revenge. Giovanna was climbing the walls, she felt like she was trapped here, forced to watch you die."

Cora stared daggers into Julian's eyes. "Answer the question."

"Once we figured out the pattern and where the victims came from, Giovanna inserted herself in the organization. It wasn't very hard, with girls vanishing left and right, this Sim prostitution ring was losing money and business by the day," Julian replied.

Clenching her jaw, the beeping on the monitor started up again. Julian glanced up at it.

"Never fear, love," he assured. "When this is all over, they'll be going down, too."

"What happened to her, Julian? Is she dead?" Cora raised her voice, cracking with every word.

Julian pursed his lips. His head cast down. "We...lost contact with her six hours ago. Johnny, too."

The monitor beeped at a furious pace. The sound like a drill in her head, Cora examined her body and pulled wires and sensors off her. Vincent flew off in the commotion.

"Hey!" Daly shouted, rushing over from his desk.

"Cora, you're in no condition to go after her!" Julian shouted over the noise.

"She shouldn't be out there in the first place! You don't know what this guy can do!" Cora yelled back, frantically peeling sensors off her skin. Daly came over, trying to grab for her hands. She weaved from his grip and pointed a finger in his face. "Touch me and you'll be the one lying here!"

Daly raised both hands and shook his head. "Bloody hell, lass! You have to give yourself time! Not as much as any of us, but some!"

Through the pain of muscles trapped in a bed for the better part of a week, Cora turned on her rear, away from Daly and Crowley. She set her toes on the cold steel floor, inches from Julian's boots. Her eyes lifted until they met his, flames still burning into him.

"Move," she demanded.

He took a step back. Cora set her weight down and stood up. As if she were walking on stilts, her knees bowed back and forth as she tried to capture her balance. Frustrated, she tried pushing through it and made a step. Her left leg gave out completely and she collapsed to the floor in a pile at Julian's feet.

Julian squatted down, resting his forearms on his knees. Shamed and frustrated, Cora met his gaze even though she didn't want to.

"You done, then? Get your arse back in the bed," he said. His eyes were stern, his tone demanding. He turned his palm up, a gesture to offer a hand he knew she wouldn't take.

Cora reached back and clutched the side rails of the hospital bed. She pulled herself back to her feet. Still shaky, perhaps even more now, she sat back on the bed, defeated. Turning to Daly, she pleaded with her eyes.

"Can you give me any idea how long?"

Daly looked at Julian for approval. As he met her gaze again, his lips curled down. "I've been tracking the rate of healing. The severed artery and breathing passages healed first. It's like your body knew which parts to go after and in what order. Damn bizarre."

"That's magic for you," Cora replied, awaiting a real answer.

She knew he had one. Barbs aside, she was well aware of how competent and intelligent Daly was. He'd also been the only doctor to spend any length of time observing her regeneration in action.

"The dermal layer, wounds, all the superficial parts started healing up in the last twenty-four hours," he said. He hesitated with some bit he didn't want to volunteer. "Judging by the rate of recovery now, I think you'd be fully healed within the next twelve hours."

She turned her head to Julian. She needed to be ready when the time came. "I need exercise equipment to use while I'm sitting here. Whatever you can find. I need all of the intel we have on Giovanna's movements and her last known whereabouts."

"Cora, slow down," Julian raised his hand. "I wasn't counting on you getting up so soon. We're already on this."

"Yeah? So you know where she is? You have a team ready to burn down this freak?"

He sighed. "Well, no, but-"

"Please get me what I asked for," she insisted. Her tone left no room for further conversation.

"Tip-top," he said, pursing his lips. He picked up his cloth bag from the floor, set it on the foot of her bed, and walked out of sickbay.

Michael lingered, motioning to the door with a hand. "Cora, c'mon."

"Not another word out of you," she said, pointing a warning finger at him. "He doesn't coddle me, he should not expect to be coddled himself. Give me a break, he was a Staff Sergeant. He's been taking orders or giving them his whole career."

She said the words, wanting Michael off her back. She wanted the whole damn room clear. The truth was more complicated. She regretted a lot of things between herself and Julian. This latest incident could go on the pile. He was still hurting, no doubt, from the loss of Merlin. Michael was his right-hand man, but they didn't seem to have the kind of personal relationship that would allow him to confide. The fact that he hated Crowley, the only therapist on Atlantis, meant his brief show of vulnerability with her a few weeks ago was all the chance he'd had to vent his feelings. She didn't want to add to that. It was why she took him off the Leopold investigation in the first place. She didn't trust herself not to hurt him.

Michael bowed his head and took his leave. At least he understood that arguing with her when she'd made up her mind was pointless. She turned her attention to Doctor Daly.

"I need my Arcadia," she said.

"I believe we have it," he replied. "I'll have me nurse fetch it."

With Daly returned to his desk, that only left Professor Crowley. She gave him a blank stare, expectant, even rude. "Anything else?"

"No, Cora," he replied, standing up. He got the message. He took a few steps toward the exit, but stopped at the foot of her bed. "I know what you're doing. Do you?"

Cora took an aggravated breath through her nose. "Shutting out the people who care for me so I can turn off my emotions and focus on tasks I've made my personal mission. Sound about right?"

Crowley nodded. "Astute. But you don't need me to tell you that you're a better leader with them turned on. And you're a stronger leader when you have allies at your side." He patted the cloth bag at her feet, making a point to remind her of it. "You may feel you have to push them away. They'll still follow you into Hell either way. But things change."

She couldn't reply to that. He sounded like her father, well-suited for leadership himself, and wise enough to dole out advice. He reminded her that in his eyes, she was still a kid with a lot to learn. He bowed his head and left the room.

Vincent flew back to her bedside. "Caw," he croaked. He didn't like that she was suddenly worried, panicked, and down. He didn't like any of her emotions at all.

"What can I say? I can be a jerk sometimes," she said.

Leaning forward, she grabbed the cloth bag and pulled it to her. She opened it up. Brown leather stared back at her from inside. She grabbed it and pulled it out. It was Richard's bomber jacket. Someone had gone to great lengths to clean it and patch it. Probably soaked and stained with blood from her fight with Leopold, somehow Julian got it looking better than it had before she ever fought him. Happy as she was to see it, her lips drew down. She turned an eye to Vincent.

"Yeah," she sighed. "I can be a real jerk."

A TURNING TIDE

Cora turned through her holographic screen, poring over data collected over the past five days. It was jarring, as if she'd hit the pause button on her life and came back to it with no idea where everything had gone. Gideon's reports to Julian show signs of a man that had dove into his work with both feet, frantically trying to find an answer.

The first thing she'd done was to properly torture herself over the latest victim, Christine Pond. Twenty-two, beautiful, she could have been a model. That was true of most of the victims. Instead, their financial difficulties and the fact that they had wet drives installed lured them into prostitution with abnormally high payouts. What Leopold had done to her was beyond anything he'd done before. Without anyone to catch him in the act, the body was posed for police. He had taken his time with her, performing surgeries on her while she was still alive. The girl had only joined the escort service a week prior. The file made her cry and throw up twice before she was done with it. Still, Cora didn't stop until she read every report, viewed every image of the scene, and blamed herself for all of it.

She was forty pages into a report on the prostitution ring, and it appeared that was the halfway mark. What she learned about the group was lurid. Every woman killed by Leopold was having trouble making ends meet. That's how the group got them, recruiting in trendy clubs where these girls hoped to turn their looks into a career as a trophy wife. Life in London was not cheap, and they were floundering. Instead of this group turning them into the prostitution lifestyle, which was legal in many EU countries, they were being offered thousands of credits for creating Sim as they took clients. The physical feelings, sight and smell, all of the data from the experience was copied from the brains of these women to removable recordings via their wet drives. This was high-end Sim, though, catering to upper-class wealth that was already devoid of thrills and new experiences long before Sim came along. If the women only knew what a small fraction they were being paid versus what the Sim was selling for, they would have unionized.

The ring had no ties to Leopold that Gideon could find. That was to be expected, as killing attractive sex workers with thirty-thousand credit wet drives was bad for business. These girls were not easily replaced, and it was likely the ring wanted Leopold dead, too. So far, the organization was only in the investigation phase. From what Gideon found on UnderNet, they had yet to put a bounty out for the killer.

As she continued, the Arcadia buzzed. The top of her holographic screen displayed a notification.

Lucius calling.

She shook her head. The gall of that dragon was remarkable. Searching around her bedside, she found her earpiece and put it in.

"What?"

"Are...are you alright?" Lucius asked, his voice hesitant. It almost sounded worried.

He caught her off-guard and made her defensive from his first words. She couldn't imagine why he'd care, but she couldn't deny that he actually appeared concerned.

"I'm not dead," she said, her voice croaking. She cleared her throat and grabbed a sip of water. "Sorry to disappoint you."

"Hardly, Cora. I want you to know - I did not approve of

anything that's happened," Lucius said.

Cora raised an eyebrow. She swiped around a few screens on the Arcadia. "Really? Fascinating, since I'm looking at a report my team put together that determined only a Tetriarch employee would have the know-how to install experimental tech like we've seen on this guy. Spare me."

"To that end...what can I say, Cora? Your man came to me. Called me specifically, the second he was back in England," Lucius said in his reverberating baritone. "I had a military project needing human trials. He wanted power to be able to fight you, in case you came after him. So, I get human testing and he goes after you with it? It looked like an obvious win."

"He's not my man. And a win? Are you kidding me? Have you seen his latest victim? That monster started slaughtering college-aged girls for sport, Lucius," Cora snapped.

Lucius sighed. "Would you even believe me if I said I wanted out when I learned of that?"

"I believe your words the first time I told you was, 'I'll set up a charity in their honor,' so no, I don't believe that."

"Posturing, if I'm being honest," he replied with a huff. "Look, I was making a lot of calls before we spoke. I had already figured out most of what you told me. We both bet on the wrong horse."

"You knew it was Leopold? You couldn't just tell me? I could have had him sooner, or been more prepared!" Cora raised her voice for a moment. It hurt too much to continue doing that. "He has two of my people."

"I know," Lucius replied. "I'm keeping tabs, remember?"

"Oh, your mole? Don't get used to having that much longer," she warned. "I already figured out who it is. I promise you, I'll be dealing with that the second this is over."

Lucius sighed. "No. You won't."

"What?" Cora scoffed. He didn't sound confident or boastful. He said it plain, with startling certainty. Her eyes narrowed to slits. "Why do I get the feeling you know how this ends?"

"Because I do," Lucius replied. "And I won't be a party to it. It's not much of a consolation, but Tetriarch London will take care of the victims' families. As for you, I've just texted a number to your Arcadia."

Sure enough, she got a text notification a second later with a London phone number. "What's this?"

"I'm not the only one that knows you're alive. He'll be waiting for you."

Cora had to laugh. There was dark humor to be mined from the fact that Lucius was playing matchmaker for a fight to the death between a five-two Native girl and a four-hundred pound metal mockery of humanity. She gave the matter some thought, and a new realization popped in her head.

"Why can't you just kill him yourself? Your tech made him. You have an entire PMC at your disposal," Cora said.

Lucius paused. "There are many variables going on that you can't understand. As it is, when my company becomes linked with the augments that a serial killer was using, I'm going to have some very difficult questions to answer. It has to be you."

"No, there's more than that," she said, clicking her tongue. "My people detected a wireless signal going in and out while I was in the house. It's him that's transmitting it, isn't it? You're collecting data from his encounters with me."

"That's how I found out what he was doing before you," Lucius explained. "I know where he is right now, and I know where he's going. I also know your people are safe, for the time being."

She tried to hide a shaky breath of relief at the news. Her hands were trembling. "So, you want out of this, but you still want the data he can provide you."

"You keep looking for simple answers where there aren't any. I told you, it's much more than that. I want to be very clear, Cora," Lucius continued. Something sounded different about him. "I thought I wanted this. I don't."

"Careful, Lucius. You're beginning to make me think you have a heart," she replied. Her sarcasm had fully regenerated.

"My heart goes deeper than you could ever understand," he said. There was a pang of sorrow in his voice. She'd never heard him like this before. "I've had to make this up on the fly, but I'm positioning your encounter to favor you. Playing both sides, if you will...or at least pretending to. I'm also sending you some schematics. One of your people can go over them, I'm sure. Perhaps they could find some weakness that you can exploit."

Cora's mouth dropped open. She didn't believe it, even as she checked her Arcadia screen and saw the incoming files. "So, you want us to fight, but you want me to win this?"

"The clock is ticking, Cora. Get your ass out of that bed and do what you do best - make a mess of everything."

Cora looked at her phone screen. There was no longer a call there. She gasped, insulted and confused. "He hung up? So, that's what that feels like."

She gathered her thoughts, combing over everything Lucius said. With a few swipes on the holographic screen floating over her blanket, she forwarded the files to Gideon. She wanted to deliver it in person more than anything. The last thing she wanted was her first contact with him to be a work order. If what Crowley said was true, Gideon had to face being alone in Atlantis for days now, blaming himself for their entire inner circle missing or dying. She must have written and erased the text a dozen times before she settled on something.

See if you can find any weaknesses. I'll be coming by as soon as they let me out.

He didn't reply. That couldn't have been a good sign of his mental state. Turning her attention back to the reports, her lip curled in disgust. If she read one more page about this international Sim ring, she'd make the disaster in the Cayman Islands compound look like a warm-up.

Instead, she grabbed an elastic workout band. Sliding her feet out from under the covers, she looped one end under the arch of her right foot. Holding the other end fast with both hands, she counted off reps, stretching her leg to full extension. Even if her regeneration would do most of the repair, anything she could do to speed things along would let her see Gideon sooner. She pumped her legs until her thigh cried out in exhaustion, then switched.

"Excuse me. I hope I'm not bothering you," a man said to her side.

Cora found George standing in the doorway to sickbay. Out of his usual duster and hat, he still managed to give off the cowboy vibe in jeans and a plaid button-up. She perked up and smiled.

"Not at all," she said, taking the band off her foot. She waved him over. "I heard you saved my life."

He dropped his head as he approached. Humble to a fault, he didn't take compliments well. "I think the sirens saved us both, ma'am. He had to take off before he could finish me. I got out from under that mess and crawled over to you. Got us out of there, that's all."

"What about his girlfriend? Detective Thomas?" Cora asked, rubbing her throat. While it was getting better, it still hurt to talk.

"I took the liberty on that, ma'am. I called the Detective and put him at Leopold's house," he sighed, disgusted. "I called Miss Toomes and warned her she'd be seeing them over there, but it wasn't for Leopold. I'll be honest, I hadn't told her the truth. I'm sure she's heard by now. Detective Thomas put Leopold's face all over the news."

She couldn't fathom what that poor woman was going through. Of all the victims that died, Andrea Toomes had to live with what Leopold had done. Cora looked back at her Arcadia. "So, you've heard who Leopold became, I'm sure."

"Yeah," George replied. He stuffed both hands into his pockets and sighed. "I'm real sorry, ma'am. I didn't want to believe it, myself."

"Well, whatever spirit took him over, it doesn't matter," Cora said, resolute. "I'm dealing with it and I'm getting my friends back. What he did...I'm not trying to 'bring him in' or get him arrested. I'm going to put him down."

George nodded. "Like a rabid dog, ma'am."

"You're never going to call me Cora, are you?"

He replied with a snicker and fingered his mustache. "I suppose I could keep trying. Force of habit, that's all."

"Keep trying?" Cora raised her eyebrows. "I would have expected after all this, you'd want to return to your old life. I'd imagine Doc Holliday would want that, too."

George threw his hands up. "After what I've seen? No. I don't reckon I could do that now. If this was just one man, a single soul that was intended for Lucius, there's no end to the trouble his people are about to cause. You need me. Frankly, I think I need this."

All she could do was shake her head. She was overjoyed, to be certain, but it came with sadness, too. He was condemned to be a part of her war and her life. He'd be in harm's way until the bitter end, yet he shut down every escape route she'd offered him. She sighed and stared at him in awe.

"I was trained with soldiers. Elven masters. I work with a guy carrying around Excalibur," she said. "I think you might be the most honorable man I've ever met."

"Ma'am," he said with a bow of his head. He stood in silence for a moment, a pregnant pause as he searched for words.

"Something else on your mind?" Cora pressed.

"You said you're going after him?" George asked.

"Count on it."

He folded his hands behind his back. "I would like to be a part of that."

"Hey, I'm going to need every advantage I can get," she replied. She shifted in the bed to make sure she locked his gaze. "You stood up to him without fear and rescued me from him. Twice. I wish I could have a hundred of you. I'd bring them all."

"Much obliged," he said with a bow of his head. "I'll let you get back to recuperating. I'd say try not to overdo it, but I think I know you too well for that by now."

With a shrug and a wave she let him go. Wrapping the workout band around her foot again, Cora got back to work. Glancing up at the clock, she had ten hours of healing to go, by Daly's estimation. Giovanna and Johnny didn't have that kind of time. If she faced Leopold now, she'd scarce be able trust herself standing. Even if Lucius was telling the truth, and she was inclined to believe he was, favorable terrain and advantages wouldn't save her friends if she couldn't fight. Something had to give. She needed to buy time.

The answer clicked in her head. Giovanna and Johnny should have been dead already. The only reason they weren't was because they could be leveraged against Cora. That was a page right out of Lucius' playbook. No doubt, the dragon's advice was mixed up in there. The Ripper was afraid Cora would bring the full brunt of her arsenal against him if he killed her friends. He needed Cora dead, not them. Perhaps he believed that if the leader of their group was dead, the rest would fall apart. Julian would be too busy fighting Lucius to expend resources on a grudge. Either he was counting on that, or Lucius had poisoned his psychotic mind with misinformation. The dragon knew damn well this monster wasn't going to kill her. Now, it was only a question of what she'd lose to stop him.

She took a breath, making sure her next play was the right one. She cleared her throat and took a sip of water. Picking up her Arcadia, she dialed the number. It rang twice before the line picked up to silence.

"You tell me where. I'll tell you when," she said, struggling to make her voice sound fine.

"Take the bullet train to Edinburgh station," he replied with a mechanical, cockney accent. "I'll call you with further directions. Anyone with you, I'll send you parts of Mister Clean over here. You'll just have to wait to see what I do with the Italian."

Cora checked the clock. Ten hours was too long. He sounded impatient. She swiped through screens as he made his threats. The bullet train out of London left in six hours. She'd have two more on the train to recover. That would have to do.

"I'll be on the three o'clock," she replied.

He paused. If he tried to get her to take an earlier trip, there was no way she'd be ready. Fear gripped her as she held her breath.

"Be seeing you," he said, sounding as though he spoke through a smile.

She couldn't close the call soon enough. Tears filled her eyes. She'd never been so afraid of anything or anyone, not even Lucius in his true dragon form. She panted, trying to catch her breath. George's request would have to fall on deaf ears, along with anyone else that wanted to join her. They'd never let her go alone. They'd tell her she'd be crazy to try. That it was suicide. That there had to be another way. She was too used to doing everything herself, too willing to sacrifice.

They would be right about all of it. She was still going. She just couldn't tell them.

FAREWELL TOUR

Four hours remained before she left. She walked into the computer room in a rock shirt, jeans, and bare feet. She still needed a shower, but this was more important. On all six monitors at the other end of the room, video played back. It took her a second to realize what she was seeing, but all of her friends sat around a table. Then she noticed Leopold. Subtitles, charts and graphs appeared over the playback. It was the interview video.

The door closed behind her. Gideon sat at a computer desk nearby. He turned around, startled by the sound. If it was possible, he looked more haggard than Julian, with patchy, thick hair all over his face. As he got up from his chair, his eyes met Cora and filled with tears. He took a cautious step forward.

"I'm...I'm so sorry," he pleaded, degenerating into sobs.

She dashed across the room and threw her arms around him. Much taller than her, her head pressed right into his chest. Gideon cried hard, the most emotion she'd ever seen from the normally cool, laid-back hacker.

"It's my fault," he said. He was so shaken. "I should have seen it."

Cora stepped back and stared him in the eye. "No. You didn't do this. This isn't your fault."

"It is!" he shot back, motioning his hand to the monitors

behind him. "It's all right here!"

Turning her attention to the monitors, she didn't understand all the data points that appeared and disappeared as the video played back. She knew what she saw, though.

"What is this? You, torturing yourself?"

"No," he replied, walking to the front of the room. "From the second Leopold touched that artifact, his heart rate dropped to a point lower than the baseline from the beginning of the interview! His voice was one octave lower! The pacing and meter of his words changed completely!"

Cora had a pretty good memory of that day, and she'd watched the video with George. Her brow furrowed. "Gideon, is any of that detectable by the human ear? Even cochlear implants?"

"Well, no, but-"

"So, I was right," she said, waving a dismissive hand. "You're sitting here torturing yourself."

Gideon shook his head. "It's not like that. George said something about what happened to him in the Cayman Islands, how the spirit in his artifact took him over. Julian, Michael, Madeline, and Tesla all said it's happened to them before, as well."

"Me too," Cora sighed. "It's like we switch places. The spirit takes us over, and we get moved to a corner of our mind."

"With Leopold, I think that happened almost immediately," Gideon replied. He pointed with both hands to the screen. "I analyzed the video and my biometric readings taken at the time. The details were so small, but I would have seen them if I knew what to look for."

Cora walked around the desk and joined him at the front of the room. She grabbed his hand and held tight, even as she felt the metal carpal bones beneath his skin. She gnashed her teeth against the urge to picture hand surgery.

"That's what you're going to beat yourself up over? You didn't know what you didn't know. We're all learning this as we go."

"He almost killed you! He has Gia and Johnny!"

Cora deflected, shaking her head. "Don't let her find out you called her that. I think Johnny is the only one that gets away with that nickname for her."

"Cora..."

She raised her hand. "No. This shit on the screen? This is the past. We can't change the past. I'm going to get them back. Tell me what you've found."

He tapped his foot. "I'll tell you what I haven't found - I haven't found the bank account he's using to pay for these girls, or for the surgeries to put this tech in. It's like..."

"Like he had a double life," Cora nodded, solemn. "I think the Leopold we saw and the one we ended up with shared more in common than they didn't. None of us saw it."

Gideon hesitated, running his fingers back through mussed, unkempt hair. He choked up, on the verge of tears again. He crossed his arms.

"Look at what he did to you," he said, pointing at her with an open hand.

Cora touched her neck. She could feel the stitches that once held her throat closed, but there was no sensation attached to it. Like a glove, it was foreign to her body now. Still, she could only imagine she looked like Frankenstein's monster.

"This? I'm healed, Gideon. It's like a scab," she said. Trying to make it seem like it wasn't a big deal probably wasn't working. "When I shower in a few, this layer of skin is going to peel off. It's going to be gross, but I swear I'm fine. Hell, when I sent you that text, my voice sounded like one of those boozy, tobacco smoking lounge singers from the 20th. I'm fine now, or I will be."

He sighed and stared at the ceiling, frustrated. "But you want to fight him again. You want me to tell you how."

"Yeah," Cora nodded, deadly serious. "So, make sure I win."

She waited until his eyes met hers. He needed to see how serious this was, to get his head back in the damn game. He may not have known it, but that confrontation was coming much sooner than he realized, and she needed every advantage she could get. His eyes stayed on hers before he relented, defeated. He walked over to his plush leather recliner and got himself situated. Cora looked away. She hated watching him put the data jack in his skull, or seeing his body fall limp as though he died.

"Alright," a mechanical replication of his voice played through the speakers at the four corners of the room. "Let's start with how did you get these?"

"Unimportant," Cora replied. "What have you learned?"

Gideon sighed. The six monitors changed from the video to technical schematics, a different one in each screen. They rotated in three dimensions. "If all of these parts are in him, I don't even know how he survived. He's basically a torso and a head wired into a tank. There's more Tetriarch than Leopold in his body."

"Having been face to face with him, that sounds about right," Cora said. She took a seat on the edge of the nearest desk.

"All four limbs were completely replaced, and his pelvis," he explained. Cora shuddered. "His spine has been grafted with a bleeding-edge version of wired reflexes, and then reinforced all the way to the throat. Parts of his lower jaw were replaced, along with reinforced plating around his skull. That part is the most delicate and takes the longest to heal. He's not wearing bandages, he's wrapped in Keoline Nanofiber, the same stuff Stitch-Patches are made of."

"So, he's not finished healing?" Cora asked.

"No way," Gideon replied. "He got these implants three weeks ago. He'd still be paralyzed in a hospital bed trying to relearn how to feed himself if it wasn't for this."

The upper central monitor changed to a zoomed-in view of a computer chip attached to the dark-blue circuit boards used for implants.

"This thing is out of left field," Gideon said. "This chip, if I understand the reports correctly, is processing brain inputs and converting that into a digital signal to move his body. Basically, until his brain builds the pathways to operate the implants itself, it's doing the work for him, only better. This is the thing I've spent the most time looking at, and I still can't believe it. There's virtually no lag in the signal. He thinks it, it's already doing it. In the cybernetics community, this kind of technology was thought to be at least five years away."

"Tetriarch, the future is now," Cora quoted acidly. "These implants...they're all military applications?"

"Without a doubt," Gideon replied. "The control chip alone would allow a wounded PMC soldier to have an implant performed and return to the battlefield within days."

Cora crossed her arms and looked at the hideous prosthetics. Carbon fiber and metal, they weren't even trying to imitate looking human at all. "Who would want these?"

"Every single PMC and government that could afford it," Gideon replied. "You forget, in Tetriarch's infancy, the UNS was one of their first investors during the Second Civil War. Where Lucius can't make up magical advantages, he'll even the playing field with machines. Everything from the Mexican Revolution to the elven eco-terrorists in France, if a PMC gets involved, Tetriarch stock goes up."

Somebody needed to add war profiteer to the list of Lucius' titles. Looking at the images on the screens, things were bleak. She sighed. "So, you've found no weaknesses or design flaws?"

"That's not entirely true," Gideon replied. The central screen again changed, this time to something resembling an armored breastplate. "The biggest flaw is that it still relies on the human body. Since vital organs are imperative to keep the human components alive, he still needs to breathe, eat, and so on. This armored chassis was designed to safeguard the ribcage and all vital organs. It can take a shotgun blast at point-blank range."

"Could magnetically propelled Rhino bullets pierce it? What kind of ordinance are we talking about that can penetrate that?" Cora asked.

A series of calculations appeared on the screen, text and numbers moving so fast she couldn't process a single word. After a brief wait, it vanished. "Given the design and construction of the plating, I think he'd go into shock from internal bruising before even a Rhino round would penetrate it."

Cora rolled her eyes. She got a fair amount of the outlawed

bullets a while back. Banned by every country because of the vile way they ripped through armor and tore through body parts, it never lived up to the hype for her. Both Lucius and now Leopold would shrug off the most dangerous bullets known to man.

"But, it's not hopeless," Gideon said. The image of the chassis rotated until Cora was looking down the neck hole. An arrow pointed at both shoulders. "There's an anchor point above the collarbone, where the chest plate meets the back plate. It needed to be laid out this way to hold them in place, otherwise they could compress and crush the organs they're protecting. It's also the thinnest, weakest point in the armor."

Her eyes narrowed. "I'd need to break the mooring, rip off the chest plate, and shoot inside it?"

"Either that, or make him eat a bullet," he replied. "The only thing I can't figure out with these schematics is the power source."

"Explain," Cora replied. She didn't know enough about cybernetics to understand how they worked.

Another monitor displayed a man's arm. In three dimensions, the skin became transparent and showed a metal skeleton that replaced the human one. A network of wires intermingled and danced around veins, all the way up the arm. It filled Cora with nausea looking at it.

"In a normal person, an implant can operate off the same amount of electricity that the human body generates for a regular limb," Gideon said. "For someone with this much tech and less than fifty percent of the body left, there is no way to internally power it. And that's before we even talk about the energy shield emitters on his chest and back. In short, this monster has to have a power cell in him somewhere. Based solely on the schematics, I can't tell where it'd be, though."

"Alright," Cora said, holding up her hand. "That's what I needed to know. You did good, Gideon, as always. We'll start talking plans with Julian in a few hours. I need to wash up and I need to talk to Andrea Toomes. She deserves the truth."

Cora headed for the door in silence. As she reached for the handle, Gideon called her name. She turned around to find him getting up out of the chair. He struggled with it. Normally lanky, he was now sickly thin. She pretended not to notice, for his sake.

"Was there something else?" she asked.

He took a step forward, eyes cast down as if he were trying to find the words. "You're going alone, aren't you?"

Cora laughed him off and shook her head. "Of course not. That would be suicide."

"These plans came from Tetriarch," he replied, taking another step forward. "You had two calls since you woke up - one from Lucius...the other was only thirty seconds long. It was him, wasn't it?"

She fumed and blew out a breath from her nose. It felt like a violation, but he was the communications master of the station. He could have easily tapped into the calls and listened for himself if he wanted to. Everything routed through systems he managed. Cora took a step back into the room.

"If I don't, he'll kill them," she said. "He wants me. Alone. So, he's going to get me."

"You just said you know it's suicide. You're going to do it anyway?"

Cora nodded. "Yeah. And I'm about to put you in a really shitty position. I need you to keep your mouth shut about this. Giovanna and Johnny's lives depend on it."

"Oh, Cora," he sighed, hanging his head.

"I'm going in there, getting them both and hitting the emergency transport," she said, holding up her hands in defense. "Once they're out of harm's way, we can use every trick and weapon at our disposal to make sure he never hurts anyone again."

Gideon stared at her, trying to read her. He wasn't good enough at real-world human interaction to tell if she was lying, but he tried real hard.

"Julian isn't like us, okay?" she insisted. "He's one of those big-picture type of strategists. He'd view them both as acceptable losses compared to be putting me in danger. I don't get special treatment, and I don't leave men behind!"

"I know," he said under his breath. He cleared his throat. "I'll cover for you, okay? Don't make me regret it."

She stepped to him and waved him to bend down. Grabbing him by the back of the neck, she pulled him further and kissed his cheek. He understood her. He'd been there since the beginning. He might not have been a soldier, but he understood brotherhood. Every time she was near death, near the end of her rope, or just clueless, he was there. He violated a presidential pardon to save her. Like Johnny and Giovanna, what they had went deeper than family.

She walked out of his computer room and headed to the crew quarters. Once she was back in her room, she stared at the cloth bag with Richard's jacket sitting on her bed. Her clothes were still packed in suitcases. She never really lived here, it was always just a visit. Something horrible was going to happen when she went back to London. It wasn't a fear of death that came over her, but a sudden realization Atlantis wasn't her home. Like a once-over of a nice hotel room, she surveyed the living quarters as if she'd never see it again. Stripping down, she walked past the mirror without glancing at herself. She didn't want to see what Leopold had done to her, even if the marks were now superficial.

The steam coming off the water fogged the mirror out in due time. Her muscles relaxed under the hot stream. Cora turned her back and shut her eyes, letting her hands guide the soap down her form. Bits shed off her like washing away glue. Some of it was medical adhesive, but the parts around her neck came off in coiled ropes, pinching at her new skin as it pulled away. The last time she'd been in the same situation, in the wake of a horrific battle, she recalled weeping in a ball on the floor of the shower. This time, all she could feel was anger and determination. Her friends were coming home, and she didn't care how savage she had to get to make sure it happened.

"I know you didn't have magic to rely on, back then," she whispered to herself. Sitting Bull awakened in her mind, aware of her words. "But I need to draw more power than I ever have. Help me find the strength to avenge these women, and put right what I've unleashed on this world."

Like a prayer, she knew she was heard. The spirit within her stirred. The ball of magic in her belly roared like fire, warming her all over. The tingle danced up and down her spine. She'd be ready.

She stepped out of the shower and toweled off. She wore a shirt of the Man in Black, and pulled on her jeans. Her body still felt like she'd just gotten out of a car accident, but the strength she'd recovered was still deadly. She grabbed a Predator and her last three magazines of Rhino rounds. Against the corner of the room rested her Master Hidori katana. Even with its molecularly sharpened blade, she doubted it would prove much use. Besides, she could hide her Predator, but she couldn't exactly explain away a blade strapped to her back that was almost as long as she was tall.

Once she had donned Richard's jacket and rolled the sleeves to her elbows, she stood in the doorway and took a final look at her quarters.

"Just another hotel room," she said as she shut the door behind her.

ABSOLUTION

"Julian, I'm going to London for a short bit," Cora said as she made her way to Tesla's lab.

"What? No."

"I need to see Andrea Toomes," she insisted. She rounded a corner and walked down the final ugly green hall. "I can't sit here knowing she's hearing these horrible things on the news and wondering. I have to tell her."

"Cora, need I remind you this maniac attacked you across the street from her house?" Julian replied.

"It's two in the afternoon in London, Julian," Cora scoffed. "Cops have been crawling all over that area. I have nothing to worry about. Look, I have to do this, okay?"

Julian paused and huffed. "At least take someone with you."

"No need," she said. "Tesla will be on standby with the emergency transport protocol. I'll have my tracker on me. Be back in a bit."

She ended the call before he could argue the point. He was probably back in his office throwing slurs around the room about what a stubborn, difficult woman she was. He wasn't wrong. Holding out her arm at her side, Vincent phased through a wall and perched.

"Ready to go, buddy?"

"Caw," he replied. Unease slithered along their tether.

She shrugged. "Me too. We're still doing it."

Inside the transport lab, three knights bustled around the room. Madeline sat on the edge of the transport platform. Her eyes opened wide when she saw Cora and raced over. Madeline was never one to show much in the way of affection, but she hugged Cora so tight she had trouble breathing. Cora smiled and patted the back of the girl's head, shaved stubble, scars and all.

"I thought we'd lost you, mon ami!"

"Who knows? Maybe Saint Joan was watching over me, making sure I didn't end up like her," Cora replied with a wry smile.

Madeline guffawed. She made the sign of the cross on her chest. "You...you heard me?"

Cora nodded. "I did. Thank you. You know, you're the most badass teenager I've ever met."

"You saying goodbye?" Tesla said from his computer desk. "That's what it sound like."

She replied with a fake smile. She hated lying to either of them. "Only for a little bit. There's something I have to do. I need you to get me back to Lindley Street in London. I'll have my tracker on in case of emergency, but I should only be there a couple of hours."

Madeline grabbed her by both arms, her grip so tight it hurt a little. "You are coming back, right?"

"Yeah," she said with a huff. "Of course I am! I'm only going to talk to Leopold's girlfriend. To tell her the truth."

Madeline nodded. "She must be a mess. You want backup?"

"No," Cora shook her head, trying to spin a story. "I made a vow to her. She needs to hear it from me. I'll be back soon enough."

Tesla stared at Cora with a disapproving eye. If he knew better, he wasn't saying anything. He moved through holographic screens, all the while his eyes remained on her. "Lindley Street, London. Coordinates are in. Clear the platform."

She'd never tried it before, but Madeline was French. She bent down and kissed each cheek. Madeline responded in kind and smiled. With the goodbye, she finally released her vice-like grip. Cora stepped up to the transport platform and turned to face Tesla. He was still glaring at her. She gave him a nod and shut her eyes.

With a flash of light, Cora waited for the vertigo to pass. She opened her eyes to an alley near the corner of Lindley Street and headed out. Looking about, there weren't any bystanders nearby that might have witnessed her emerging from a bolt of lightning in broad daylight. The sky overcast, it was another gloomy day in London.

Her lie had a shred of truth to it. She purposely left early to stop at Andrea's house. After all the woman had been through, maybe she could give her some closure. It was the only mercy in all of this bloodshed Cora could afford to spare. She hoped the plain, bookish woman would be home. Being four in the afternoon on a Sunday, she didn't imagine Andrea having big plans. Arriving at her flat, she knocked on the door.

"I have no comment!" a voice shouted from the other side of the door.

"I'm not press, Miss Toomes. It's me, Kathleen," Cora replied, raising her voice.

She heard a deadbolt, a chain, and a biometric lock release before the door opened. Andrea opened it a crack and peered out, her eyes narrowing at the light outside.

"I thought you'd given up," she said, her tone bitter. "After you came last week, the both of you just vanished."

Cora hung her head. The next part was never going to be easy. She let out a heavy breath. "I know, and I'm sorry. I'd like to explain everything to you. The truth."

Andrea stepped back, swinging open the door. Cora stepped inside. At least if Leopold was watching and waiting for her in Edinburgh, she wouldn't have to worry about him interfering. Their time was rapidly approaching. For now, she wanted a simple, painful conversation.

The interior of the house was dark. All the windows had the blinds drawn and dark curtains covered over them. Not a single light was on anywhere in the living room or kitchen. Not even the holovid monitor illuminated the room.

"I'm sorry," Andrea said. "I'll get a light on. I don't want those vultures knowing I'm home."

There wasn't a single car camped outside her home, no news vans, nothing. Cora knew it was a lie, but there was no need to press the issue. Cora's mother thought she was turning into a mole after her father's death, sitting in her room all the time, alone in the dark. She remembered those bleak days, back when losing someone she cared about was a new feeling.

The light came on, and Cora got a look at Andrea. She was wearing the same silk pajamas as the last time she saw her. Her eyes were puffy and red, her hair a tangled mess. Cora motioned to her couch. Once Andrea sat down, Cora rested on the opposite side.

"I know you've heard a lot of things," Cora said.

Andrea teared up from her first words. "They're saying he murdered those women! Not Leopold. We've been friends for years. They don't know him like I do!"

Cora sighed. "About four weeks ago, Leopold left unexpectedly for a trip. Did he tell you why?"

"No," Andrea shook her head. She sighed. "I mean, he said something about a family member or something, but I knew it was a lie. He wasn't very good at lying."

Cora stood up. There was no way she could tell this story sitting down, pretending to be calm. She shuffled her feet on the living room rug, trying to figure out where to begin.

"Leopold felt a calling, from a spirit," she said. "His search brought him to me. I'm engaged in a secret, magical war. A select number of artifacts from the past, containing the spirits of those that once held them, are the weapons of choice. Both sides are in a cold war to amass them and get them into the hands of those they belong to."

Andrea raised an eyebrow. Next, Cora was going to tell her she was a fortune teller and ask for a hundred credits to tell her future. Cora pointed to the holovid monitor.

"The armed men that broke into Buckingham Palace a few months back? They stole Excalibur."

"Excalibur is a myth," Andrea replied, rolling her eyes.

"Dragons were a myth thirty years ago," Cora replied. "Magic. Elves. You can't even go on a cruise ship now without learning safety precautions against Siren songs on the water. Look, I know you're a woman of science, but you have to know there isn't any belief since The Awakening that can't be questioned."

Andrea shifted in her chair, uncomfortable. "Why did Leopold go looking for you? He was never into magic."

"It wasn't me he was looking for," Cora replied, trying to assuage any fears or jealousy. "I have several artifacts that have no owner yet. He was drawn to the one that belonged to him."

"What was it?" Andrea asked.

"A 19th century leather medical bag," she replied.

Andrea's brow furrowed. "The souvenir he brought back? That was an artifact?"

Cora nodded. Her head dropped. Now, things would get ugly. "I didn't give it to him right away. We gave him a medical evaluation, then we interviewed him. On the surface, everything looked fine. There is a phenomenon that happens to those of us that have been bound to these artifacts. The spirit can take us over for short periods, like giving over our body's driving wheel to them. For Leopold, this happened immediately, and I don't think it ever stopped."

Andrea covered her mouth. "Oh, God. He's trapped inside his own mind by this spirit? Who was the owner?"

Cora walked forward and squatted down in front of her. She shook her head, eyes apologetic. "I don't think he's trapped. I think the weak, passive man you knew held a rage in him for a long time. He hated his own weakness, how he couldn't even tell you how he felt about you. A stronger, more grotesque personality suddenly dominated his mind, and wanted to take that anger and rage out on the world. Against women, in particular."

"What?" Andrea shouted. She grew furious. "Leopold hates

women, now? So, what, he just sat back in his mind and let this spirit control the puppet strings, murdering young girls?"

"I know it's hard to hear, but-"

"Hard to hear?" Andrea shouted. She got up from the couch with a start. Cora weaved back, almost falling on her rear. The woman put distance between herself and Cora, all the way back to the kitchen counter. "Hard to hear would be that he gets his rocks off to prostitutes, not that he carves up girls old enough to be his students!"

Crowley would probably have a field day dissecting the implications of that statement. Knowing greater detail than Andrea did, there was probably something to that line of thought she was on. The time for analyzing Leopold and what happened to him was over, though. Andrea needed to understand that, too. Cora put her hands in her pocket and sighed.

"I have to go after him, now," she said, sorrow in her voice. "I gave him that artifact, and I had no idea who it belonged to. The people I've worked with are imbued with spirits like Joan of Arc and King Arthur. I'd never even imagined what the other side looked like. That falls on me. This is my responsibility."

Andrea put a hand on her hip, choking back tears to keep hold of her anger. "Are you going to kill him?"

"I...I can't let him continue like this," she said, unable to keep eye contact. She didn't want to watch her heart break, even if it was the price she knew she had to pay.

Andrea huffed and turned her head. A single tear fell down her cheek. "What did you come here for, Miss O'Malley? You want my blessing? Forgiveness?"

Cora took a step toward her, then thought better of it. "I owed you the truth. It's not the one you wanted to hear, I know. I was desperate to find he'd been kidnapped. I...I never imagined the killer and Leopold were-"

"Don't!" Andrea raised a finger in warning. She looked Cora right in the eye, filled with fury. "Don't you even say the words. Just...just get out!"

She lingered a second longer. The guilt piled on. Cora wanted to help, even if she was the cause of all this.

"Please!" Andrea shouted.

Cora nodded and made her way to the door. She left without looking back. Vincent swooped down from Andrea's roof and landed on Cora's shoulder.

"Caw," he said.

He meant well, but Cora still took her share of the blame. No one was going to take that away from her. Her father's words turning in her head, leaving her blameless, ignorant, or naive, they melded with her own feelings on the matter. The truth lie somewhere in between. Either way, Andrea would be Leopold's last victim.

As she walked down the road, every step brought her closer to the train station. Her emotions were solid and she had control. There was no sadness, no tears left to shed. This monster had two people she cared about. Once they were safe, it didn't matter what happened to her, or Leopold. One of them had to die, and she was going to make damn sure it wasn't her.

The bullet to Edinburgh was a two-hour spectacle, showing everything Britain and Scotland had to offer. From the neon and hologram-laden downtown London, to the emerald green countryside of the Northern York Moors, it rushed past at speeds rivaling a plane. Vincent did his own thing, preparing for battle by perching on the roof of the train and letting the wind beat against him. He was never so contented as when he was riding on the wing of a plane or the roof of a bullet train. Maybe he had speed envy. Whatever the cause, his contentment made it easier for her to meditate and center herself. She channeled magic from the ball in her gut, making it spread throughout her whole body. The fire Sitting Bull helped light in her was a pool of power to draw from as strong the darkened flip side, without the threat of corrupting her. It was a wellspring open to her, she need only ask.

When the train came to a stop, Cora was only three steps onto the platform before her Arcadia rang. It was him. She tapped her earpiece and kept walking.

"Where am I going now?" she asked.

"Take a cab to Arthur's Seat Museum," he replied in his mechanical, cockney accent. "Be waiting for you there, love."

The line went dead. She had to laugh at both the choice of locale, and the name. Of course it was Arthur's Seat. Unwittingly named for his mortal enemy, the inactive volcano served as Lucius' lair. He had buried himself inside of it at the end of the Second Awakening in the Middle Ages. Since emerging in 2056, the site had become a tourist trap. There wouldn't be anyone there, though, she knew that much. If Lucius had as much a hand in this as he alluded to, the place was likely cleared out. They would have a massive chamber to battle each other, away from prying eyes on the ground and by satellite.

Somewhere in all of that, Leopold's tech would be transmitting data from their battle to Lucius. The information about his military augments tested in battle against a magic user would be priceless. No doubt, it would be the trump card that kept Lucius from a UN inquiry. The only thing she couldn't figure out was why it had to be Cora that fought him. Lucius could have quietly brought Leopold somewhere and had him killed. He risked more by letting Cora do it, forcing him to admit his augments were used by this killer instead of controlling the narrative by destroying all evidence.

She walked out of the terminal and onto the street. Hailing a cab, she continued her path to its natural conclusion. The whole ride, she pondered the unspoken twist in Lucius' plan.

THE LAST VICTIM

With her hands on her hips, Cora stared at the mountain with disgust. Arthur's Seat was the epitome of the commercialization of nature. Tunnels drilled into the base robbed the basalt crags of their structural integrity and natural beauty. As such, hideous metal support frames were built around the mountain. To distract from the god-awfulness of it all, trees were relocated to obscure the bad areas, while neon and holograms blinded anyone looking for the worst. An animated Lucius hologram perched above the main gate leading to the interior.

"He's actually a couple meters shorter," Cora said, staring up at the dragon.

The path to the tourist park was a cement walk paved through lush grass on either side, another blighted scar on the flawless land. The peak, 250 meters above the city behind her, was now so unstable that the corporation owning the land would no longer allow visitors to ascend. Cora's mind swarmed with visions of people in suits directing construction vehicles to burrow into Heaven's Crest. It gave her chills.

The entrance to the park walked through an enclosed building before the mountain proper. Outside the front doors, four well-armed men leaned against the hoods of two Jeeps. Wearing black Nomex bodysuits beneath gray, plated riot gear, there was no mistaking Bauer Security soldiers. She rolled her eyes as she approached them. Being Bauer meant they were a part of the most elite PMC in the known world, and every one of them acted like it.

Vincent took off from her shoulder and flew for the peak, a small bit of silver in his talons. Cora motioned to the door. "Don't mind me, I'm going in there for a battle to the death."

"You're clear," a soldier said. "Proceed."

The interior enclosure was the home to the welcome center and the all-important gift shop on her left. After all, everyone would want to remember their trip with a commemorative pencil set or Lucius plush doll. The welcome center, like the parking lot, was a ghost town. There was not a single employee in sight. Only a pair of Bauer soldiers stood between her and the door to Lucius' bedroom for the last 750 years before The Awakening.

One soldier tapped the comm button behind his ear. "Guest has arrived," he said. The two guards started for the exit. "Returning to perimeter."

Cora glanced behind her as she reached for the door. The soldiers were already gone.

Dim track lights illuminated a path through the tunnel carved into the mountain. Ahead, Leopold stood in the center of a circular chamber a hundred yards away. Behind him were two figures on their knees. Cora walked through the tunnel of smooth rock until it opened into the lair. At either side, interactive computer stations invited her to come and learn the history of the world's most famous dragon. The consoles stretched along both walls. At the halfway mark it switched to thick glass cases that housed artifacts of the dragon himself, circling the other half of the chamber. Cora's eyes turned skyward. The fading light of the sky above poured through a massive hole in the ceiling of the mountain, seven hundred feet above her.

Leopold's frightening green eyes glowed in the distance. The rest of his face still hidden in bandages, somehow she still knew the bastard was smiling. Behind him, Johnny and Giovanna didn't look too banged up, with only a few scrapes on Johnny's face. It was weird seeing him without his shades, though. Giovanna's dress was filthy and didn't suit her, intended for a much younger woman.

"First things first," Cora shouted across the space between them. She pointed at Johnny and Giovanna. "You let them go. This was about me, not them."

"Don't think so," he replied, taking a step closer. He pointed at Giovanna. "This one posed as a whore, tried to trick me. When I'm done with you, I think she'll be my next bit of work all the same."

Cora knew he wouldn't play honorably. She counted on it. Now, she needed to buy a few seconds. She took another step into the chamber.

"There is no part of Leopold left? Andrea...she still asked me about you," she said. Her magic pulsed throughout her body, pumping through her extremities like blood.

"That's a proper woman, there," Leopold replied. "You don't get to mention her name. Can't go back to her now, not like this. But maybe for the old boy's sake, someday we can make her understand our work."

Vincent landed on Giovanna's shoulder. His talons let loose the silver object he was holding. With a quick peck, he took off as fast as he landed, sailing through the air to Cora's shoulder.

"Caw," he screeched at Leopold. He also let Cora know that he did his job.

"Before we start, I have a few words for my friends," she said.

He glanced behind him and checked on his hostages. "Not much point. They'll follow you where you're going real soon."

"Johnny," she started, turning her attention from Leopold. "I just wanted to say you were right about American football. It is better, because it's a contact sport."

Johnny's eyes narrowed. He knew she was feeding him a code. He waited for the order.

"And Giovanna," she said, pausing. Locking eyes with Leopold, she continued, "You've got the ball."

Johnny dove to his side. Leopold spun and moved toward them. Before he could take a single step, Johnny tackled Giovanna to the ground and laid on top of her. Cora reached up and tapped her comm button.

"Expat."

With a blast of lightning, Tesla's machine locked on to Cora's tracker, affixed to Giovanna's dress. In a heartbeat, they were gone. Leopold grabbed for them, but found only air. He growled and wheeled on Cora.

"It's only us," she said. She pulled energy to her hands, the swirling magical dust forming dual Stunbombs. "Come and get me, you sick son of a bitch."

Leopold roared and ran for her with blinding speed. She tossed both Stunbombs in his path. The resulting burst of energy and resulting shockwave kicked up a cloud of dust. Leopold dashed right through, an energy shield glowing a few inches from his chest.

Cora returned his rush and ran at him. Pushing magic to her legs, the scant seconds it took for them to clear the distance between each other was enough. She jumped into the air with a blast of energy from her feet. Beneath her, Leopold struggled to halt himself. Cora sailed a dozen feet over him, twisted, and landed on a knee. His back to her, he was already in motion to about-face.

Her Predator snapped out of its holster. Hands came in line with where her eyes already aimed. He turned around. Cora double-tapped the trigger. Leopold stumbled backward. She stood up and double-tapped again, center mass. He reeled back another step. She moved forward and fired off another two. This time, Leopold braced and leaned into it, letting the Rhino rounds strike him in the chest plate.

With a running start, servos whirred and hydraulics huffed from his legs. He leaped into the air, barreling toward her. Both hands above his head, he meant to drop both of them on her like a hammer. Off-guard by his speed, Cora jumped backward. She readied herself to take the basalt ground hard with her shoulders. She slammed down, narrowly out of harm's way. Leopold's hands struck the floor with explosive force, cratering the rock into a pothole the size of a manhole cover. Pebbles exploded and peppered Cora like hail.

"Cora!" Gideon shouted in her ear. There was such pain in his voice. "You said you'd come back!"

Apologies would have to come later. Leopold recovered faster than she did, moving like a gorilla as he jumped again and smashed down with both fists. Unable to put distance between them, Cora rolled away. In the dash to get out of the way, she released the Predator from her grip. Leopold smashed into the rock beside her, pelting her back with debris.

"...five minutes until coil reset," Tesla said. She tuned out the radio chatter. With as fast as he moved, either her or Leopold would be dead before that coil was ever reset and she wasn't wearing her tracker, anyway.

Vincent asked for power, and she opened herself to him. Leopold was already digging his fists out of the hole he made in the rock. His eyes fixed to hers, she needed to get to her feet. High above them, a glowing orange ball appeared in the raven's talons. He let it go. Leopold's wired reflexes gave him only enough time to look up. The ball shattered on his forehead, between the front and rear energy shields.

Leopold's eyes flared wide. The shockwave exploded between his shoulders. His head jerked to the side violently. Gears screeched and whined. His body twisted, trying to find balance. Cora swung her legs out and kicked up to her feet.

With one hand to the sky, Cora summoned another ball of magical energy to her hand. She watched the sway and movement of Leopold's body. The control chip struggled against his own equilibrium to steady him. His synthetic eyes crossed. Cora imagined a spark, the fire in her belly given life. She channeled that thought as magic siphoned and coalesced into her palm. She screamed, a cry to war from the spirit inside her. The ball in her hand ignited in flame.

She pitched it high, over Leopold's chest. Vincent had taught her a valuable lesson about the limits of his tech. The ball exploded on the side of his face. The bandages caught fire as if soaked in gasoline. Leopold screamed and clutched at his face, tearing at the synthetic cloth. Cora somersaulted toward him as he flailed, her hand sweeping up her Predator from the ground.

At point blank range, she took aim on his head. He roared, pulling his arm up to his face. She emptied the clip, but his forearm deflected the rounds. He lashed out with everything he had, his arm like a club. Cora didn't have time to dodge. He hit her full force. The magic surging through her suddenly burst out from her skin, absorbing the hit like his energy shield. She flew through the air backwards from the force. Her back smashed through the glass case of exhibits lining the wall. The resulting contact with the base sucked the wind out of her. Other than that, she was shocked to find herself unharmed. Richard's jacket protected her from the glass at her back, and the magical shield prevented his strike from shattering bones.

Ten paces ahead, Leopold cast scorched bandages to the ground. He turned around. His face bare, the hideous sight threatened to send Cora into a panic. The skin of his face distended, stretched and pulled back to accommodate the added thickness of his skull. Plates protruded out like bumps, surrounded by bruising and stitches. Burned skin mingled with it, her contribution to the mess that was his face. His mouth stretched wide, pulled back towards his cheeks. His brow furrowed. He extended his arms backward, letting his smoking trench coat fall into a pile behind him.

"Gonna pay for that," he warned, stalking over to her.

She pushed off the base and got back to her feet. Cora wouldn't be taken by his speed this time. Turning to her side, she pushed magic into her foot and snapped out a kick. Inches from his face, her foot froze. He held her by the ankle, spun, and tossed her like a discus. She twirled and spun through the air before crashing to the unforgiving ground in a heap.

Wincing, she felt every bruising part of the impact. Even after she hit the ground, head spinning and disoriented, she continued to roll another few feet. Her eyes opened to the basalt floor. Between the two holes Leopold had punched into the ground, a crack had formed. She got up to all fours above the second crater. A golden glint of metal shone back at her. Like a rod or staff, something was buried in the rock beneath.

The sound of gears and servos whirring moved toward her, along with his clomping, heavy footfalls. They sped up, running at her like a charging bull. She threw both hands into the hole, grabbing hold of whatever was buried there. Even if it was a pipe, she'd take any improvised weapon she could get. As she pulled, the handle came with her, giving only the most minimal resistance. He was almost on top of her. With a yank, she pulled on whatever she was holding and swung it in the direction of Leopold. It came free, larger and more unwieldy than she envisioned.

The full length of the staff was taller than her. Leopold reacted by halting himself and rearing back, but the bladed edge clipped the side of his cheek. He reeled with a hiss, grabbing at his face. Holding the staff by the very end, the front-heavy weight made it clash on the ground with Cora's motion. She pulled it toward her, readjusting her grip at the middle and stood.

At the end of the golden staff, it split like a pitchfork into three separate sharpened blades. It was a trident. Cora's mouth fell open in shock. No spirit was conferred to her, yet somehow she knew Merlin's last request was now fulfilled. Her sudden reverie was broken by Leopold coming at her again. She hopped backwards, snapping back to the task at hand. Both hands gripped the haft tight.

Cora flooded magical energy to her arms. She needed to strike as fast as him, to make him fear the blade, or else his wired reflexes would snatch it from her hand. She poked at him, forcing him to adjust and block from range. He was only dangerous in close quarters. She forced him to face her on her own terms, keeping him out of reach. She moved backwards in a circle, stabbing to keep him off-balance.

Vincent swooped down from the sky, releasing another Stunbomb. Leopold jumped backwards, letting it explode between himself and Cora. The shockwave blew Cora's hair back.

A cloud of smoke erupted, obscuring her view. Shutting her eyes, Cora cleared her mind. His next move became obvious. She threw her weight to her back leg and leaned, bracing herself. As she predicted, Leopold burst through the cloud in the air, arms above his head as he pounced.

Cora threw her weight forward. Channeling the magic in her hands, she let it pulse out into the trident and thrust. Leopold froze, his expression dumbfounded. All three points pierced his armor, to the vital organs underneath. His mechanical, chortling breaths came out like gasps. He pulled himself backwards, wrenching free of the blades. Blood poured out of the wounds and trickled down his stomach. He looked lost as he stepped back, struggling not to trip over his own large, metal legs. One hand grabbed at his stomach. His face was a mask of utter disbelief.

It wasn't enough. Cora gathered more magic still, pushed it into the trident, and threw it with a scream. It sailed across the distance, but Leopold's reflexes kicked in. His hand wrapped around the shaft. He gasped. As he fell backwards, she could see he was too late. The three prongs had sunk into his chest a second time. His back collided with the ground. A frightening crash echoed throughout the whole chamber.

Leopold gurgled and choked, reaching to pull the weapon free. Looking all around her, Cora found a rock bigger than her head, broken off in the crater his fists had left behind. She didn't care if it was too heavy. Summoning more power still to her hands, she grabbed it up and spun about. She yelled as she ran with it over her head. She aimed for the weak spot, above his collarbone, where the back and front plates interlocked. She smashed down with the rock as he fumbled for the spear while trying to deflect her attack.

Unsatisfied from the first hit, she pulled it up and screamed again. Then again. Leopold crossed his arm to cover his shoulder, opening up a clear line of sight. With another cry, she pulled up the rock again, changed trajectory, and smashed it into his head. His cybernetic eyes rolled from the blow. Giving in to her most base instincts, she went for another, determined not to stop until she crushed his face into the floor.

Leopold used his free hand to yank the trident out. It fell to his side with a clang. With the other hand he threw a punch into the rock, pulverizing it before Cora could strike. With blinding speed, another punch smashed into her face. Even with magical energy emanating from her body, the blow still crushed her nose with a loud crack. Her eyes slammed shut on reflex, tears coming right behind. She reeled back, both hands clutching her face. Blood poured from her nostrils. She shuffled on her knees until she could get back to her feet.

Struggling to pull magic to her face that would allow her to endure, she could only hope he needed a moment to recover as bad as she did. The incessant comm chatter in her ear caught her attention.

"Coil in place," Tesla said. "Transport in five, four..."

Cora tried to make sense of it. Unless there was some new tech Tesla had designed, there was no way to retrieve her without the tracker she put on Giovanna. He couldn't take her away now. She needed only a few moments longer. Leopold could not leave this battleground.

Magic burst to her face as her regeneration got to work. Her eyes fluttered open. Tesla reached the end of his count. A bolt of lightning struck the northern end of the chamber. In a flash, Julian, George, Madeline, Johnny and Giovanna appeared, all holding hands. In their other hands, they each carried a Apex RK-202 rail rifle.

"No!" Cora shouted. It was worse than she thought. With each of them recovering from the transport sickness, they'd be vulnerable, and Leopold stood between her and them.

Leopold, already back to his feet, spun on her team. Whether by adrenaline or sheer will, each of them recovered within a second from the transport and took aim.

The monster took one step forward. The team unloaded their rifles at him. The roar of all that weapons fire made Cora clasp her hand over her unprotected ear. Leopold threw up his arms to defend his face. Even as he took a knee, the team kept firing on him until they emptied their magazines. Cora called on the magic again, this time creating a ball she tossed to the back of Leopold's head.

"Down!" she shouted through the deafening silence that followed the last bullet.

With a burst of energy and gust of wind, the monster was once again obscured in a cloud of dust. Cora got back to her feet and circled around the chamber toward her people. Everyone else was getting up, too, all waiting to see Leopold finally finished.

Yet, before the smoke had even cleared, she could see his silhouette, still on one knee.

"Bloody hell," Julian said.

"He survived all that?" Giovanna gasped.

"You've got to be kidding me," Johnny groaned, dropping his rifle and reaching inside his suit jacket for a pistol.

As he stepped forward and took aim, an arc of blue lightning burst from the cloud. Johnny jumped back from it. The bolt struck the golden trident on the ground beside Leopold. It vibrated on the ground. Dust cleared. A clang of metal struck the floor in front of Leopold. His chest plate fell before of Cora's feet.

Leopold kneeled with the exposed, frail, bare chest of a much weaker man. Pockmarked with bruises and bleeding stab wounds, the most repulsive feature was the Y-shaped incision that crossed from both shoulders and down his stomach. Stitched together and holding his organs in place, a pocket of skin was open at his belly. A wire wound from the incision to a glowing blue power cell mounted inside the chest plate. It was ruptured, sending arcs of electricity between the plate and the trident. Akin to a lightning rod, the trident absorbed every bolt that exploded from his body.

Chortling, wet, mechanical breaths came from Leopold. His sinister, disgusting mouth of metal teeth curled into a smile.

"My greatest work, it seems," he laughed. Locking eyes with Cora, he said, "The whole bloody lot of you."

His hand reached up, a clenched fist ready to smash down on the power cell. Highly volatile, ruptured cells could cause an electrical explosion. His hideous mechanical fist threatened to crush down on it, intending to blow himself to pieces.

Cora saw the play. It wasn't even a thought. She dashed forward, intending to tackle him and take the brunt of the explosion. In the first step, something moved in the corner of her eye. By the second step, she realized the arcs of blue lightning continued to strike the golden trident, even as it levitated in front of her. By the third step, everything went white.

CASUALTIES OF WAR

Even with her eyelids open, everything was black. Then, blue text appeared in the corner of her left eye.

Electrical error.

System reboot.

Welcome back, Giovanna.

The temporary paralysis was terrifying. Giovanna's nerves were still alive to feel everything. Her whole body throbbed hot like a burn. She still sent commands to her cybernetically-enhanced limbs, but they couldn't respond until they were back online. The cochlear implants, though, they were the first to return. She heard the groans and the coughing. Then her eyes, staring up at the sky through a hole in the mountain above. A cloud of dust swirled above her head.

Once her limbs responded, she rolled off her back. To her right, Johnny kneeled over George, while Madeline kneeled over Julian.

"Gia, can you hear me?" Johnny shouted with his back turned.

"I hear you," she replied, coughing out dust.

"We got wounded and my comm is fried," he said, his tone urgent.

Getting up, every muscle in her body tingled like a sleeping limb. Beside her, a pile of blackened, gnarled metal components splayed out in the shape of a man amid a pool of blood and gore.

To her right, Johnny lifted George to a sitting position. The tall, rugged cowboy cradled his right bicep as blood poured from between his fingers.

"Really, sir, I'm alright," George said. He motioned to Julian and Madeline. "Check on them."

Spinning on his heels, Johnny wheeled to Julian. Giovanna walked past George, taking another glance at his wound. He must have been clipped in the arm by shrapnel from the explosion. As she stood above Julian, however, the situation was far more dire. His eyes closed, he wasn't responding to all the commotion and shouting going on. Johnny barked orders at Madeline, advising her to keep pressure on his chest.

Giovanna gasped when she saw it. A shard of metal as long as a knife jutted out from the center of Julian's chest. His Army uniform and the shirt underneath were saturated in blood, his face white as a ghost. Johnny turned to her and yelled something, but she was still too disoriented to process it.

"What?" she asked, disoriented and stunned.

"Do you have comms? We need to get him back to Atlantis!" Johnny repeated.

Shaking the cobwebs from her head, she reached back. Two fingers moved past her thick black hair and tapped a comm button behind her ear.

"Doctor, we need emergency transport, do you read?"

The line came back with static and distortion. She'd need to have that implant replaced. "...just sent you there! I need...at least four minutes!"

"Call me direct when you're up," she replied. Kneeling beside Johnny, she got a closer look at Julian. "We're at least four minutes to coil reset."

Johnny shook his head. "I don't know if he has four minutes. Keep the pressure even, kid. Christ, we're gonna lose him."

Giovanna checked over herself, but didn't find any wounds. She looked left, then right. They were the only ones in the chamber. "Wait, where's Cora?"

"She wasn't here when I got up," Johnny replied.

George grunted behind her. "She ran at Leopold before the explosion..."

Johnny got to his feet with a start and paced. He checked Julian, he examined Leopold's corpse. Back to Julian, then Leopold. He pulled his custom 9mm from the ground and emptied three rounds into what appeared to be the charred remains of Leopold's skull.

Giovanna startled with every bullet fired. She got it, though. After what they'd been through the past two days, it was the only catharsis Johnny was going to get.

"This piece of shit!" he shouted, his voice reverberating through the chamber. He stepped forward to the team. "Where did she go? There's no body, nothing. She was point blank before he exploded. She should be on the floor, dead...or at least hurt real bad!"

Giovanna looked around the chamber. Her eyes fixed on the other end of the chamber, and her shoulders dropped. "She's gone."

"Gone?" Johnny shouted, incredulous. "Gone where?"

Giovanna pointed across the chamber. Vincent stood on the floor, pecking at the ground.

"Caw," the bird shrieked. If an animal could sound forlorn, he nailed it.

"Her bird didn't follow her," Giovanna said. "Wherever she is, he can't reach her."

Johnny threw his hands out to his sides. "What the hell does that even mean? We're basing that on a bird now?" He paced again, then checked on Julian. Squatting down, he checked for a pulse. He nodded to Madeline. "You're doing good, kid. Keep it up, he's still kicking."

George got himself up and walked to Giovanna. Still holding tight against his arm, blood trickled down his hand. "Was it magic? I don't understand."

She groaned, moving her fingers back through her hair. The tingling throughout her body had changed to a sharp ache in any muscle she tried to move. From what she understood about battlefield first aid, she was suffering from the effects of electrocution. She probably needed medical attention, as well, but she'd be at the back of the line in comparison to Julian and George. She let out a heavy breath.

"I don't know enough about Cora's magic to say," she replied. "Richard was the one that brought her around the globe training her, not me. When she left for Heaven's Crest to learn from her uncle...well, I wasn't there for that, either. What I do know is that we researched magical teleportation when we were chasing after the French girl. Cora said it couldn't be done."

George looked down at the ground, and found his hat a few feet from Leopold's body. Reaching out with his wounded arm, he fetched it and put it back on with a hiss of pain. Somber, he stared at the remains. "What do we do about him?"

Giovanna had many opinions, none of them good. The psycho held her and Johnny in an abandoned warehouse on the outskirts of London for the past two days. She was starving, cold, waiting for him to murder her at any moment. She spit on the ground beside his body.

"Leave it," she hissed. "It's Lucius' tech, Lucius' park. It's his problem."

Huffing, she grew impatient. Any second, Johnny would turn around and tell her they lost Julian. She tapped her comm button. "Doctor, how much longer?"

"You take best assistant!" he shouted back, his voice crackling with static. It sounded like he was hammering metal in the background. "Make...transport five people! I work...put coil in...MACHINE! THIRTY SECONDS!"

"Medical...on standby," Gideon relayed over the comm.

Giovanna nodded. "Alright, everyone fall in. Thirty seconds."

The group gathered around Julian, each one touching him. Giovanna turned her head and whistled at Vincent. He perked his head up.

"You coming with us?" she said. She had no idea if the stupid thing knew a word of English, but Cora never stopped talking to him.

"Caw," he shouted back, pecking at the ground.

She shook her head. The bird didn't budge. Cora was gone. Nothing felt right. Now, she was going to leave Cora's spirit animal behind. She choked back tears, clenching her jaw. Leopold was more frightening than she had ever imagined. Being around him was a constant threat of getting tortured and murdered right in front of Johnny. She wanted to be saved. The sight of Cora coming to her rescue was the biggest relief she'd ever known.

With a last look at Vincent, she watched him peck at the stone ground, aimless.

"Three...one," Tesla said.

"The cost was too high," she whispered to herself.

A PLACE TO REST

Cora sat on the green grass and moved her fingers through it. Shutting her eyes, she took a deep breath through her nose. The air was heady with nearby livestock scent. Her feet dangled over a basalt crag. The drop beneath her feet was a thin ledge a few yards below, then off the edge of a cliff that fell forever. From here, she could look out over all the tiny shacks and homes of the city below. Women prepared food outdoors, the plumes of smoke from the many fires sailed into the sky. Men banged hammers and toiled on the farmlands to the west.

The scene was idyllic. Perfect, even. The only thing she couldn't get used to was the itchy quality of the linen dress she wore. She hated dresses. She hated the color orange. This was both. Over it, she wore a peplos, an outer dress that hooked to her shoulders. The darker brown with the orange underdress made her look like a damned Thanksgiving decoration at a department store. She pointed up her toe and looked at her motorcycle boot. At least she could still wear these without anyone batting an eye.

"Ker-da!" a man's voice called out behind her.

She turned around to see the older man approach. In his late forties, he was the oldest man anyone could find for miles. His hair was dark brown with gray streaks, a sign of great wisdom in these parts. He called her name again with that funny accent.

228

Only, when he started speaking, her eyes opened wide, completely clueless to a single thing he said.

"Wait!" she said, raising a finger. She gestured at her ear.

The old man rolled his eyes and shook his head. With a sigh, he walked to the edge of the cliff and sat down beside her. He scratched at his bushy beard with an expectant stare. She shut her eyes and reached into the ball of magic in her guts. It took much more effort to perform the magic as Merlin had taught her. More complicated than anything she'd ever done, she shaped the magic as she brought it to her ears and tongue, giving it design and purpose. Once she moved it into place, she released the energy and let it go to work.

"There, can you understand me?" she said.

"I can, now that you've remembered to cast the spell," he replied. His lips moved with his native Welsh tongue, yet she heard him in English. It was like watching a dubbed foreign film, though stranger to get used to in real life.

"You know, you're a crotchety old wizard," Cora said with a smile. She loved that about him.

He grumbled. The countless times he'd referred to her as headstrong, stubborn, or difficult over the past two weeks, she could have mistaken them for her name. It was hard to remember all the little details and rituals he wanted her performing. Waking up every morning feeling like she had a cold was hard enough. Her regeneration fought against dozens of diseases and bacteria that didn't exist in 2082.

"Are you planning on going out today?" he asked.

Cora picked up a few small rocks and pitched them off the cliff, watching each one until it vanished from view. "Nope."

"Are you not curious where the trident has gone?"

"I know where it went," she said, motioning to the sky. "It was moving ahead of me, pulling me along. I broke free of the ride, it kept going. So, now I'm here."

"Cora, I enjoy our time together, of course," he started.

She raised a hand to stop him. "I must respect the river of time. Yeah, I know. Look, I haven't interacted with anyone in town, I never leave this place, I wear these horrible clothes so I fit in. What more do you want?"

"Put simply - I want you to go home, Cora. Before you do any damage. You don't belong here," Merlin said. His eyes said he regretted the words.

She didn't need to hear it. This gorgeous mountain was a hollowed-out tourist trap in 2082. This view of what would become Edinburgh was unattainable. There were wild animals here that would be extinct in the next few centuries. There were no corporations, no commercialization of the land, and most importantly, no war with a dragon. Her brow furrowed.

"Where is Lucius, anyway?" she asked.

Merlin raised an eyebrow and stroked his beard. He was uncertain he should answer.

"I'm not going looking for him," Cora said with a huff. "I'm the one who can't tell you things about the future. You can tell me whatever you want, this is all ancient history to me."

Still unsure, he waved her over and got up from his seat. They walked away from the cliff, back to the castle that loomed over the land in all directions. It still took her breath away to see Camelot in its prime, when it was still in use. As far as she knew, the castle was not only missing from her time, but it was only theorized that it was ever there. All traces of it were gone by the time humans began recording history. She couldn't say any of that to Merlin, of course, he'd sooner use his magic to rob her of speech before letting her tell him any more than she already had. She stared up at the battlements, where knights in chain shirts kept watch over the area.

Merlin said nothing as he walked beside her, his heart heavy. She knew he wanted her to leave, to return home. She wasn't even sure how she got there, and found herself even more clueless as to how to leave. One moment, she was in 2082, fighting a cybernetic serial killer. The next, she was in 6th century Scotland wearing a t-shirt and jeans. Fate had told her she'd travel back in time eventually, but no one ever said how she got back. All that she knew for certain was Pops' vision, where a final battle between her and Lucius awaited her in the future. Only, she didn't want that future anymore. She wasn't sure she ever did.

They walked through the torch-lit halls to a large room with a massive table. Spread out over the table was a map of Europe, much more sophisticated and accurate than the history books said was possible. There were normally wooden figurines on the table, marking military units, but a small boy was using them to make war in the corner of the room. She smiled when she saw him, lost in his imagination. Duran was a sweet boy, and she was grateful so much of Arthurian legend was purposefully muddied by Merlin and the Illuminati that she didn't know the fate of the heir to Camelot.

Merlin grumbled at the boy. He pointed on the map to what would be southern France. "The last sighting of Lucius was here. Gallahad's forces should be there soon, if they are not already. I will divine them tonight, to see how they fare."

Cora stared at the map. Her thoughts returned to the impending war and the 687 souls that were forever in danger as long as it continued. She'd lost so many already. If Leopold was only the first taste of what Lucius' forces would look like when this war came to a head, she couldn't bear it.

She'd gotten used to the empty, cold feeling without Vincent there. She missed her mother more than anyone, as she was the only person she'd never spent time with like it was her last. The last time they spoke was on the phone, and it was unpleasant. She couldn't even remember the last time they'd seen each other in person. Her father was more than capable of watching over Heaven's Crest with Sitting Bear at his side. Julian could take his rightful place as the bloodline that fights the dragons. No one needed her anymore. They were better off without her.

"I'm not going back," Cora said, her voice soft.

"What?" Merlin gasped.

She pointed to the boy. "Duran is still young, this kingdom has no king, Gallahad is off trying to murder Lucius...I could just stay here, out of history's way."

Merlin turned, pulling Cora to face him by both shoulders. His grip was firm, his eyes stern. "No! You can't possibly imagine the damage you could do in a single lifetime!"

"I know, the Butterfly Effect and all that," she said. Looking away, her eyes filled with tears. Her chin quivering, she fought to hold back all the sorrow of a year spent watching friends and family die. "You don't know what it's like. I can't live with anyone else's blood on my hands. I can't!"

Try hard as he might, the wizard couldn't stay angry. His eyes softened. "Cora...you don't belong here."

She broke from his grip. Stepping back, she shook her head.

"If I stay...everything is preserved," she said, her eyes to the floor. The tears came freely. She tapped on the side of her head. "Everyone I love gets to stay right here, where I can remember them. Nothing will happen to the ones I have left. They're all alright. I could stay here with you."

Merlin chased after her, stepping forward. Gone was his taskmaster demeanor. He placed a hand to her shoulder. It was the sweet, gentle old man she knew. "No one lives forever, Cora. Not even me."

If only he knew what a horrible, loaded statement that was. She started bawling.

"I think she should stay," the little boy spoke up. He stood up from his toys. Cora perked up, shocked from her tears to see Duran smiling back at her. "I like her, Merlin."

Duran ran over and hugged Cora around the leg. She had been nice to him, of course, but she didn't know he cared. She put her arm around him and squeezed.

"All you're trying to do is run away, Cora," Merlin insisted.

She took another look at the fatherless boy at her side and smiled. His mother could care for him, Merlin could educate him, but no one could teach him to be a warrior like she could. All of his father's knights were off on some forsaken crusade to find and destroy Lucius, an endeavor she knew was doomed to fail. Duran could grow to be the king he was meant to. Screw the timeline. She could live a full life and die here, in this place, and that would be okay.

"You're wrong, Merlin. I'm home."

THE END

ABOUT THE AUTHOR

The Master of Kung Fu and Friendship was born in the smog-wastes of New Jersey, then journeyed to a mountain in Asia. There, he learned of the power of friendship, and knowing is half the battle. The other half is Kung Fu.

He now resides in a dojo in North Carolina, where he has sired a future champion with his Mistress of Friendship. He writes of fantasy and humor, strong women and dragons.

Thank you so much for reading this far. If you liked the book, please leave a review here!
http://getbook.at/SpiritsUnbound

Keep up to date and read more about The Dragon's Dream Saga!

Facebook: http://facebook.com/dcfergerson
Youtube: http://youtube.com/dcfergerson
Twitter: @DCFergerson
Blog: http://artofthearcane.com

PREVIEW OF BOOK 5, SHADOWS OF OLYMPUS

GREENER GRASS

Hurtling through empty space was a comfortable ride. Cora almost didn't realize what was happening. Before she opened her eyes, the sensation was like floating in water on her back. Bobbing up and down in gentle waves, the effect calmed her. It would have been easy to go back to sleep. When she looked, her heart rate went right back through the roof. Rays of light surrounded her in a cylinder, streaming by in every color of the rainbow. She tried to shift and move, but all she did was spin around in the cylinder as though trapped in a coffin.

Towards her feet, the wake beneath her boots saw the light rays fade into nothingness. Only darkness was left behind. She craned her neck up to see ahead of her. The cylinder, and every beam of color with it, intersected at the tip of a golden trident. Whatever was happening to her, wherever she was moving, that damned artifact was leading the charge.

Panic kicked in, fueling her to move on instinct. The claustrophobic nature of the tube made Cora press her hands to the edges and touch the light. A streak of red before her, a color without source or substance, resisted the pressure of her hand like a wall. It would not bend or move as she pushed against it with everything she had. The smooth caramel complexion of her skin shifted to yellow as light emanated from her palm. The warm well of magic in her guts had almost depleted, but she had enough left to experiment.

Power channeling through her hand, she hammered on the beam of light with a closed fist. To her surprise, the wall of light gave way for a moment, a break in the ribbon. In that split second, the darkness around her flickered to green grass and blue skies. The darkness returned, and the moving ray of red light became an unbroken line again. That was enough information to act on. Whatever was happening to her felt like imprisonment, and she couldn't abide it a second longer.

Bending at the knees and drawing her arms in, she curled herself up. The light within her pumped hot through every vein, worming through her every extremity and filling her with power. If it failed, she'd likely not have the strength to try again without resting. Shutting her eyes, she took a soothing breath in through her nose. When she exhaled, she let out a roar. Throwing her arms and legs out, she let all of the magic within burst outward. The whole cylinder, light show and all, shattered like glass. The world flickered into view once more, though the ground was farther than she imagined and coming at her quick.

There was enough time to throw her arms in front of her face and prepare for the inevitable pain of a high-speed fall. She slammed down with enough force to cause her to tumble and roll sideways. The chill of damp, dewy grass hit her first. Then came a pop from her nose, causing her eyes to reflexively squint. She came to rest on a patch of soaked grass. Clutching her face, she used her elbows to help her up to her knees and throw her head back. Blood poured into her hands in a torrent.

"Dammit!" she shouted to the skies. "I just healed this five minutes ago!"

In her haze of shut eyes and throbbing pain, she reached out for the tethers of magic that bound her to Vincent. Without her spirit animal perpetually worrying about her, she felt hollow and alone. Nothing came through the connection except a feeling of loss on her part. Wherever she was, Vincent was beyond her reach. She wondered if maybe she was just in too much pain to feel him.

Resetting the bone was pointless. Within a matter of seconds, it readjusted itself with a wet crack. Her nostrils filled with a thick, clogged sensation that forced her to sneeze crimson onto the ground. With that nastiness done, she opened her eyes. The skies were gray, though it appeared to be midday. That was par for the course in the UK, as it hadn't stopped raining in weeks. The first thing her eyes settled on was a man in a chainmail shirt stalking toward her with a spear. He came with two friends, one on either side of him. They both brandished swords and regarded her like she was a feral animal. They stepped with caution and a strange gait, using the balls of their feet to take each step.

"Where the hell am I?" she muttered to herself.

Though she had no idea why they were dressed that way or walked so strangely, she threw her hands up in surrender. They walked a step closer, with more confidence. Cora got to her feet and bowed her head. She didn't need another fight so soon after the last one ended. The man gasped and held out their weapons.

"Easy!" she said, trying to dial back from angry to soothing. "I'm already surrendering. Lower your weapons."

The man at her left replied to her, but she couldn't understand a word he said. More than that, she couldn't even recognize the language he spoke. Lyrical and heavily accented, she couldn't decipher meaning out of a single word. She examined the men closer as a perplexed look washed over her face. They were white men, northern European perhaps, though the lot of them were a bit short. The largest man, on her right, only had a few inches on her, at best. Cora kept her hands raised and shook her head.

"I'm sorry. I don't understand you. Do any of you speak English? Deutsch? Lavolla? Nihongo?"

The men were as confused as she was, only more upset about it. They separated, trying to surround her. Cora rolled her eyes and sighed. It wasn't meant to be. A moment's respite to get her bearings wasn't on offer.

"I'm only going to warn you once," she said, knowing they couldn't understand her. "One step closer, and what happens next is on you."

She looked them up and down. Other than the chainmail shirts, their protection came in the form of shields strapped to their backs. Where the metal shirt ended, they wore brown, rough linen pants and leather shoes that resembled slippers. It was a pretty lazy day at the Renaissance Faire - these guys weren't even trying that hard. Her mind filled with questions, like where the hell she was and who were these guys, but that would have to wait. The angry faces and crooked brows didn't look like they were in the mood to answer questions.

The man with the spear stepped forward. Whether to threaten or stab her, the tip came too close for her liking. Cora weaved to the side, her arm snapping out and grabbing it by the haft with her left hand. Looking right, the next man to approach her held his sword above his head. A rookie mistake, to be certain, but not a single man before her was out of their teens. She threw out a kick, aimed low into his stomach. He gasped out all the air in his lungs and doubled over.

Her spearman wanted his weapon back, but she wasn't done with it yet. The last man, coming up from behind her, was the most immediate threat. She pulled the spear toward her, yanking its owner with it. Throwing one leg up as high as it would go, she sent herself into a standing backflip, twisting in midair to face her attacker. Adjusting her grip on the spear, one arm went behind her back to maintain her hold. So stunned by her athleticism, the swordsman stopped his forward momentum with his jaw hanging open.

Another kick, this time a roundhouse, and her motorcycle boot clipped his wrist. The sword tumbled to the ground. Drawing her knee back to her chest, she cocked a front kick to his chest, throwing him backward.

The spearman gave a mighty yank, the rear-facing points of the tip sinking into the soft flesh of Cora's palm. It stung enough to release his weapon, with plenty of range to mount a stab. Cora somersaulted away, toward the swordsman. Wrapping her hands around the leather-wrapped grip of his weapon as she rolled through, she rose up with an equalizer to combat the spearman. The make of the sword was no Master Hidori, but the workmanship was still outstanding. She turned and assumed a fighting stance, letting the spearman know how comfortable a sword felt in her hand.

"Atal!" a commanding voice shouted.

Cora's eyes shifted to the source. A man approached from a dozen yards away. Dressed unlike any of the attackers, he wore a gaudy purple shirt and tan breeches. His long, dark hair and thick beard put him decades older than any of them. Cora held her stance, even as the spearman yielded to the older man's orders. Both of the swordsmen got to their feet and joined their friend.

The older man took his time to join the group, but they didn't move a muscle. As he got closer to Cora, she pivoted to keep him in her sights. He froze as she let him know he was too close with a simple twitch of her weapon hand. The man held up his hands in surrender and recited a few words she couldn't make sense of.

"What language are you guys speaking?" Cora groaned in frustration.

The older man held up a finger and paused. Shutting his eyes, Cora felt a tingle in the air. The hairs on the back of her neck stood up. By the time she realized he was casting magic, he'd finished. She rushed forward, sword at the ready to plunge it into his chest.

"Please, wait!" he shouted.

Cora locked her muscles, pulling back before she committed to the thrust.

"You came from the light in the sky?" he said, pointing to the air behind her. Each word hit Cora's ears in English, even as his mouth moved much different from the words he spoke.

"You...used magic to understand me?" she replied, still undecided if she needed to kill this guy. She certainly wasn't about to look behind her at the whatever light he was talking about.

"I did," he replied.

Cora looked around. Far behind the older man, the green grass traced a path up a hill that sloped up forever. At its peak, some eight-hundred feet above, a rock outcropping formed a cliff that looked out over a town of wooden shacks far across the plains ahead. Behind the edges of the cliff rested a castle made of dark gray stone. White banners with a red lion draped down from the battlements. The whole region carried a strange sense of familiarity, but she'd never seen such a castle.

"Where the hell am I?"

The older man raised a single eyebrow. "The Kingdom of Camelot. From where do you hail, stranger?"

Cora took a long breath. Her heart leaped into her throat. Somehow, that damn trident made her travel back through time. The wizard Merlin and his journal, the Pendragon Codex, detailed her traveling to the past. Even the realization that it was true seemed a farce. Time travel wasn't possible, even with magic. The wizard's words tumbled about in her head, warnings to respect the river of time, as he called it. The disasters that awaited her future could not be understated.

"I...came from a far-away land," she said, choosing her words carefully. She fixed her eyes to the older man. "I must speak with your king. Arthur, yes?"

The man's eyes narrowed. "Indeed. Walk with me, stranger."

She didn't move, holding fast to her attack stance. He already used magic she was unfamiliar with. She couldn't afford to take any chances. As though sensing her hesitation, he motioned to her hand.

"Keep the sword," he offered with a kind smile. "I promise no harm will come to you, but hold onto the sword if it will help."

Cora relaxed, but only enough to walk to him. The spearman and remaining swordsman were no real threat, it was this magic-user she had concerns about. As she approached, he turned and set out for the path up the mountain. His long, dark hair danced about his shoulders as he walked. It reminded Cora of her father and the way he never tied back his flowing, jet-black hair.

"Tell me, stranger," the older man started, grunting as the walk turned into a climb. "The clothes you wear...I've never seen their like."

Tipping her view down, she could only shake her head. She wore the bomber jacket of her mentor, Richard, over top of a rock shirt featuring the Man in Black. He was long gone before her grandfather was a toddler. Yet, if memory served, he wouldn't be rocking at Folsom Prison for another fourteen-hundred years. She was already polluting the past. Although as far as she knew, nothing was damaged by this trip. To Merlin, it had already happened by the time she found out. She decided to err on the side of caution and say little.

"These are garments from...the place I come from," she replied.

"Do you have a name?"

She sighed. "My name is Cora Blake. I can't say anything more. I must see the king."

The older man nodded with understanding. Perhaps it was the way he looked at her, but the eyes staring back were more than just familiar. She shook her head, unable to imagine why she hadn't realized it sooner.

"You're Merlin, aren't you?" she asked.

He stopped walking and turned. The guards behind her, knights of Camelot, froze in step with the wizard. The older man motioned toward the castle with a cock of his head. "Get back to the castle, men."

She couldn't understand the reply, still coming in that lyrical, jumbled mess of strange words. Despite that, she knew a protest when she heard one. The spearman gesticulated wildly, his reply animated and upset. He was right about whatever he said.

She is dangerous - absolutely.

She shouldn't be trusted - Cora didn't even trust herself to make the right decision in this place.

The older man raised his hand. He'd heard enough. "I'm aware of the risks. Now, go."

Shaking their heads, each of the knights walked past Cora and made their way up the winding hill to the peak. Once they were out of earshot, the man raised an eyebrow to Cora and looked her over.

"You're not from any lands I'm aware of, yet you know my

name," he said. "You're not a traveler from far-away lands. Your clothes, language, the way you walk...you come from a different age."

"What gave me away?" Cora joked. Though he was younger than she recalled, this was the man she'd spent most of her days with since meeting him three months ago. Two weeks ago, the son of a bitch had to go and die on her. After a long line of people she'd lost over the years, losing Merlin to old age was a novelty. Even so, the wound was still raw.

Merlin pointed at her shirt. "You have the soul of a man trapped in your dress."

Cora looked down and laughed. "Johnny? It's just a picture of him...like a painting."

"I see," he replied. "What business have you with the king?"

They continued walking up the hill. It never grew steep, only sloping upward enough to make the thighs burn. She contemplated what she could say against what he'd already know.

"Arthur fought the dragon, Lucius?" she asked.

Merlin nodded without a word.

"I am still fighting him where I come from," she continued. It was a cover story, but one she imagined she could get away with. "I need to know what he knows. Perhaps I can find an edge."

The wizard didn't reply. Instead, he became reserved and pensive, eyes straight ahead. At the summit, Cora stood before the glory of a castle that would not only be gone from this mountain in her time, but its existence erased from history altogether. Hundreds of men in chain shirts bustled about. A unit of twenty young men trained with a scarred old veteran in swordplay. Others tended to horses at a stable adjacent to the castle. What she didn't see struck her as odd.

"Where are all the women?" she said.

Merlin pointed to the cliff's edge, overlooking the village that would someday be called Edinburg. "The men's mothers, wives and children are down there. The castle is no mere seat of power. It overlooks all of Arthur's kingdom, ever vigilant of invasion. The only people here are soldiers...and the royal court, of course."

"Of course," Cora replied.

It wasn't too long after that the knights noticed her. Gasps and murmurs spread like wildfire. All eyes went to her as a hundred men stopped what they were doing to examine this strange and exotic visitor with foreign clothes and dark skin. Without a doubt, she'd be the subject of much talk and rumor for quite some time.

"Ignore them," Merlin said, pressing forward. "Follow me."

He took her through an archway beneath the battlements, to an interior area laid out like a city block. Stalls lined the interior, where blacksmiths toiled at their forges. Plumes of black smoke spread into the sky, joining each other to make clouds that blocked out what little sun visited them this day.

The stone building at the center of the interior reminded her of old manor homes dotted around the Southern Confederacy. She always imagined castles to have existed as she saw them in her time, with massive holes for windows and entrances. Instead, she found shutters and doors, like any other house. White banners with red lions were everywhere, the proud symbol of their kingdom. Merlin lead her to a door at the centermost building, the grandest within the castle walls.

The door to the interior building led to a large, sprawling area. The inside was lit by sconces on the walls every few feet, but no fire burned from them. Instead, glowing amber stones twinkled bright. It resembled candlelight, but was the furthest thing from natural she'd ever seen. Merlin's magic went into their design, no doubt, but Cora had never seen a magical item before, save for the artifacts.

To her left, a massive table served to display a map of the known region, with small wooden figurines representing armies in different colors. Men on horseback in red to the south, swordsmen in white to the north, each one depicted the various factions of the area. Then there was another that caught her eye. A black, winged creature like a serpent on the southernmost portion of the map. Lucius. It had to be.

"Come, now," Merlin insisted, waving her back to his side.

Cora followed him to a room on the opposite end of the great hall, a room lined with handwritten volumes of books and scrolls. A desk rested in the middle of the room with chairs on both sides. She held her breath. The Pendragon Codex sat on his side of the desk. She'd seen it too many times for it to be anything else. Within the next few days, he'd write down his observations on the time he spent with her, information he would relay as she met Julian Penel, the current wielder of Excalibur.

"Sit down, my dear," he said from behind her.

Without the sight of his face, his words and voice came back to her. It was like he had been brought back from death, rejoining her for a game of chess. Her jaw clenched, holding back a tear. She let out an exasperated, emotional breath and sat down. She rested the sword against his desk. She had no use for it now.

"There is much we need to discuss," Merlin said, taking his seat. "How did you come to be here?"

"It was an accident," she replied, running her hands through her jet-black hair. "There was a trident...you told me to find."

"Me?" Merlin awed, pressing a hand to his chest.

Cora nodded. "Yeah. During a fight with a very bad man, I found the trident buried in the rock beneath our battleground. The trident activated somehow, with these pulses of electricity-"

"Electricity?" Merlin stopped her, raising a hand.

"Lightning," Cora corrected to a concept he'd understand. Merlin nodded understanding. "The point is, one second I was in my time, the next the trident was pulling through this tunnel of color and light. I used my magic to break free of it, and I literally landed here."

"The lights in the sky appeared a few minutes before your arrival," Merlin explained. "I thought it a dangerous omen. Are you dangerous?"

"We're friends where I come from," Cora replied, biting her tongue. She almost used the past tense. "I would never hurt you."

Merlin sighed, reaching across his desk. He picked up a clear, faceted gem like a diamond. As though trying to get something from it, he clasped it in his hand and shook his head.

"I had truly hoped you were lying," Merlin said. He held up the gem between his thumb and forefinger. "This crystal darkens when lies are spoken in its presence. If you're telling the truth, this complicates things a great deal. I cannot let you speak with Arthur."

Cora's brow furrowed. "Why not?"

"You've come too late, my dear. Arthur is dead."

Printed in Great Britain
by Amazon

63799588R00142